FINDING MAY'S COUNTRY

KAREN MARIE WHITE

ISBN: 978-0-9756565-0-1

DEDICATION

To Geoff, my most exacting critic, my best friend, my life love.

"The future depends on what you do today".

– Mahatma Gandhi

ACKNOWLEDGMENTS

In the spirit of reconciliation and healing I acknowledge the Traditional Custodians of Country throughout Australia and their connection to the land, sea and community. In doing so, I pay my respect to their Elders both past and present.

The completion of Finding May's Country would have been impossible without the assistance of my much-loved daughter, Jasmine D'Antignana Director, Momentum Design. Jasmine provided ongoing support, advice and when the time was right, drew out the soul of my story with her beautiful cover design of the Flinders Ranges.

To Diane Hester, Eyre Writers, thank you for your encouraging words and great expertise offered in relation to sentence arrangement and composition in those early days when the manuscript was still taking shape. To my editor, Ingrid Waltham, your essential advice on structure and final line edit was completed with exceptional competence and professionalism. Finally, to Mary Gudzenovs Eyre Writers, your critical know how applied at the right time, enabled the book to be taken over the line to reach the final stage of publication.

PROLOGUE

The story that had to be told. My escape and near-death experience in the arid lands has stayed with me all these years, infiltrating every sphere of my existence.

Some might say that luck was with me, keeping me alive when I ventured north, encountering unexpected danger at every turn. Others might say I should have heeded the warning signs that were there right from the beginning ...

Chapter One

Hopelessly lost out here, but I can't go back now. If they manage to capture me a second time, my life will be in imminent danger.

I've reached the summit, expecting … I don't know what. Despite the exhaustive climb and overwhelming tiredness, I am deeply moved by the rugged and yet ethereal beauty of these panoramic mountains, millions of years in the making. I feel as though I am standing on top of the world. Far below in the distance, spectacular deep gorges and misty blue-grey ridges loom; a remote wilderness that seems to stretch on forever and ever.

This is May's country.

Eight days earlier

There was a lot of jostling and friendly competition in the office to get the nod to head north to write a cover story about one of the largest and most notable cattle stations in the state, Mirna Springs Station. Initially, Callie – my boss and the editor of *The New Times* – had flagged her interest in fellow journalist and co-worker, Paddy; the Paddy who won awards for his overseas reporting in war-torn areas such as Syria and Afghanistan. In fact, some of Paddy's work had propelled him into literary stardom. Perhaps it was only after Paddy refused the job for personal reasons that Callie gauged my interest in travelling bush to take on this assignment.

So, second choice at best, yet I jumped eagerly at the chance to take on the assignment. Callie knew I grew up in the bush, and in my heart there always remained a yearning to go back to that rugged landscape I remembered so well.

They didn't need to tell me how high the stakes were, either. Although I'd been working in the field for a couple of years I had yet to contribute to a full-page spread in the paper. If I was lucky, the story might launch me into a new level of respectable journalism, which somehow had eluded me so far.

The assignment seemed simple enough. Producing a snapshot featuring the current owners, including the day-to-day running of a large Australian cattle property. The McCallum family could trace their roots all the way back to the original pioneers who courageously left their place of birth in northern England for unchartered waters, making this vast and unknown country their new homeland well over a century ago. My article would include noteworthy facts about the original family who settled on the land, building the foundation for the property as people know it today.

The ownership of Mirna Springs Station continued to remain with the McCallum family despite all the hardships and challenges they faced over the decades.

Then there was the other matter of course, also part of my brief. The case of a missing man, presumed deceased, but enquiries were still ongoing. Almost twelve months ago to the day, a thirty-six-year-old man, travelled north on an information gathering trip. An amateur historian, he was seeking information for a book he intended to write about the early settlement of Australia. Following his reported disappearance, extensive searches were carried out in the local area. To date, there were no new leads that might assist police in their attempts to solve the puzzle. Although numerous theories were on the table, there was still a great deal of uncertainty about what had actually transpired in the lead-up to the man's untimely disappearance.

*　　*　　*

I left town early next morning, relieved to be finally heading north. The last glimpses of the city I called home, with its enticing emerald-green seacoast, faded quickly into the distance. The usual markers surrounding the mussel and tuna farms in the middle of the bay were a familiar sight. Further out, Cos Island, its steep rocky hills rising high out of the ocean, the perfect nesting site for sea birds, was now bathed in early morning light. I would be staying at Mirna Springs Station for five days, and interviews had been already organised with the owners. Australian cattle stations are often thousands of square kilometres in area, and the geographically remote Mirna Springs was no exception.

Finally, the rolling green hills disappeared and rocky outcrops appeared spasmodically on the distant horizon; ridges on the ranges sprinkled with a crown of grey-brown granite rock. The first signs of the outback. Sparse grey saltbush grew in the sandy red dirt, alongside low-growing mallee and the occasional swathe of thin she-oak trees. The normal flow of traffic was reduced to the occasional four-wheel drive or truck, and as the hours ticked by, even they became less frequent.

Two hundred and fifty kilometres up the track, the 'Welcome to Osborn' sign stood out like a sore thumb. The original placard - probably made by one of the local handymen - may have served a good purpose in its time, but it was now peppered with bullet holes, and graffiti covered the original lettering. The sad looking remains now tilted drastically sideways, pointing north towards the never-ending highway. Decades ago, this tiny settlement was a bustling hub. The town was bypassed by the railway and many people decided they would have to move on, in an endless quest to find work. Some houses had been boarded up, abandoned by their owners years ago.

No stop for a coffee break here, then. In the centre of town, a derelict petrol station, green and yellow sign still advertising bygone business, sat on the edge of the highway, windows caked in grime, doors broken, walls covered in graffiti. Tall strands of brown grass forced their way through cracks in the cement around what would have been the building's main entrance. The business was long closed, staff having moved on to bigger and better things many moons ago.

Further north, a familiar scene as smoky blue ranges loomed large, dominant against the clear skyline; a tantalising trail that twisted and turned closer and closer to my destination.

Over the next big hill, hundreds of wind turbines dominated the surrounding landscape. Churning slowly in the morning breeze, the turbines looked like giant aliens anchored into the brown hills, arms commanding the clear blue skies above. Displaying almost a hint of menace - for those with an imagination - these gigantic interplanetary creatures now lay claim to more and more parts of our world. A newly built powerline perched high above the road would be the lifeblood for energy of the future, supplying electricity to many rural and metropolitan areas throughout the state.

Finally, the unrivalled beauty and mystery of the Flinders Ranges seemed to reach out to touch me. So very close … yet the smoky hills always calling for you to get closer.

The 'Welcome to Dillalong' sign reflected some innovative metalwork; a rural scene portrayed windmills, cattle and sheep all cast in the same rusty tin. Underneath the sign a fire season update informed visitors the fire season was still in place. I pulled off the highway and slowed to a crawl.

At the urging of Callie, I had promised I would let someone in the local area know my whereabouts over the next five days. I made a mental note to check in at the police station, to relay the details of my stay at Mirna Springs Station. I also needed to establish that the road out there was not too hazardous.

A small outback town with a population of less than two thousand people, Dillalong was one of the last towns before the desert to the north. To the east was the larger town of Simpson Creek, some two hundred and fifty kilometres away.

It soon became obvious the long drought had been relentless up this way. Furious heatwaves had continually scorched the land, killing livestock and wild animals. The land was littered with countless casualties, on the sides of roads, paddocks and scrub - animals too weak to survive another day, or roadkill skeletons laying wherever they had dropped.

An added burden for the townspeople still coping with the severe drought was the roll-on effect of high unemployment, a common fact of life for many now.

Driving slowly along the dusty streets told a story. A few shops dotted here and there, some houses appearing well looked after, sporting a coat of bright paint, others old and dilapidated. Sadly, some houses built in much more affluent times now in partial ruin.

Into the heart of town I spotted a distinctive greeting by the roadside. Colourful bunting tied between buildings in the main street, and brightly painted signs spread along several streets, advertising with pride: 'Welcome to Dillalong. Celebrating our 150th Year Anniversary.'

The local police station, circa 1960s, with pale brown brick and chipped wooden window frames, also looked like it had seen better days. The Australian flag, hoisted high on a pole set in a tiny, neatly manicured lawn, fluttered faintly in the breeze. I climbed the front steps and rang the doorbell, before pushing the shaky old wire screen open with a shove, entering the office more abruptly perhaps than I would have liked. From behind the small wooden desk two pairs of eyes suddenly looked up in a show of mild interest.

The older man, red hair and beard, greeted me first with a

friendly nod, rising quickly out of his chair. 'Hi, how are you today what can we help you with?'

'Hello, my name's Sarah Wills, I'm a journalist from *The New Times*.'

The younger cop, who towered over his superior, introduced Sargent Faulkner and then himself, Constable Jamie Landers. Constable Landers gave a big smile, his cordial approach easing the atmosphere somewhat.

We all shook hands and I promptly informed them of my plans.

'Just thought I would touch base to let you know that I'm heading out to Mirna Springs Station tomorrow to interview the McCallum family for a cover story. I'm wondering how the road is out there and if there is anything I need to worry about – I have a four-wheel drive, so figure I should be OK.'

Did I detect an instant mood change following that last comment?

Constable Landers was first to speak.

'Thanks for letting us know you'll be travelling out to Mirna Springs, but…' he questioned me with a surprised look - 'you say you have already arranged with the family to go out onto their property, and they have agreed?'

'Yes, it was organised last week by the paper's editor, I believe they spoke to Mr McCallum directly and made the arrangements.' A look passed between the two of them as though they were carefully assessing what I was saying.

I noticed Sargent Faulkner jotting down a few notes as I spoke.

'So you are definitely planning on returning next Monday?' he inquired.

'That's the plan at this stage, job finished hopefully, and headed down to the city again.'

'Perhaps you could call us when you arrive at Mirna Springs, so that we know when you have arrived safely,' the tall cop said.

'Of course, I can certainly do that.' I wondered at the same time what the phone reception would be like out there.

Constable Landers peered out through the window to see what sort of vehicle I was driving.

'Yeah, the road is a bit dodgy out that way, so you might want to be careful. There's been a drought up this way so there's lots of dust on the road and a few potholes, but you should be fine if you take it slow. Are you carrying extra water in case you break down? We've had some pretty consistent forty-degree days here over the past month, it wouldn't do to get caught in the middle of nowhere without adequate water.'

I knew these were standard questions for anyone travelling into remote areas. I told them I had a twenty-litre container in the back of the four-wheel-drive in case of a breakdown.

A large map of the district was pinned on the wall behind

the desk and the older cop, who was probably the sergeant in charge of the local area, pointed out specific directions to the property. Using my phone, I took a quick shot, zooming into the Mirna Springs location.

My attention was also drawn to a poster on the far wall. Noticing my interest, the sergeant mentioned the disappearance of a man out this way, at a similar time last year, whereabouts still unknown.

'Don't 'spose you heard any information on the news about the disappearance down your way? He was reported to have told someone he was visiting the McCallum property, but they claimed that he never showed up.'

Sarge didn't wait for an answer, he had busied himself realigning the crooked poster and re-attaching it to the wall. I had read several news items and all the follow-up information I could find in relation to this missing man, by the name of Chad Dimitri. Reports suggested search parties failed to find him after extensive efforts that took place over a number of weeks, curiously, his car had never been located either.

There had been some talk of foul play, but I was unsure how far investigations had progressed and if any breakthroughs were on the horizon. I gazed back at the poster. A black-and-white photograph of a youngish-looking man with a friendly smile, short tousled darkish hair. So, this was what Chad Dimitri looked like. On the bottom of the A3 print, there was further information about the missing man and his date of disappearance in the local area. I noticed a reward of $100,000 for any information that would help police to locate him.

Reluctant to immediately reveal I was also here to gather information regarding this man's disappearance, I did slip in a few questions before I left.

'Are there any new leads in this case?'

'Not at this stage. We have put a lot of effort into an extensive search of the whole area, and interviewed everyone who had contact with Chad on the day, but as yet we've not been able to ascertain if he actually arrived at Mirna Springs, or if some incident prevented him from reaching his destination.'

'So the owners at Mirna say they didn't see him in the area?'

'No, they allegedly haven't seen sight nor sign of him. The only witness on the road that day reported seeing a car matching the description of Chad's car about ten kilometres from the station heading in that direction.'

'What would be the next step then?'

'Well, we can't reveal at this stage what we have decided to do, but I can tell you that because we suspect foul play, we have enlisted the assistance of Adelaide detectives who are helping us with this investigation now.'

'I wouldn't mind keeping in touch, in case there are any

new developments. Am I able to request that you make contact with me if there happens to be a breakthrough?' I handed him my business card.

Sarge hesitated. 'Well, yeah, we might be able to arrange that, obviously it needs to run through the correct channels before we can disclose details to the media. I'm sure you'd understand that.'

'Thank you, and yes,' I said with a smile, 'I do understand where you're coming from. I really appreciate any information that might help me to put together a story that could help the public to remember any details on the day of the disappearance.'

They politely followed me out to the car, giving the white Toyota Prado with the large red NEW TIMES sticker on the side door the once over. I assured them the photograph of the map would certainly prove valuable as I made my way out of town. Sarge gave a final kick of the front tyre and wished me a safe journey. All was arranged then. I thanked both men for the helpful information they had provided and waved goodbye.

Heading into town I started to wonder how the family of this man would be coping, not knowing what had happened to their loved one and if they would ever get answers explaining how and why he vanished into thin air, with no current clues to his whereabouts.

Following the street signs back to the centre of town, waves of heat shimmered above the bitumen road, the smell of melting tar heavy in the air, a constant reminder of the intensity of the season. The streets looked empty; there were few people around even at this time of the day, I guessed it was thanks mainly to the heat.

Most of the shops and businesses were in Wilson Street. I desperately wanted to stop for a coffee break, sit somewhere cool and stretch my legs.

Out of the blue I picked up the unmistakable sound of voices, perhaps even a crowd, at first distant but getting louder by the second as they moved closer, their shouting in unison disturbed the still morning air. People were stopping in their tracks to look. It sounded like some sort of coordinated chant. I heard the same words repeated over and over again, getting louder, it must be coming from the adjoining street. Ah, so that's where all the people have been hiding. I craned my neck at the next street corner. At first, I couldn't see a soul, but then was suddenly overtaken by a large group of about a hundred people marching in unison who turned into the same street I now stood in.

Some were walking along the footpath carrying placards.

SAVE OUR WATER!

WHERE ARE THE JOB OPPORTUNITIES YOU PROMISED US?

WHAT HAVE YOU DONE TO HELP THIS TOWN, TIM GRANT?

I watched with interest as the group marched towards a large historic-looking brown building at the end of the street. People started to congregate around the steps. An official-looking sign with intricate logo near the main entrance informed anyone who may not have known, that this was the Local Government Offices Dillalong. I followed the crowd now, intrigued to know who they might be waiting for.

Just ahead, a young woman popped her head out of a small shop, looking this way and that way along the street. An ornate sign above the door announced in bright gold lettering that this was Macey's Hairdressing Salon. The local hairdresser - pixie haircut tinted with silver and purple highlights for wow factor. She was yelling excitedly to her customers and passers-by urging anyone who was listening to 'Come and look at this!' She was quickly joined by some of her clientele and I approached a group of them standing at the door.

'Excuse me, I've just arrived in town and I'm wondering what the march is all about?' Many piped up with answers, from the general gist I gathered a local Member of Parliament, Tim Grant, was in town for a rare visit.

One of the customers quietly confided in me. 'Everybody wants more action and less talk from Tim Grant, we all think he has become just one more bureaucratic fat cat and doesn't care about the electorate that voted him into office in the first place.'

I followed the crowd milling down the street, joining in with the locals. There was a certain edginess within the group; some were quite vocal about what they believed had 'to be fixed.' The journalist in me thought this was an unusually large and very organised gathering for such a small town, and it could be a good move to capture their story – whatever it may turn out to be. If the story had some merit, Callie may be interested in picking it up.

The heat was overwhelming. Flies buzzed around the waiting faces and settled on the backs of those gathered in the crowd.

Finally, the appearance of Tim Grant. I craned my neck to get my first glimpse of a stout, middle-aged man stepping up to the podium dressed immaculately in a pale brown business suit and pink tie. Mr Grant appeared somewhat overdressed for such a stifling day in the outback.

He was obviously under the impression that he might still be the darling of the moment, but those days were long gone it seemed, judging by what the community were now saying to him. The errant politician stepped up to the microphone and proceeded to present a mundane speech regarding his perception of what he has achieved over the past few years for the townspeople and the district.

I took out my mobile phone, opened the camera app and

started clicking, also setting up video record as Grant commenced his speech in order to capture the moment.

No more than five minutes into what seemed to be a very short - lived speech, rumblings erupted across the assembled crowd, and in spite of the MP's best intentions to soothe troubled waters, the mob quickly got out of hand.

Some official-looking people standing near Grant looked on in horror as the scene continued to unfold. Security guards stepped forward and stood between Grant and the surging horde. The MP's voice was drowned out by a general rowdiness erupting with some regularity, people were starting to advance forward chanting, 'broken promises, broken promises.'

From the front of the throng, a tall woman with short grey hair wearing some sort of official badge used a megaphone to pull the rabble into order.

'Scuse me everyone, a bit of quiet now.' Her raucous voice rebounded throughout the street and the volume of the chanting subsided. 'We have a lot of questions we are hoping you can provide the answers for, Tim Grant.' By this time Grant looked completely rattled. His jelly-like double chin was shaking uncontrollably, and his pudgy, Canberra politician's hands waved meekly at the onlookers as if to stop the noise and aggression. The hecklers had obviously taken him completely by surprise. Why, this was just little old Dillalong, nothing much out of the ordinary ever happened out this way!

In usual politician speak, he attempted to side-step questions, informing everyone in a hurried tone about the wonderful opportunities that were still coming their way. The crowd were not buying it.

Mobile held high, I edged to the front. Grant made a final attempt to appease the protestors, telling them about pending deals that would benefit the local community.

'Like what?' asked a disgruntled man who had also stepped forward.

Tim Grant hurriedly replied; 'We might open up mining out here again, I'm negotiating with some local station owners.'

This answer seemed to set people off again, and someone shouted, 'Yeah, like the sweetheart deal you did with John McCallum and the mining companies last year - some people will have no water on their properties, thanks to you and your arrangements with the Federal Government.'

There was a sudden blur of movement to my right. In less than a split second, a man who had already asked Tim Grant many questions but received no reply, was making his way through the throng with almost superhuman speed. As the crowd spilled apart, he lunged forward and grabbed the unfortunate politician by the scruff of the neck. Everyone now mesmerised by the scene that was unfolding in front of them.

The unknown man clutched his victim in a vice-like grip,

moving close to his face shouting; 'Yeah, and I am one of those people! Deal with crooks and you are just as bad as them. You are just a useless piece of shit and we want to see you gone.'

I sensed the seriousness of the situation as the security guards, who up until now were standing on each side of the large gathering, rushed in and removed the man with such force that he was pushed backwards, falling heavily on the ground.

Tim Grant, face and neck turned a deep red, was visibly shaken. With hands to his throat and making no further attempt at appeasing anyone, he was ushered to a safer place inside the building by security.

The assailant surrendered without a fight. I gazed at him, seeing visible frustration and anger in his face. As I continued to stare as an interested onlooker, I briefly glimpsed a sigh of resignation and even a fleeting shadow of what could have been deep melancholy settled momentarily into his features. I wanted to know why this man decided to attack a local MP. Was it worth it after all that? It could mean an assault charge and even jail time.

Wandering up the street with the remnants of the group, I asked one of the young people if he knew the man who attacked Mr Grant.

'Oh, that's Connor Edwards, he owns a property near the edge of town. He's had trouble with stolen stock and people wanting to buy his property. He says he doesn't want to sell.'

Another woman piped up. 'Connor says he has had death threats made against him.'

'What is the name of Connor Edwards' property? I asked them.

'It's called 'Beyond Yonder', about a kilometre along the north road, on the right-hand side, you can't miss it.'

Right then and there, I decided I would hang around town and see if Mr Edwards would be willing to talk to me - if not tomorrow, then on my way back through town.

In spite of the issues and concerns raised by the community, Mr Grant had not planned to stay for any extended period. He had already 'left the building', hastily catching a taxi to the airport with his entourage.

Checking the footage later, I decided this could potentially be a scoop story for the paper. There didn't appear to be anyone else there who might have reported on the protest, so I called Callie, who was immediately interested in having a look at the footage.

She called me back within twenty minutes. 'I am impressed with your footage, Sarah. This might even make the headlines, Tim Grant's performance as local MP has been under scrutiny for some time now. I'll arrange with the team to edit this and put it together for our media drop. This could well be on the national news, particularly as it involves a local MP. We'll also run the story in the paper tomorrow. Good on you for being in the right place at the right time! So look after yourself, but don't forget to call me if anything untoward happens and we'll see you next week.'

I also filled Callie in about Connor Edwards during that brief call. Callie thought it may be worth the follow-up visit - if Mr Edwards wasn't locked up in the local cells, that is. She recognised the importance of trying to interview Connor even if he was incarcerated, and asked me to seek permission from the authorities.

I decided to hang around, as this could conceivably be an important part of the story and give me an insight into the inner dealings of the McCallums at Mirna Springs Station, particularly if they were involved with some sort of sweetheart deal with Tim Grant.

Sitting in the local cafe I noticed staff chatting amongst themselves about the march. I gathered from the conversation there was talk of mining being opened up in the local area, but farmers didn't want mining operations on their land so the matter was controversial.

A local named Pip had a brief chat to me. Her uncle had owned a small farm near Dillalong for fifty years, and the family were offered an exorbitant sum of money if they would sell their property.

'Uncle Harry said his stock had been gradually declining due to the drought and he had also reported a number of sheep stolen last year.'

'Where is your uncle now?'

'They moved to the Gold Coast and retired; they had a daughter living up that way and I think they moved near her.' I asked Pip if she knew who the buyers were, and for some reason she whispered her answer.

'One of the larger enterprises, apparently they don't live locally but are linked with locals.'

Later on, I got talking to one of the girls employed at the cafe, Kiana Fraser, who told me she had lived in the town for much of her life. She talked with pride about the town celebrating the big One Hundred and Fifty Year anniversary this week.

'It's great you happen to be in town this week, there'll be lots of activities, including the official opening of events this afternoon at the town oval. Lots to look forward - a band, food stalls, sideshows, and the big event of the year, the dance in the town hall tonight. Everyone's welcome to join the celebrations - and guess what? My brother Ben's lead singer and plays bass guitar in the Banjo Bush Band. They're setting up in the hall tonight, if you'd like I can pick you up.'

I had intended to stay in town that night but learned from Kiana all accommodation in the town was booked out some weeks ago due to the special celebrations.

Luckily, I had brought my swag along for the trip, so I decided to bed down in my car for the night.

Kiana arranged to meet me when she finished work at five.

She was obviously close to her brother, who dropped in briefly before leaving for the town hall to set up equipment. I noticed Ben Fraser's huge engaging smile and similar mannerisms to his big sister, both friendly outgoing country people.

Ben gave a wink as he was leaving. 'We'll see you both tonight then.'

Kiana looked amazing, long dark hair styled, flashing that charismatic smile. She was ready to party! At the urging of Kiana, I changed out of my jeans and shirt into a pale blue number, the only dress packed for the journey. One quick look in the mirror and we set off.

We glanced briefly at each other, newly found friends, both in anticipation of having a good night out, as we strutted across the freshly cut and watered lawns along with dozens of other visitors, excitement now hanging heavily in the air.

We walked into the hall, not unsurprisingly already jam packed with people. The ancient old building had been really spruced up for the special occasion, the smell of fresh paint still hung in the air. Lavish decorations took pride of place along the stage; white and purple streamers and silver balloons with 'Dillalong 150th Year Anniversary' printed on them.

The mayor, dressed in his official robes, stood centre stage and made a long speech about the town, and his pride in what the town had achieved, particularly in the last twenty years. He touched on the many setbacks the townspeople had lived through, like the bushfires that had ravaged the national park and houses on the eastern side of town last year.

It was an encouraging speech, and the mayor finished with a toast to the town and its people, followed by lots of applause, cheers and laughter. There were even a few tears from some. The event, now officially opened, was well attended, with perhaps four or five hundred people milling around both in and around the outside of the hall.

The evening reminded me of a bygone era, similar to events we attended when I was a kid. Like all good country get-togethers, many young ones were having as much fun as the adults, dancing to the music and playing hide-and-seek outside in the bushes, and everyone brought a plate of supper to share. The band was synced ready to go, and suddenly music filled the still air. Yahoos, whistles and cheers filled the hall, and throngs of people jumped up to move to the beat, determined to enjoy this rare night.

My connection to the bush goes back a long way. My parents lived and worked in a small country town where my younger brother Josh and I grew up. My father was the local accountant, my mother a nurse who worked part-time for an old doctor up until his retirement.

On the weekends we often went bush. My parents loved camping and my love of the great outdoors came through them. Dad would show Josh and I how to climb a gum tree, peeking inside a hollow to see if we were lucky enough to see any baby galahs before they fledged. Mum and Dad had a special place that we often travelled to, a dam with lush vegetation around the edges. We would lie quietly watching the wild ducks, bronze wing pigeons and sometimes herons and kingfishers at dusk. We didn't kill the wild birds - Dad didn't believe in killing the wildlife, he just wanted us to see nature at its best.

The band had everyone fired up, more people were joining the throng and some were already cutting loose near the front of the stage. Amongst the crowd Kiana, dressed to kill, dancing with a young guy wearing what would be regarded around here as everyday country attire - blue jeans, check shirt and black Akubra hat.

Minutes later I noticed a young cowboy, grinning from ear to ear, skidding across the wooden floor before stopping abruptly in front of me.

'Hiya, name's Hoss, care for a whirl?'

I introduced myself with a cheesy smile and we cruised across the hall floor and started to strut our stuff to the beat of a very groovy Australian version of *Crossroad Blues*.

At some stage I looked across the room and noticed someone over the other side looking right back at me. I didn't recognise that face immediately, but soon twigged – it was the tall cop I met earlier today at the police station. He continued to watch from across the room and as soon as the band stopped for a break he swooped in with a grin as though he'd been waiting for an old friend.

I took a step back, a bit surprised by the bold greeting.

'Hi, remember me?' he said, with a great rush of confidence.

I did remember of course, so I answered honestly, 'Yes I do, but didn't catch your second name.'

'It's Jamie Landers,' he said with a cheeky smile. 'How do you do, again. It's Sarah, isn't it?'

My very friendly partner had thanked me by then and moved on, leaving Jamie and me standing there. It felt a little awkward for a few seconds, but then Jamie cracked a joke about the mayor looking really overdressed wearing his thick robes for such an event. Standing where we were, we could see perspiration glistening on the mayor's face and we both had a chuckle. Suddenly, the ice was broken, and we were chatting about the celebrations and what was happening in town. He was easy to talk to, conversation came naturally, he wasn't afraid to reach out to people and judging by many of the locals who came up and had a chat to Jamie, he was obviously well respected.

I started to feel at ease talking to this tall, amazingly good looking stranger. We stood near the entrance to the hall; even the slightest breeze wafting through the open door provided a bit of relief from the relentless evening heat, that is, to those lucky enough to be standing near the entrance.

The bar was in full swing with locals shouting their mates a beer or two. Jamie bought some drinks and we hoisted ourselves up onto a couple of hay bales scattered around the hall as seating.

I listened intently as Jamie filled me in on snippets about his own career.

'I've been working in Dillalong these past four years, originally from Adelaide, but there's a family connection to the place. My paternal great-grandfather was born on a property near Dillalong, he was one of many labourers contracted to build the railway that runs all the way up through the ranges and eventually links up with the track to Adelaide.'

Jamie was offered the post out here and decided to take it up. He wanted to re-trace his great-grandfather's footsteps, having a great interest in the history of the place. Jamie said he recently located the house his great-grandfather was born in, and the current owners had kindly let him visit.

'At the request of the town I've been working on a part-time basis with troubled youth in the area. I take a group of them out for a week at a time to a few of the outlying stations. We have an agreement with some owners who house the boys and offer both work and recreation if they are interested. It's the last chance for some of them to pull themselves out of serious trouble and make a new start.'

'How successful is the program? Do you think some of those long-term goals are working?'

'There have been some great achievements so far, and that's what continues to motivate me to keep going. A few of the boys are now working on the stations, and have been offered permanent work because of their ability to learn and do the job properly.'

The program was impressive based on what had already been accomplished. I recognised the value in his work, and the positive spin-offs would be gold. I had heard many examples of chronically unemployed people - both young and older - getting themselves back on track, deciding to further their studies or entering full-time jobs. Jamie said publicity was important, not only because it reminded the community of the positive changes happening for some of the troubled youth in the area, but it also helped with funding. The program relied on government and private funding.

'We've got another group leaving for Yingali Station on Monday,' Jamie said. 'I don't suppose you'd have time to come along and observe the program?'

I felt immediately struck by his enthusiasm, and answered quickly. 'Thank you for the invitation and yes, I'd love to come! I return from Mirna Springs next week, so you can count me in!'

But as soon as I put my hand up to go on this trip, I realised it would be dependent on my boss Callie being willing to give permission for me to go.

I had an extra day to catch up with townspeople before heading out to Mirna Springs Station. I would touch base with Callie in the morning, I suddenly felt ambivalent about the likelihood of me really going, it all hinged around Callie, she might not be so willing for me to cover this new story.

Later I found myself telling Jamie a bit about my own life, including an outline of my current plans.

'You asked about my role as journalist and how long I've been working with *The New Times*,' I said with a smile. 'It's getting on for three years now since I started as a junior journalist at the paper. This assignment means a fair bit, I'm hoping it will give me a chance to prove to myself as well as my boss that I'm capable of getting to the bottom of a good cover story. I need to make sure this story is a winner.'

Jamie chuckled. 'Well, that sounds like a tall order to me, but I've got a feeling you could crack it.'

We talked about my past connections with the outback, growing up in the bush. I recalled the strong link with my past experiences.

'I guess the seeds were sown during my childhood, much of it spent growing up in some of these arid areas. Country is still close to my heart.'

Jamie seemed intrigued. 'So you lived in the outback for most of your younger years?'

I smiled, remembering some of those happy memories. 'I lived in a town similar in size to Dillalong. We would go out on weekends and camp in the creeks. My love of nature came from my parents, who always taught us not to harm the creatures that lived out in the wild but to learn from everything around us.'

Jamie nodded and grinned in agreement. 'Some places up here, as remote as they are, can claim a piece of your heart, which always makes a return visit pretty special.'

Our conversation changed direction then, and we chatted about the town. It seemed a natural transition and avoided the discomfort of any further disclosure about our personal lives. I also had a real interest in the anniversary celebrations in the town. Jamie knew a fair bit about the history of the area and had borrowed a couple of books from the library to find out more.

He told me that in the early years, the town prospered. But after a series of events that included two World Wars, rabbit plagues, severe droughts and a lack of available work, many people in the area became destitute. Some businesses went bankrupt - or close to it - and some sold up and moved.

After the railway line bypassed Dillalong in the 1950s there was talk the place might eventually end up a ghost town as there weren't many stable businesses or industries that could keep it afloat.

'Perhaps what saved the town was the fact that many World War Two soldier settlers were offered land by the government and took up farming. New industries also opened up in the local area.'

We touched briefly on the events in town earlier in the day, and when I asked Jamie about some of the issues the townspeople are upset about, and whether they are real problems or perceived, he said there were things happening in the area that could be benefiting a few, but most people were not getting a fair go.

I knew Jamie would be aware of the earlier incident, but I realised that for confidentiality reasons he couldn't discuss the arrest of the person who assaulted Tim Grant. I sensed reluctance on Jamie's part to talk about it, so I dropped the subject.

I was surprised when I looked at my watch and it was nearly midnight. The hours had slipped by so quickly. Even though the band was one of the best I'd heard in a long time, we had spent most of the evening talking!

We strolled outside and stood together in the still summer night. Sparks from the fire drums circling the hall rose up through a dark sky sprinkled with a million bright stars. The smell of burning gum leaves mixed with the fragrance of cut grass lingered in the air. It had truly been a totally unexpected but ultimately captivating night. I had really enjoyed my time here and didn't want the night to end.

Happy laugher and cheers rang out as people gathered in small groups outside the hall. Gradually the voices died down. Those camping for the night started to roll out swags and settle into the backs of their utes or on the grounds of the oval. The band were busily packing up their equipment and loading it onto the truck for the journey home. Soon the lights went out and quiet settled over the hall and oval.

Jamie reminded me again about the trip next Monday morning. He mentioned he would have to be up early and packed ready to collect the group of young men scheduled to travel with him. I would be following along in my own vehicle. Would I be okay with the early start?

I nodded. A moment of easy silence passed. I thought how content I was having spent this time with Jamie. It was just by chance we met today, and yet it already felt like we were friends. That's how easy it was between us.

Until now Jamie hadn't mentioned my trip to Mirna Springs Station, but when he did, his tone was serious.

'Be careful out there, Sarah. You don't know this country, and - not to frighten you or anything - but there is a guy still missing in this area. It can be very harsh if you don't take the right precautions.' He lightly touched my arm. 'Travel safe, and we will catch up next week.'

A friendly hug, a final glance and another cheerful grin and we went our separate ways. *I actually do know this country well, Mr Jamie Landers,* I thought. *But all the same, I'll keep your advice in mind.*

Chapter Two

I woke early and immediately made the decision to drive out to Connor Edwards property, on the off-chance he might agree to talk to me. I packed up my swag and waited in the queue with the other campers for a one-dollar shower in the hall. The showers were fitted with three-minute timers now, due to the drought.

A battered old Rav 4 did a half circle and pulled up near my car. Kiana, looking very lively for someone who hadn't had a lot of sleep, had kindly popped out to see me before I left. We chatted about the celebrations, agreeing that it was an exceptionally good night.

I thanked Kiana profusely for inviting me, telling her it was the best country event that I have been to in a long time.

'By the way - who was the good looking guy that you were dancing so much with?' Kiana shook her head and burst out laughing.

'Would you believe he's really keen to see me again, but I'm not so sure. Said he's going to give me a call this week.'

Kiana turned to leave, then changed her mind.

'Ah, Sarah - you spent a bit of time with Jamie last night. Did he mention that he has a girlfriend? A nurse who works at the local doctors' surgery, I think her name is Jess.'

'No, he didn't mention it. We were just chatting, and he made me feel really welcome.'

I felt a brief twinge of disappointment at this snippet of information about a girlfriend. And then, self-reproach - after all, I was just passing through this town. Having recently come out of a long-term relationship I had convinced myself I wouldn't be looking for another relationship with anyone right now. All the same, it was a pleasure to meet such a warm and friendly guy. I put the thought of Jamie behind me.

It was a reminder though, of one of the recent low points in my life. I'd come out of that relationship six months ago. In the beginning I thought Taj and I belonged together, we had so much fun. Sometimes things can turn sour without you even noticing - or perhaps pretending not to notice. It took me a long time to face the reality that we just weren't happy anymore. In fact, I started to dread going home from work. Maybe he felt the same way, but like me, he didn't want the truth to get in the road until there was a major crisis in our lives and we had to talk about it.

Taj had a big problem with alcohol. Not being able to say no to a drink took over his life to the point that he started taking big risks - drink driving, staying out all night and not remembering next day what he had been doing. Eventually, in those final months, Taj was regularly late or did not turn up to work all. It was the road accident that finally changed everything.

In spite of what happened between us, there was an element of sadness and deep regret on my part. This is where the "what ifs" and the "maybes" come in. I know grief has a bargaining cycle, with times you're just not ready to face the truth. There is also the strong dip in the cycle, when you feel anger and resentment.

I had certainly felt that emotion over the months. It would be easy to lay blame, but I decided I was also part of the relationship and needed to come to terms with what happened and move on with my life.

By ten o'clock I was headed out of town, travelling north-east looking for a sign that might lead me to the Edwards property, Beyond Yonder. My timing could be all wrong but I decided to take a risk and drive to the property unannounced; Connor Edwards was probably still in custody, but I hoped someone at the property would be willing to talk to me.

I pulled in to the rusty gate decorated with a wooden sign hand painted in irregular black letters. Beyond Yonder. I took a deep breath and drove straight in, down a track past a large old stone homestead. As I drew closer, I could see the house was now derelict, possibly abandoned some years ago. The rusty tin roof that would have been red in its day was now partly collapsed; the nearby outhouse had fallen in on its side. Long dry grass and tumbleweeds grew through the veranda boards and around the sides of the house. This was obviously the original family homestead; it looked as though it could be close to one hundred years old.

Five hundred metres further down the track, set among gum trees, was a small, newer looking cottage. Most likely built in the 1980s or 90s, it was a transportable home. Affordable and easy to erect, these homes were often used by couples who had moved onto their parents' property to work on the farm. I couldn't imagine that the newer house would stand the test of time like the old stone homestead. It looked quite forlorn; there was little greenery to be seen apart from a few straggly westringias and acacia bushes nearby. Dust blew across the paddocks and swirled around the sides of the house.

An older model white Toyota Hilux was parked next to the house. A truck and other equipment in the shed near the house reminded me that this was a working property, perhaps carrying sheep or cattle. A black-and-white border collie greeted me with a couple of excited barks, running around the car in wide circles. I cautiously slowed down, hesitating for a few seconds before I got out of the car. I noticed the front door open and someone was quickly making their way across the yard.

I knew I was taking a risk rolling up at a stranger's house and expecting them to talk to me about their personal issues. I hoped I wouldn't regret my decision.

'What can I do for you?'

I instantly recognised him. It was Connor Edwards, the man who assaulted Tim Grant. There was a menacing air about him, and I was wary as I stepped forward.

'Oh hello, my name is Sarah Wills, journalist from *The New Times*. I was at the march yesterday and saw what happened. I wondered if you would be happy to talk to me about some of the issues that you raised with Tim Grant.'

Connor Edwards face darkened, his mood rapidly reflecting indignation; the same distinctly set face I remembered from the rally. He started to repeat the words he called out at the protest march.

'I've had enough of corrupt politicians and unscrupulous people, some of whom live in this district. Even if I go to prison I am going to fight for my rights - I'm out on bail, you know and I face court next month.'

Strangely, I didn't feel threatened by Connor Edwards. I sensed the same air of sadness, perhaps even resignation, that I picked up yesterday.

'How do feel about having a chat about what's been happening, Connor? Would you be interested in talking to me?'

He hesitated, appearing unsure about whether he wanted

to allow me to stay.

A second person was walking over to join us. I stepped forward and introduced myself; this was Connor's wife, Jane. It turned out to be an icebreaker; Jane was quite open to my visiting the property without prior notice.

Connor lit a cigarette and started to pace the driveway whilst I talked to Jane.

'Would you like to come inside and I'll make a cuppa?' Jane had a calm presence about her. She had not attended the march, but obviously wanted to voice her opinion on the matter.

We entered the house. Everything appeared neat and clean, although it was obvious little money has been spent on furnishings, the lounge looked comfortable and inviting. A fan whirred back and forth, providing some small relief from the unrelenting heat. Jane put the kettle on and invited me to take a seat. Connor busied himself getting milk from the fridge and arranging cups.

A faded wedding photo sat on the sideboard. I peered more closely. There was Jane as the pretty bride, and a much younger version of Connor holding her hand, smiling happily. Their two children featured in several other frames. Jane explained Marcus and Cindy had grown up and moved to the city years ago.

'We really miss them, but we do get down to the city every few months to see them. There wasn't enough income from the farm for the children to want to stay and help. We're happy though, because they have good jobs and have built their own lives now.'

As we sat down together, I became acutely aware of the need to be sensitive in what questions I posed and how I gathered information.

If what the people in town said was true, this was a family who had been having a really tough time, and it was obvious they were still suffering ongoing stress from the pressure that they have been put under.

Jane presented as the more trusting of the two. I sensed she may have decided that by talking to the media, people would gain a better insight into what had been happening to them, and even that some sense of justice might eventually prevail. I wanted to help their plight, not hinder it, but I knew their version of what had happened could have a negative impact on them as well. On the other side of that coin, this story should be told. The public had a right to know things like this really do happen out here in the bush.

Jane watched in some concern as Connor casually popped a pill with his cuppa. 'Blood pressure tablets,' he explained. 'The doctor said I have to stay on these for now, due to the stress I've been under over the past year.'

Jane grew quiet, taking a back seat to allow Connor to tell me his account of events.

He continued, talking now without hesitation. 'Well I guess you're wondering about the property. It belonged to my parents. Beyond Yonder has been in the family for almost fifty years.

'Over time the property has carried both sheep and cattle. I've been able to run the property successfully since my parents passed away some years ago, but sadly, in the last four years there have been multiple issues to deal with.

The drought affected many landowners in this district. Some forced to sell stock earlier than they would normally have, while others won't be able to restock. We've had people knocking on our door wanting us to sell up.'

I listened intently as Connor's voice suddenly became strangely quiet, each word spoken more deliberately, the conversation obviously spoken with careful consideration.

'There are rumours circulating around town about associates of John McCallum and his son Tom buying up small properties in the district with support from Tim Grant, he happens to be a friend of the family. A neighbour of ours has already sold his property to John McCallum and an unknown business associate after packing up overnight and moving to the city with his family.'

Connor told me he'd heard this small talk which could be just a bit of gossip at the local pub.

'Well, some are saying there's a lot of shonky stuff goin'

on out there at Mirna Springs Station.'

That pricked my interest. 'What sort of shonky things?'

Connor wouldn't elaborate further, and when I pushed for information, he declined to give it, saying decisively, 'I only want printed the truth about what is happening if that's okay with you. Some of this stuff could just be hearsay.'

'Fair enough,' I replied. 'I'm all for reporting the truth on matters as well.'

This was a true statement. I hated "gutter snipe" journalism, where an exaggeration of the truth or even total lies and sensationalism not only give the reader the wrong impression, but it also makes the journalist and the organisation that they represent appear untrustworthy.

Jane told me Tim Grant recently announced he had made a deal with a mining company, as part of that deal they would have direct access to local water. The only source of water in the area was a river running directly past Connor's property. The family had been using the river for generations to water their stock. Connor and Jane had been informed this water would no longer be available once the company started mining. When they advised John McCallum's agent they would not be selling, they were told they might "regret it". Not long after, Connor started receiving anonymous death threats. He had heard vehicles on his property during the night, and one morning found a horse shot through the head.

The few head of cattle he kept were stolen about three months ago. Police were involved but to date, no suspects were ever identified.

'Put it this way - nobody seems to be able to get to the bottom of the death threats and stealing stock, but I have a pretty good idea who's behind some of this shady stuff.'

'Are you prepared to name anyone at this stage?'

'No, not until I've got substantial proof, but I'm working on that. The other issue that's still facing some of us out here is who would you normally go to in a situation like this, apart from the police? Yep, the local MP - which in this case would be pointless because of the connection Grant had with both the mining company and the McCallum family.'

I didn't tell them I was leaving for the McCallum's property today and would be staying there until next Monday. In retrospect, if I had, they may not have shared their personal information so readily. Maybe they would have warned me to be careful.

I was ready to leave. I reassured them both I would keep them updated on any news. Similarly, Connor said he would let me know if there were any significant developments. Passing my business card to Jane through the car window, I thanked them both, reassuring them I would stay in touch.

They didn't have much, they were in dire straits

financially, and faced the very real prospect of losing their farm. Yet they made me feel welcome and shared their incredible story with a stranger.

43

Chapter Three

The heat was stifling. I set off on the road again, knowing this final leg of the trip would take about two hours. The first few kilometres newly laid bitumen, then dirt the rest of the way. The dusty old road looked as though it hadn't been graded for months. It paid to stay alert in order to dodge the large potholes and manoeuvre through dry creek beds where small but razor sharp rocks could easily puncture a tyre if hit hard enough.

It reminded me that this country still had many very primitive access roads, some not much more than rough bush tracks. The creeks showed signs of previous floods; trees that had been uprooted during a wet season were washed further downstream, lodging high in the branches of another tree, waiting until the next major flood. That's the legacy of the outback. Years of drought replaced overnight by life-giving rains, resulting in swathes of wildflowers and native grasses covering the plains.

I stopped and checked my GPS, making sure I was still on the right track. Minutes later, a stroke of luck - I spotted a mobile phone tower perched high up on one of the bigger hills near where I would be staying. It looked like a new addition to the landscape, a narrow, newly graded road led up to the side of the tower. My phone would be my lifeblood, a necessity to keep in touch with my family and of course Callie, who was always looking for regular updates.

Suddenly before my eyes, a vision of the missing man, Chad Dimitri. I clearly recalled his face from the image on the poster at Dillalong. The police said he disappeared on the way to Mirna Springs Station. I wondered if he, too, travelled along this road. What really happened to Chad Dimitri?

Despite the drought, the land remained as beautiful and mysterious as ever. Deep gorges and creeks wove throughout the property. These ranges were home to the rare Yellow-footed Rock-wallaby, and emus wandered slowly, small stripy chicks in tow, still plentiful on the open plains.

The early settlers knew little about weather patterns and the harshness of the Australian bush. Properties were overstocked with sheep and cattle, often leading to the demise of thousands during droughts. Over time, many properties were abandoned. Only the hardiest and more astute pastoralists were able to survive this land. The family on Mirna Springs appeared to be a classic illustration of long-term resilience.

Painted in glossy black paint, the sign on the gate announced I had almost reached my destination. Mirna Springs Station.

By the look of it, the ancient wooden sign had been touched up with fresh paint numerous times, the thick paint now cracked and peeling. Underneath another newer looking sign in bright yellow and black letters.

WARNING! Private Property.

If found on the property without permission you will be prosecuted.

A third sign, smaller and rustier, simply said, 'Shut the Bloody Gate.'

Once out of the car, I struggled with the catch on the gate. The barbed wire - which felt like an ominous warning - was difficult to manoeuvre without sustaining a cut to the fingers or hands. Eventually I pulled it up, the gate squeaking loudly as it swung backwards.

The top-heavy four-wheel drive swayed uneasily as I passed over not one, but several cattle grids. I drove through a wide valley, noticing in the far distance a wide hill with the dominant outline of a building set on the very top. Mirna Springs Station homestead.

According to local records, Mirna Springs Station had been owned and operated by the McCallum family for a hundred and twenty years. In its heyday, Mirna Springs carried over two thousand head of cattle. Old Edward McCallum and his father before him built up quite a dynasty through hard work and sheer determination; they were the pioneer graziers who made history in this unforgiving country. The generations who have followed can only look back and reflect on those achievements and give thanks for the prosperity that they now enjoyed in this beautiful country.

But times still remained consistently tough. Regular droughts, fluctuating beef prices and increased wages meant it was harder to find people who were able, or willing, to run a successful enterprise like Mirna Springs.

The current owners, John McCallum and his son Tom, ran a smaller operation. It was my job to find out if they were succeeding, and how. My story would go into the paper's Financial and Business section; the assistant editor owned a rural landholding himself and was keen to run the story of a successful outback business that was surviving despite the odds.

Not much had been documented about the station hands, including the Aboriginal stockmen, who worked on these stations. But it is known that Aboriginal stockmen were generally paid a smaller wage - if any - in comparison to their fellow white stockmen.

These Aboriginal stockmen were often the backbone of a cattle operation, knowing the lay of the land better than most simply because it was their land before the white man came. I was curious to know whether these 'new' owners were giving their workers a fair go.

It was late afternoon when I pulled up outside the homestead. I paused to look across the surrounding area. The sun was setting over the ranges that loomed in the distance, the air was still and warm. The homestead bathed in golden light, deep shadows creased the land where the surrounding gums grew. The road led directly to the front of the homestead. A track wound down to the cattle yards below, while to the left, another road snaked its way through the gorges. An earlier Google search showed me that this was a very old track, perhaps made when the station began a hundred and twenty years ago. The Old Mine Road.

The homestead itself was typical of those I had seen many times before, an Australian version of an Edwardian style, perhaps completed at the turn of the century. The cream and red brick exterior was embellished with wood detailing around the doorway and a very tall chimney on one side. To add to the charm, ornate stained-glass windows were set on either side of the front door. A wide veranda skirted the house, white wicker chairs and matching table set near the front door. Despite the drought, rose bushes and a few straggly flowers grew near the front iron gate and along the slate stone path to the house.

The whole household had turned out to greet me. I introduced myself and received a welcome handshake from John McCallum and his son Tom. The housekeeper, whom I later found out was John McCallum's stepsister Ronda McCallum, a thin middle-aged woman with a seemingly permanent frown. The housekeeper announced she would serve afternoon tea for everyone as we made our way inside.

An elderly Aboriginal lady had stood back from the group, and I couldn't help but notice the shy smile she gave me. I later discovered this was May, who had been working for the McCallum family for many years. She was the cook, and had lived with the family since she was a young woman. Also in the mix that day I noticed several station hands, all young men who had probably gained employment after leaving school and were responsible for helping run the cattle station.

I had gotten off on the right foot with the family, or so it seemed. I was ushered through the old hallway to my room by May, who told me I could use the bathroom in the hallway, and that dinner would be served in the dining room at six each night.

I put my bag down in my room and looked around. In keeping with the appeal of the house, the bedroom had an enchanting aura; pale yellow plaster ceiling featuring ornate decorative roses, timber cornices and skirting boards - a standard finish for many houses from this era. A French door that led out to the veranda could be a later addition, judging by the different timber around the door frame. Peering outside, I could see for miles, beyond the property and out to the distant ranges that stretched across the horizon.

I carefully placed most of my clothing in the lined drawers of an old hand - carved dresser, which, by the look of the ancient wood, may have been brought over by the original settlers. I could smell the faint soft fragrance of cedar oil, and had a feeling the room had been recently cleaned in readiness for my visit.

At dinner that evening I was seated between John and Tom McCallum. The three of us were served the evening meal perched at the very end of a beautifully preserved polished oak table. The grand old table was obviously created to suit a large family as well as perhaps entertaining a considerable number of visitors. There would have been a demand for tables such as this one back when it was built; now it seemed almost comical to contemplate these two men taking their evening meal at this gigantic table each night.

While we were being served, I had a chance to really observe my hosts. The senior McCallum had quite rugged features, looking not dissimilar to his ancestor, old Edward McCallum, whose photograph was part of a collection of family members hanging high in gilt frames on the dining room wall. Gaunt features with a jutting chin, pale blue eyes and near-bald palate. Tom, probably thirty years younger than his father, shorter and a lot heavier in build, but the same shade of pale blue eyes and balding palate. A noticeable similarity between father and son.

We started the usual chitchat about how dry the season had been and how my journey went.

'So how was the trip out here? Did you have any trouble getting through that rough area near the last creek?'

'Well, I must admit I took it really slow, it's a bit of a dust bowl in places.'

'Yes, well, it's about time the bloody council got their act together and graded the roads again. Drought or no drought, we still need to have decent roads to get from A to B out here.'

I found conversing with Tom McCallum nothing short of difficult. He appeared to be making an effort to be present; probably instructed by his father to be hospitable to the 'journo from the city.'

'So Tom, I'm guessing you've lived out on the station for most of your life? Did you travel to Dillalong for your schooling? I guess School of Air would have been another popular option out here?'

'No, neither,' Tom replied gruffly. 'I was sent away to school and returned when I was sixteen.' He aimed a sideways scowl in his father's direction.

'Well it did benefit you in the long run, you've learned enough about maths to run the station accounts now,' laughed his father.

The younger McCallum appeared uncomfortable with the dinner arrangement. Right from the word go, this man did not want to make direct eye contact with either myself or his father, and steered well clear of engaging in friendly dinner table conversation.

We were served our meal by the equally sullen housekeeper Ronda McCallum, who appeared nervous and edgy. I wondered if she was flustered because a guest was present, or was it because she was worried her employer had high expectations of her. Or perhaps there was some entirely different reason for her anxious behaviour.

It was also disconcerting that father and son didn't appear to have a friendly relationship. I commented on the stunning oil painting set opposite the dining room table; I wondered if perhaps the artist had stayed for some time on Mirna Springs during the completion of this intricate work. John McCallum looked up from his evening meal, looked briefly at the painting, and said it was completed in 1938 by well-known landscape artist Hans Heysen. The painting took on a life of its own: a gleaming black buckboard placed strategically in front of the homestead, a grand gentleman seated at the wheel – probably McCallum's grandfather, who commissioned the painting. I gazed at the details; it was as though time was suspended in this masterpiece. Even from where I sat I could see the fine, soft paint strokes of the maestro, enduring through the ages.

The younger McCallum had stopped eating, and focused on the precious work of art, unexpectantly cut through our conversation.

'Why don't you sell that damned painting, we could do with the extra cash right now.'

There was a brief few seconds of awkward silence before John McCallum responded to the sudden demand. After briefly glancing in my direction, he said in a low tone, 'Tom, we'll talk about this later, not now, okay?'

Tom McCallum shook his knife in the direction of his father. A threat? His father put his hand up in a silent signal to his son. There was a palpable tension in the air that lasted several seconds. The knife was lowered.

It was on that first night, as a newly arrived visitor, that I became acutely aware of the aggressive behaviour and excessive demands Tom McCallum constantly made of his father and others around him. This weird outburst in the midst of dinner was unsettling, but I remembered I was a stranger in this house. Who was I to judge these people and what I thought to be their communication shortfalls? But then the second unsettling event happened, only minutes after the first.

Atop the most beautifully ornate sideboard that I had ever seen, looking to have been carved from the same rich wood as the dining table, was a modern touch - a large television, which looked out of place in this setting. The television was obviously switched on each night while the father and son -

and any guests that happened to be present - were dining.

The evening news began, and we ate and chatted while catching up on the news. As Ronda was serving us dessert, a breaking news announcement appeared. It was in reference to a protest that occurred in the local township of Dillalong. The story immediately grabbed our attention.

My footage of the incident in town yesterday had been expertly edited and I was feeling quietly enthralled with my story. I assumed the footage had gone to air after negotiations with the national television channel by the owners of the newspaper that I worked for. The speed in which this footage and reporting was edited, put together and broadcast on national television surprised even me!

Captured by the scene on the screen I put down my spoon, seeing once again the crowd gathered in the town, including Connor and the violent struggle that occurred near the end. Reality struck sense into me as my concentration was shattered by a violent jolt forward by John McCallum, who had banged his fist hard on the large table when he heard his name on the news. A crimson tinge spread rapidly across the elder McCallum's face and neck, a nervous tick involuntarily pulsing above the right eye.

Luckily, they did not see a connection between the news story and me. Not yet, anyway. They were too busy identifying some of the locals who attended the rally.

The earlier wrangle involving the Hans Heysen painting long forgotten, John McCallum angrily addressed his son.

'I'm going to get to the bottom of this scandal, I will find out who's behind this rally and when I do, they'll be sorry. Some of these people think that they can get away with whatever they please. It's time they were put in their place.'

No signs of wrongdoing or self-reflection on his part at all, just a strong need for reprisal. Perhaps the McCallums had been unfairly targeted as the culprits of some of the underhand deeds in the local area after all.

Tom McCallum didn't appear daunted by the outburst and gave a small grunt of agreement before he stood and headed out of the dining room without bidding anyone goodnight.

I decided it was important to finish dinner while presenting a level of composure and acting as normal as possible.

Later, I experienced a surprisingly strong sense of guilt. As a guest staying with this family, it was my reporting to the media that had ultimately angered them. I pondered my role as a journalist from many angles. On the one hand, the story may have been picked up by anyone present on the day, but it just so happened I was in the street and witnessed the protest firsthand. In the end, I chose to draw on one of the so called "ethical philosophies", maintaining truth telling as an important moral aspect. I also realised this story could give me some leverage for the interview I had planned with John McCallum the next day, though pushing this line with no background information could prove to be a very contentious move.

After dinner I was shown some family photographs collected over the years; some had pride of place above the mantelpiece, others on the walls in the dining room and sitting room. I noticed a photograph of a very beautiful young woman dressed in a long gown and was intrigued.

'Who is this young woman, John, is she a relative of yours?'

John McCallum gazed out the window.

'Well, that's actually Tom's mother, Alice McCallum. She hasn't lived on the property for almost twenty years. She decided station life was not for her and moved to the city to further her own career.'

He voice had an air of bitterness as he retold the story about his estranged wife and the mother of Tom.

'I insisted she leave Tom here and as that was my only demand, she agreed. To this day, we haven't seen sight nor sign of her. She's never even bothered to write or give us the occasional call.'

It sounded as though the relationship with Alice McCallum showed little hope of reconciliation - at least, not in the near future. Perhaps they both were happy to leave it that way. There seemed to be no love lost in that direction, at least from John McCallum's point of view.

I was handed a well-preserved sepia photograph of an elderly man and woman. Judging by the style of dress the photograph must have been well over one hundred years old. He proudly told me this was his great-grandfather Thomas McCallum and his first wife Anna. Thomas lost Anna during the birth of their first child, but he later remarried and fathered eight children.

The McCallums immigrated from northern England and, after looking around in the eastern states, decided to settle in South Australia. With eight children, there would no doubt be many descendants living throughout Australia.

John went on to tell me that life was harsh for the new settlers, each family having to locate a steady source of water and find enough food to feed their very often large families. Women gave birth at home, far away from any medical help, and it was not uncommon for women to die in childbirth. This was the fate of Anna McCallum, who was buried on Mirna Springs along with many other family members.

Medical assistance was usually far away, and it could take days by horse and cart to get to the nearest help. Many children fell victim to diphtheria, scarlet fever and other maladies, for which there were no effective treatments.

I learned Thomas McCallum enlisted the assistance of a local builder by the name of Charles Stuart who, like many others before him, had immigrated from England in search of a new life. Plans were drawn up for the homestead that were very grand for the time. While staking out the land, the McCallums lived in simple canvas tents and later, a pug and pine hut was built for the family on the very hill where the current homestead now stands. Pug and pine homes being a unique piece of South Australia's architectural history.

History tells us that during this period of colonial rule, the settlers fought with the local Aboriginal people who had lived on their land for thousands of years. Many were imprisoned, murdered or had their children sent away, much of their traditions, languages and culture were destroyed. This dark shadow in our history still looms large for many. I was interested to pursue this with the family, wondering if they had ongoing contact with some of the local people over time, and if so, what had transpired.

I queried John and was surprised to learn about some of the earlier family members and their working relationships with some of the local people.

'Old Thomas had a soft spot for May's grandfather, Henry, who was the number one stockman here for many years. Henry worked well into his sixties before he finally went back home to his own country. Those two had a special friendship; old Thomas always sought Henry's advice with respect to various aspects of the cattle business. When Henry died the McCallum family paid for a granite headstone for him.'

This sounded like it could have been a rare and quite genuine mutual friendship. I asked to see photographs of Thomas and, if there were any, of Henry. John McCallum promised he would look through the old memorabilia and albums in storage, he had a vague memory of seeing such a picture as a child.

Back in my room, now my haven, I reflected on a most eventful day, much of it totally unexpected. I had started to gain valuable insight into everyday life out here; but there was so much more to find out over the coming days. My information gathering had started the ball rolling, I decided tonight I wouldn't work on the laptop. Just get a good night's sleep to be ready for an early start next morning.

Chapter Four

At the back of the homestead, old May was hanging the washing out on a primitive clothes line that stretched almost halfway across the homestead. Bent and crooked wires, leaning down at a precarious angle were held up by a handful of aged pine logs that had been warped and buckled by the weather over time. Could this ancient relic really be the original line? If so, it had done well to survive through the generations of living.

The warm breeze fluttered through May's snow-white fairy floss hair and sent small shimmers through her bright floral dress. I approached her slowly, being careful not to startle her.

'Good morning, May, would you like me to help you with the washing?'

'Why yes, my girl, if you like.' She gave a little giggle.

She had considerable trouble bending down to the wash basket.

I handed her the washing and she slowly pegged each item.

'So May, where did you grow up? Around here?'

'Yes, my girl, I was born on country, I've lived on these

lands all my life. My people, they live way over yonder, that's our community. Sometimes I go there, see everyone, they say May, you are one of the elders now, when are you gonna come back and stay with us for good?' She let out another chuckle.

May had a wistful look on her face when she described her younger days. She told how, when she worked for the 'old McCallums' she would walk from the homestead back to her mob, who often camped by the huge creek; the ancient watercourse that was formed many thousands of years ago, weaving its way through hundreds of kilometres of rugged terrain. The same creek that, for as long as anyone can remember, has been the lifeblood to humans, animals and other creatures that knew of its existence. In times of drought, May's family knew - just like the kangaroos and emus - to dig deep in the creek bed to find the precious water.

But that was a long time ago. These days some of May's family still live on country in the local community, but they drive into the big town for stores, relying less on their hunting skills and the old ways. May said sometimes she feels sad for her people; however she still has much hope for the future and the generations that will come after her.

Afterwards, May invited me into the kitchen, asking, 'Would you like to help me? Today we make fruit scones for the men working in the stockyards.'

I gladly hung around to give a helping hand. We shared a comfortable connection. There were some humorous moments, especially when May asked me to, 'Roll out the dough, my girl Sarah.' Somehow, there was more flour through my hair and on my face than on the benchtop. May laughed along with me. That morning, as I discovered the warmth and generosity of this elderly lady, I decided that even if I didn't succeed in my quest to write the perfect story, I would remember this moment in time long after I had left Mirna Springs.

As she worked the dough, May recalled how she learned from her mother about what food was edible in the bush, and how to prepare the food they gathered. She described how her people had been making damper for thousands of years.

'My people would collect the native seed, always learning from the old people what plants we could harvest in every season. We crushed the seeds, made dough and baked it in the coals of fire.'

'Ah, May now I know why you are such an expert in the kitchen,' I said with a big grin.

Up this way, the native acacia, or wattle tree, has been an important source of food. Growing up, May had observed that when the seeds are ready to be harvested, they are placed on rocks and beaten with sticks to get the precious seeds out. May said that some of her people still made damper the traditional way, but when the settlers introduced white flour to her people, they had foregone some of the old ways of making damper. Unfortunately, this had led to many health problems.

Much later we sat in the garden, on a well-worn wrought iron and wood garden seat placed under the shade of a spindly gum tree. I carried the wooden tray out into the garden; on it sat an oversized, very chipped brown enamel teapot. It reminded me of the teapot my grandmother used back when we were small children. May and I quietly shared a cup of tea with scones and jam while the elusive homestead cat sat watching us from the corner of the house, her large green eyes checking for any tasty crumbs that fell on the ground.

May's old hands were wrinkled and calloused through years of hard work; her gold wedding ring was worn down to little more than a thin wire. As she smoothed her floral dress and relaxed back into the seat with a deep sigh, she appeared glad to have some company – and the rest.

I got the impression she didn't get many opportunities to just sit and relax, she was too busy cooking and cleaning for the McCallums. I also sensed May had enjoyed talking to me about her life, her family, and her history, and I felt privileged to be able to sit and hear her personal story.

There was a sense of presence about May that to this day is still hard to describe. Her beautiful weathered face creased with deep wrinkles whenever she smiled, and I sensed the wisdom in those dark eyes. I recognised then that I was looking at someone who could have lived for a thousand years; her very existence was bound to this country, and she could trace her ancestors, who also lived on this land, back through the centuries.

May spoke with pride about her late husband Willy, who she met as a very young girl. Willy was a great hunter in his time. May and Willy's three children moved into the bigger towns for work and are now married with children of their own. May was overjoyed when her grandchildren started to arrive. There were now six, and another one on the way. May wanted to see her family soon; she missed them. I wondered if there was an important link between May choosing to stay on for so long, and her grandfather's relationship with Thomas McCallum. Surely May could go home of her own free will? She hadn't said she *has* to stay here. She did say she will want to go home one day, and then she would not return to this place.

'Soon my time will come, then I go home for good.' May spoke softly, and I listened, feeling both happy and sad for her at the same time.

I asked gently, 'May, when will that time come?' It was then she helped me understand why she was still working at the station.

She spoke in a more solemn tone, glancing down in the direction of the cattle yards, almost as though she could see her grandson from where we sat. 'My eldest grandson Joe, he works here you know. I stay to make sure he's gonna be alright.' She added quickly, 'I want to make sure nothing happens to my grandson now.'

The next question I thought to ask could well have been answered as Tom McCallum marched past, heading in the direction of the windmill, obviously with some pressing purpose in mind.

May spoke in a hushed tone. 'Watch out for this man, he's a bad one.'

I found May's disclosure quite unsettling, and contradictory in some sense. She obviously had good memories of her past employer - it was clear from her conversations about the family that her favourite McCallum had been old Edward, who passed away some twenty years ago. But she clearly didn't trust the youngest McCallum.

May revealed she had wanted to go home years ago, but old Edward had begged her to stay on and help with the domestic tasks, telling her she was the most loyal, hardest worker on the property. Apparently old Edward ensured May had her own room and was always treated with respect by the station hands and other domestic staff. Based on what I had already witnessed, I wondered about how the current McCallums treated their staff.

Afterwards, I sat in my room and contemplated the conversation I had with May, especially the warning, whispered in hushed tones, about her employer. What has she seen or heard that might make her feel compelled to tell me, a complete stranger, this information?

I certainly had experienced those inner warning bells when communicating with the younger McCallum, which fortunately didn't seem to be often. If it were possible for someone to radiate a message that they were not to be messed with, it certainly was this man. Still, I was only staying for a few short days, and I intended to get as much information as I could about this enterprise and make the story mine.

We organised an interview for that afternoon. I was to use a pad and pen to take notes; John didn't want to be taped during our conversation.

At the arranged time, Ronda ushered me into a private lounge area where more old family photographs covered the walls. These were of great interest to me, and I planned to ask about them if given the opportunity. One of them was of Thomas McCallum and Henry standing next to a horse-drawn buggy, with Henry holding the reins. Old McCallum looked as though he was about to leap on board. I took a photo of it; I wanted to include this historical image in my story about the family.

John McCallum arrived. We observed all the pleasantries, sipping tea from fine bone china cups and munching on homemade cake while we made small talk. He was a tall man,

I guessed he was probably about sixty years old. With large muscular arms and weather-beaten hands covered in deep scars from past mishaps, his presence dominated the room, and he seemed out of place holding a delicate cup and saucer in place. His forbidding presence alone told me he would not be a person you could argue with. Just like his son Tom, his word was the law out here.

He ended the small talk abruptly. 'Well, where do you want to start? Have you thought about what you would like to ask me today?'

'Well yes, I do have some questions ready, we can start right now if you like. Are you happy for me to go through the questions one by one?' The answer didn't surprise me.

'Well, yes and no. If the questions are suitable, then I will answer them, if not, we will move onto the next question, okay?' Right from the beginning, John McCallum led the conversation. This was definitely a man who was used to being listened to, and giving the orders. Over the next twenty minutes or so, the interview progressed to a point that might be described as distinctly uncomfortable - probably more for the man sitting before me, but I also felt some awkwardness. Apparently some of the questions I posed were not the sort of questions McCallum appreciated having to find an answer to. In particular, around the subject of the political rally and the protests against Tim Grant a few days earlier.

'So John, what was your take on the rally in Dillalong the

other day? Did it come as a surprise that you were named by someone in the crowd, or was this something that you expected?'

He drummed his fingers on the armchair, hesitating then for a few seconds as though contemplating that next comment.

'I'm not interested in what someone in town has to say about me. My father lived and worked this station as his father's father did before him. This land has been in our family for well over one hundred years.' He moved forward on his chair, his huge body emphasising the intensity in which he spoke. 'We have faced drought, the loss of our stock, recession, and at times been driven by necessity just to survive, disasters anyone who doesn't live in this part of the country would ever understand or care about.'

I nodded my head in quiet agreement as I continued to jot down notes. I asked what the family would particularly like readers to understand about the family operation at Mirna Springs Station.

'What I'd like readers who pick up the paper and read your article to know is that we do it tough in the bush. However, we'll never give up on this land and our livelihoods. Cattle farming has been in our family's blood for generation after generation, and we intend to persevere and continue to do what we do best.'

Some questions I posed during the long interview were

ignored; others just received a quick 'yes' or 'no' in response.

I asked a direct question. 'John, can you tell me how the station is surviving, with the current drought and other impacting factors? Judging by what Tom said yesterday about the need to sell your painting, I wondered if you are facing some financial difficulty.'

This question didn't go down well. He didn't answer straight away; he looked challenged about what he thought I might put down on paper.

Laughing uneasily, he eventually spoke, but with a lot less confidence. 'Well, we have survived droughts in the past and we will survive this one. Can I just say though, that you people think you can write whatever suits, am I right there?' He didn't wait for an answer.

'The main reason I agreed to allow you to come out here was to show people we really are running a legitimate cattle station, just going about our business like all of the landowners around us. Our money is in the cattle, and drought or no drought, we need to get them to market in good condition. That's when we make our dollars.'

I continued to write my notes, other questions burning through my mind. Why do you feel the need to constantly justify yourself? What are you inferring by telling me you are running a legitimate business? Of course, for fear of a complete shutdown of the interview, I didn't pose those questions.

Much of the information I required for the feature would be gained when Tom took me on a guided tour to meet the stockmen and find out more about the cattle run and the inner workings of the station.

Nearing the end of the interview, I broached the subject of the missing tourist, who had supposedly been travelling to the station.

John McCallum was abrupt. 'Look, I've already been through an interview with the police and I don't want to discuss the matter further. This has nothing to do with why you are here, you need to stick with what you are supposed to be writing about.'

It occurred to me that the television news report could have set something off with John. I wondered what inner demons he was grappling with. Perhaps he was worried about his reputation and deeply resented the fact that he had been personally named in the national news item. Finally, I broached the delicate question regarding the rumours relating to the family and unknown cohorts buying up other smaller operators. Although his barely controlled anger was now clearly evident, during these last few minutes I caught a flicker of ... what? Hesitation? Uncertainty? I guessed there was more to this account than McCallum wanted to reveal, especially when he terminated the interview by standing up and saying, 'Where do you people hear such wild talk? Some of your questions are totally immaterial to the article you are saying you are going to write. I think we've talked enough for today. Tom will make the necessary arrangements for you to go on the tour of the cattle yards to complete the remainder of your story.'

There was to be no more small talk. John strutted out into the kitchen. I could hear him barking orders to the embittered housekeeper - she could now clean up the afternoon tea dishes, and he would not be present for dinner as he was heading into town for business. Even though I had only been a guest in the homestead for a short time, I had noticed that Ronda was tightly controlled and treated with contempt by both father and son. I wondered what motive, if anything, kept this woman from walking out the door and not ever returning. Did she have a vested interest in the property?

I walked back to my room and considered the interview carefully. There was so much that I still wanted to know, but it was doubtful now if I would ever get another opportunity for a further audience with John McCallum. Could it be that these people were actually threatened by my presence? If anything, I felt a bit disappointed the interview ended so abruptly, but I could bide my time. I knew there was a lot more information that I could still potentially gather - but what I didn't know was that I would never have the opportunity to speak to John McCallum again.

Chapter Five

Dinner that night was a strained affair. The senior McCallum had gone into town and wasn't expected back for a few days, so it happened to be just Tom and I. He sat on the same side of the dining table as me, but at the other end - he clearly didn't want to communicate and there was very little eye contact to speak of. He seemed restless and didn't stay long. I couldn't help but notice the furrowed brow, the clenched fists and guarded movements.

I tried in my own way to keep the small talk flowing to ease the tension.

'How has your day been, Tom? Have you been down at the cattle yards all day?'

He answered in grunts, and after gulping down his evening meal he stalked off, having spoken no more than a few words. Even after he left, the atmosphere felt tense, as if he had managed to dial the tension up a notch without even trying.

The housekeeper, Ronda, reappeared to curtly enquire if I would like a tea or coffee after my meal. I asked for a pot of tea so I could drink it at a leisurely pace.

Nobody had bothered to turn on the television in the

dining room that evening, but I felt comfortable just sitting there. I sat in silence, sipping quietly on my tea, contemplating the past twenty-four hours and what I had learned so far about Mirna Springs and the people who lived there.

Later, I heard soft footsteps outside in the hallway; I had the impression I was being watched. Perhaps the housekeeper had been ordered to keep an eye on me.

I recalled the initial welcome I received upon my arrival. The group on the hill included many station workers, who had seemed genuinely happy to meet me. On the other hand, McCallum's initial agreement with the paper and his accepting me as part of the household has clearly been a thinly disguised veneer. I felt like an unwanted guest, a thorn in their sides. I was unsure why I was being treated with such hostility.

I didn't go directly to bed. It had been a long day and I was tired, but I felt a strong urge to write an outline of my interview with Connor and Jane Edwards and forward it to the editor for further discussion. I had a vision of them waving goodbye to me when I left Beyond Yonder. They had placed a lot of trust in me, and I wanted them to feel confident that justice might prevail if their story was eventually revealed to the wider public.

Engrossed in work, it was nearly midnight when I next

looked at my watch. Feeling satisfied with what I had written, I decided to call it a night. As I was preparing to go to bed, I again heard light footsteps this time outside my door. A woman coughed. Someone was definitely listening …

Early morning brought a slight breeze from the north, but it fizzled out quickly. The day was going to be hellishly hot again. I tied my hair up in a ponytail and plonked on my hat. A sort of discovery tour of the homestead was planned, and I was looking forward to what I might find along the way. After breakfast I amused myself by wandering around the homestead and taking photos of the house and garden.

Propped against the wire screen on the windowsill was an ancient old radio, complete with silver shutter and large brown dials. I could hear Troy Cassar Daley's *Take a Walk in My Country* belting out across the still morning air.

I was fascinated by the old laundry behind the homestead, connected to the veranda by flagstone steps. The ancient cement floor looked as though it was part of the original building; huge cracks lined the floor, large chunks missing near the doorway where thousands of footsteps would have crossed back and forth over the years. The building had retained its original cladding of corrugated tin, now rusting through in places. Timber slats, possibly made from the native pine growing in the nearby gorges, had been installed as window openings in the walls to let cool air in on hot days.

Out in the yard I could see an old, abandoned copper, the common method of cleaning clothes before washing machines, generators and electricity were introduced to the country. As I took pictures of the homestead and the ancient outbuildings, I imagined the women that were here before May. They must have gathered firewood and placed it under the copper to get the water really hot for wash day.

My grandmother told me that washing for a large family using not much more than soap and a washing board could take a full day, the last items not hung out until nightfall came.

A little further down the hill was an old long-drop dunny. These were the original toilets, built outside of many Australian homes. The walk in the middle of the night when in need would have been a challenge in itself. When Mirna Springs Station modernised the homestead and installed inside toilets, it was no doubt to the relief of everyone who lived there.

Someone had tended the garden over the years, and although there was an acute water shortage I assumed that water supply came from the well sunk near the creek. A few rose bushes grew along the back of the house, while oleander - a hardy shrub from the other side of the world - was planted along the side of the homestead.

I spotted an ancient mulberry tree so large the branches spread out and reached the ground, taking up a large portion of the yard. It was probably brought out to this country as a young sapling by the original McCallum family. Just like the people and animals living out here, the tree had endured good and bad years, always riding the wave of the seasons.

Standing there looking at the old tree I felt some sort of familiarity between the tree and the past generations now long gone, facing all the odds to provide a stable and secure future for those that would come after them.

I could hear the crank and pull of the windmill in the still morning air. I decided to walk down the slope and onto a small track leading directly down to the windmill.

It was then that I almost disturbed Tom standing at the other end of the outhouse, speaking intently to one of his employees. The man had taken on a subservient stance, head down, hat in hand, nodding occasionally. McCallum's voice was raised, but I could only catch a couple of sentences here and there.

'I want this job done today, no mistakes this time or else. Make sure you tell the others what I want done.' He was speaking in a confrontational tone, and I drew closer. The station hand, obviously intimidated by McCallum, set off down the hill to the cattle yards.

It was clear Tom McCallum's word was law around here, and I guessed the station hand would answer to McCallum if orders weren't carried out to his satisfaction. Tom stormed off in the opposite direction - he didn't appear to have noticed my presence, or if he did, he chose to ignore me, with no regrets about me overhearing part of the conversation. I continued exploring the homestead's grounds - after all, I had been told that this area was not off limits to me. Just up ahead, in amongst the dried grass, a small white picket fence. I wandered down, surprised to find a cemetery overlooking the creek. Whoever chose this as a final resting place for their loved ones must have appreciated the view from here; the ranges loomed high above the gum-lined creek, a beautiful backdrop to the cemetery settled into the side of the hill.

A forceful push finally opened the small wrought iron gate that was rested hard against a pile of dead weeds and debris. By the look of some of the headstones, broken and writing faded, these graves were very old. Of note, the grave of Anna McCallum, dearly loved wife of Thomas McCallum, died July 23rd, 1893. Underneath was an inscription, which was difficult to read: "The Lord shall look kindly on thee." Next to this headstone was the infant son, George Thomas McCallum, died July 23rd, 1893. The inscription read: "Born with eyes closed and taken into care by the Angels." I assumed that this inscription referred to the baby being stillborn. I decided to ask John McCallum more about the history of his family when I next saw him.

Well into the distance past the cattle yards, a road veered off from the main entrance to the sheds and outbuildings and seemed to disappear into the nearby gorge. Old Mine Road, I was curious to know what was at the end of it.

Later that afternoon, standing near the kitchen window I could almost taste the sweet, yeasty aroma of baked bread wafting through the still air. May had been busily baking for some time and she waved me inside the kitchen.

Out of curiosity I asked her a few questions about the Old Mine Road.

Appearing a little perturbed, she shook her head from side to side.

'We don't go down that road, some bad people might go that way, that's the wrong way to go my girl, you know?'

I got the impression that this was the only information I would get from her, but I sensed that May knew much more than she was able - or willing - to tell me. I changed the subject.

Later, we brought the washing in and talked about May's family and her country. I was intrigued to hear her stories from the old days, how this strong young woman would walk many miles back to her community to see family.

As she spoke, she knelt in the dirt, her bony old hands waving this way and that. In what I now see as an indelible moment in time, I knelt down with May and watched her draw a map with a stick in the dirt.

'See the hill over that way,' May paused to point the stick westwards through the endless blue sky to the range past the homestead and beyond the creek.

She swept the area with her arm and spoke with pride. 'Yeah, that's my mother's country. To get to this community maybe four or five days walk, but too dangerous if you don't know this country. Yeah, maybe I'm too old to do this walk anymore, my son has to pick me up and take me home next time,' May chuckled.

Fascinated with her storytelling I said, 'But May, when you walked this land to go home, which way did you go when you left here?'

May indicates the map in the dirt again. 'Well, if you are walking from this place, this is where you go. I would go down this creek and follow over that way, you are then walking towards this hill right over there.' She drew the distant ranges in the dirt.

'When I see the big rock at the edge of the ranges, this one has a hole right through the other side, you turn there, go down that creek. That's our people's marker rock – a sign, you see? When you get to the range you can go round the other side. Too far to go over the top.' May chortled loudly.

'If I followed your way, where do I go afterwards on this path?'

May looked beyond me to somewhere in the far distance before replying. 'You will make your own path by walking, my girl.' Before I even had to time to absorb this puzzling bit of advice, we were interrupted by Ronda strutting out from the kitchen with a determined look on her face, scolding May to come inside and finish her chores.

'I thought I told you I wanted those extra loaves cooked by tonight.' Glancing my way, Ronda swished her apron, looked down her long nose and mumbled, 'This is not a garden party, the staff are all responsible for completing their jobs.'

'I see you later,' said May, and gave me a big wink. That was the end of the conversation.

Sinking slowly over the hills, the late afternoon sun continued to carry the intense heat. I spotted the station ute pulling up abruptly at a spot near the road below the homestead. I craned my neck to see who was in the car. It was Tom McCallum, accompanied by someone I hadn't seen on the property before. Tom strutted around to the back of the car and lifted out a rifle. What the hell were they up to so late in the day? I soon found out – beer in hand, they were pointing to the sky. I heard the crack of the rifle as McCallum shot his first victim, a crow that happened to be in the wrong place at the wrong time. Much laughter followed, with the visitor now taking aim at hapless birds flying home to the creek to roost for the night. Later, when they had exhausted the bird supply in the area, they lined up their empty beer cans on the wooden posts and took aim.

The housekeeper must have been observing the goings on and I spotted her, still wearing her checked apron, marching down the hill, displaying more courage than I would have imagined she was capable of. I could see her trying to implore the two to do - what? Stop shooting so near the homestead?

I heard a raised voice. Tom, with a few beers under his belt and fist clenched, was stepping towards Ronda. A menacing movement. I was shocked to see her standing her ground - perhaps she was threatening to tell the senior McCallum when he returned home? The unknown visitor walked towards McCallum and pointed to the car, perhaps appealing to him to walk away.

Engine revving loudly, the vehicle charged forward, sliding uncontrollably through the soft red dirt, round and round in ever tighter circles until I thought they would flip over and the men would pay the ultimate price for their foolhardy actions. Dust swirling up behind it, the ute finally left the homestead road, roaring down the winding track leading to Old Mine Road. Even if I were to ask Ronda, who was now stumbling back up the hill, where these two were headed and what they would be doing, instinct told me that I wouldn't get an answer.

That evening I ate dinner in my room. John McCallum had departed without further notice, still presumably away in town for a couple of days. Tom left instructions with the housekeeper that he would not be dining with me.

Eating alone turned out to be a huge relief. Tom had demonstrated on a number of occasions to be both volatile and unpredictable, which was quite unsettling. Underneath his attitude of thinly veiled contempt, I had picked up an element of aggression. I found this strange. I hardly knew the guy - does he find me a threat?

Then I got to thinking about the strange conversation with May. What was she trying to tell me about Old Mine Road? Could May have imagined 'bad people' used the road, or might this be something that she has actually found out just by being at the station for so long?

If so, who are the "bad people"? Although May would probably not be privy to the McCallum's business activities, maybe she knows more than she is willing to disclose. The winding track they called Old Mine Road stayed in my thoughts, but I realised that right now, checking this track out couldn't be a priority during my short stay. I had to let it go.

That evening I called my parents to let them know I'd arrived safely.

After the normal chit chat about the weather and everyday events, I'd told them the ranges were as beautiful as they remembered, we finally said our goodbyes. 'Yes, dear, we are all okay down here and we miss you. Stay safe, love you too.'

In the past two days, Mum and Jamie had both told me to stay safe. It's a sincere way to wish those we care about all the best, but on reflection I also realised life could be quite fragile, and really there were no guarantees that we *can* stay safe all the time. This led me to thinking about Tom McCallum's hostile disposition, and whether he had always been this unfriendly towards those unlucky enough to have contact with him.

My thoughts quickly turned to more important matters – a follow-up sequel to the Dillalong protest story, and the plight of Connor and Jane Edwards. A summary would focus on issues impacting on people living in the local area. It may grab the interest of the relevant authorities, who had the ability and resources to address current problems.

Like an unbidden shadow, a twinge of anxiety crept into the back of my mind. Would my work be good enough to meet Callie's expectations, not to mention my peers at the office? I cursed my lack of self-confidence and the way I continued to undermine my own good intentions.

In that second my mobile rang. Callie the mind reader, wondering how I was going with both the Mirna Springs story and the follow-up with Connor Edwards and his family. I flicked a copy of my interview with the Edwards family through to Callie and she looked over the notes briefly. Callie was keen to learn how the interview had transpired, especially as Connor Edwards was involved in the very public stoush with Tim Grant. Callie, also the proficient editing wizard, had already skim-read the document as we talked, and requested I expand further on some of the points I had made.

We then moved onto the other topic. Mirna Springs. Callie quizzed my progress and asked about the information I had gathered so far.

'So, Sarah, is it still viable to run the full-page spread on the station next week?'

My nervous tension returned. Was she questioning my ability to meet the deadline? Using all of the enthusiasm I could muster, I concentrated on convincing Callie I was sticking to my original brief.

'Yep, I am confident the article will be ready by the deadline.'

'So it's definitely a goer then? Great, well done, look forward to reading the story soon.'

We discussed my plans to visit the cattle yards next day.

'Make sure you capture the work in the cattle yards with lots of photos,' said Callie. 'And the interview with Tom McCallum will hopefully provide a summary of how the business is being run. That should finish off the story well, I think, yeah.'

I thought it pointless to mention that John McCallum had left the station for a few days and Tom McCallum was one of the most difficult people I had ever had the pleasure to meet. It was all about getting the story in on time at that point, nothing else mattered.

I then gingerly broached the subject of travelling to Yingali Station the following Monday, explaining the new opportunity to Callie, filling her in on the program for youth.

'Where is this place? Is it near the property you are on now?'

I hesitated before answering. Having already checked the map, I now knew where Yingali Station was, over the border in the Northern Territory.

'Er, well, no, it is some distance away, to be honest, I didn't realise how far away it was when it was first proposed to me.'

That sense of doubt again. It was a big ask, wanting Callie to release me for such an extended period of time. Travel to and from the destination involved a long day of driving.

Surprisingly, Callie seemed agreeable to the new proposal, but quick to set out her conditions.

'I want both the stories you are working on now completed and on my desk before you embark on the Yingali Station trip, that sound fair?' Excitement momentarily took over, but I managed to refrain from sounding too eager. 'Yep, sounds like a good proposal to me, thanks Callie.' Once I hung up, my eagerness gauge dropped rapidly as I contemplated the commitment. I would have my work cut out for me preparing both stories by the deadline, which was now only a few short days away.

Chapter Six

Next morning there was a sharp knock on the door at precisely eight o'clock. I had been informed at dinner the night before Tom would collect me for a tour of the station, including the cattle yards. Even before I had fully opened the heavy wooden door, the reek of stale tobacco and body odour announced Tom's presence.

Face deadpan serious, looking not at me but somewhere on the ground in front of me, he said in a matter-of-fact tone, 'Care for a tour of the cattle yards?'

Without further prompting, I quickly grabbed my hat, notebook, pen and camera. I had been looking forward to this day; it would give me a good insight into the real workings of the property.

We climbed into the old Willy's jeep, exhaust spewing blue smoke out through the still morning air as we crawled slowly down the hill.

The atmosphere was prickly, even during that short trip. It was clear that Tom would only be doing just what was required of him - to show me how the business is run. The instruction would have come directly from his father. Any hope of striking a decent conversation with the younger

McCallum was still challenging. I decided to persevere, and after a few moments gathered the courage to ask a direct question.

'So Tom, Old Mine Road leads off down into the gorge - how far does it go? Is there anything of interest down that way?'

Looking very briefly in my direction, I caught a twisted sneer with the abrupt answer.

'Old Mine Road is totally off limits to all visitors, there are sunken wells and mine shafts down there and we don't allow people to go wandering around.'

He lowered his voice and spoke deliberately.

'In fact, it could be very dangerous for anyone going down there.' The warning sounded like a threat. I was taken aback once again by how this man's menacing air seemed to affect those around him, even his own father. My interest was piqued though, not just at the thought of another road leading to who-knows-what and where, but because of the reaction I got. I still hadn't been given an answer to my question.

Minutes later we were at the cattle yards. The day was an important one as far as business operations went. Some of the herd were being rounded up, tagged and separated ready to be sent to market.

As we approached, the yipping of the kelpies and blue heelers cut through the still morning air. It was obviously dangerous work, especially when you are down on their level; a cantankerous bull often wants to have a go at someone or something. I could see them in the distance, charging around amongst the herd, the ringers sounding out commands. The dogs approached the cattle on demand, not impulse. When called back, they obediently cut through the fence and stood by the ringers. The experienced dogs were adept at jumping on the backs of motorbikes and travelling with the ringers to the next job.

McCallum launched into a spiel in an almost robotic tone. He wasn't interested in me asking too many questions of him.

'The first cattle were brought to Australia in 1788, however many of these cattle escaped, but their numbers increased rapidly until cattle farming became a commercial enterprise. Australia, as a collective, runs twenty-eight million cattle across two hundred million hectares.'

We met the leading hand Shaun, who obviously had a pivotal role in the daily management of the station. I quickly picked up an element of mutual respect between the sullen Tom and the stockman. Shaun accompanied us on the rounds. The level of experience among the workers was obvious, as the cattle were expertly chosen, singled out and brought into the yards.

I asked Tom where and when the cattle were taken.

'Most of our cattle are taken to the city markets, that's where we can get the best price,' he said self-assuredly.

'The price for lean beef is at a premium at the moment so we value the cattle that we have out here. But the remoteness of our property and getting it to market is costly.'

This was an important point. No doubt the challenge of getting the cattle all the way down to the bigger cities would take some of the cream off the top of the profits.

He proudly went on with the prepared spiel, 'Australia is one of the largest beef exporters in the world, with most cattle slaughtered and processed within Australia and then exported. The cattle industry is continually researching ways to improve efficiencies in production, and Mirna Springs Station is currently taking part in research linked directly to genetics, pastures and marketing. Our family believes the station is more intensive than our northern counterparts, and our meat is typically sold into high value markets.'

We made our way to a paddock near the cattle yards, and Tom pointed out a herd of about fifty. The cows and their beautiful young calves were curious and moved closer to the fence near where we stood talking, wet noses sniffing the air and tails constantly switching the flies away.

I sought permission to use the camera, taking multiple shots of the cattle, the stockmen and the workers down in the yards. I even snapped a few photos of McCallum himself, although it was near impossible to get a smile from that face. He was one serious character. I wondered what his childhood was like, whether he had any previous trauma in his life that made him the person he is today.

There were about a dozen energetic young stockmen, all wearing the standard ringer outfit, checked shirts, jeans, and battered Akubras. Today's job was singling out and tagging cattle. They worked quickly and skilfully; everyone seemed to know their role.

Shaun filled me in on the current plans. 'These cattle are bound for the market. This decision was made because during drought years we try to sell our cattle at a younger age to preserve what pasture we have left. Due to our limited supply of feed during drought, the supply of grains has become a big issue for our set-up.'

I met Mack Summers, the station pilot. I couldn't help but think he looked a little out of place in this setting: navy blue shorts, crisp white shirt, white socks and sandals, a very new-looking navy cap and, of course, aviator sunglasses. Mack appeared quite the dapper figure out here in the bush.

Despite that first impression, Mack was without doubt, the kingpin for this whole operation. As pilot for a number of stations in the region, his job was communicating with ringers working on the ground; he needed to locate cattle from the air, help guide the workers in the right direction to get to the cattle, who were often dispersed over a massive area.

A tiny red helicopter was a powerful mustering tool in this arid environment, saving a huge amount of time and energy normally spent driving vast distances in search of stock.

Compared with the old ways of mustering the cattle, which may have taken weeks, the same operation today can be wrapped up in days.

Whilst a small number of ringers rode horses during the muster, many station hands rode quad bikes especially developed for harsh country like Mirna Springs.

Mack talked about local feral populations, a problem to all livestock in the area. This was a problem I had not contemplated.

'So in case you aren't aware, Sarah, feral camels are a big issue in the area, there are hundreds roaming around in these remote areas. They are a very hardy animal, and pose a big threat to farming enterprises such as this one. The stockmen will shoot them where possible, but we're looking at ways we can trap them at water points. They drink water meant for the cattle, and we're already in crisis because of the drought.'

The critical water shortage had become an urgent problem for both people and livestock.

Watching one of the Aboriginal stockmen, I was amazed at the level of skill that came so naturally. He sat low in the saddle, his long, thin, muscular legs lightly touching the horse with silent commands; horse and rider looking as one as they trotted up and down the fence line. I caught his eye and walked over to the fence, asking him if he was happy for me to take his photo.

'Sure,' he replied.

With his beautiful smile, this mesmerising young man exuded a powerful confidence when he was on that horse. There was something familiar about this charismatic guy, he told me his name was Joe Miller. This might be May's treasured grandson. I asked if he knew May.

'Yeah, my grannie,' he answered with a grin.

I didn't want to miss the opportunity to talk and asked if would be okay to have a chat. Joe told me he had worked on Mirna Springs Station since he left school last year. Joe said he finished Year 12 in Dillalong and always wanted to be a cattle stockman just like his great-great-grandfather Henry, who worked at Mirna Springs Station until he was an old man.

I was intrigued to hear his story. May's family have been involved with the McCallums for generations and it seems the tradition continues. I asked Joe if he thought the life of a stockman was in his blood, and wasn't surprised at his answer.

'Yeah, I always wanted to work with cattle, I like being around them, maybe I will buy a property one day. When I'm out here I prefer ridin' Sadie than being on a motorbike. I'm happiest when I'm on my horse, she's my best friend.'

That big beaming smile again as Joe explained he has some Saturdays away from Mirna Springs. 'My girlfriend lives in town and I visit her some weekends,' he said with pride.

'We might get married soon.'

I took a couple of photos of Joe standing near the cattle

gates, holding the reins of his quarter horse, Sadie, and thanked him as I left.

It was time to move on. Tom was standing nearby, making it known I had spent enough time talking to Joe, and he needed to get back to work. As we wandered up the road, he expressed interest in my questions about cattle production in the area.

'So what's important is that beef producers will typically wean their calves at any age between four and nine months, when they are either sold or kept by the producer. It's what we do here on the station.'

'So how do you make a decision on whether you will sell or keep the calves from that season?'

'Well, once weaned our calves enter a stage during which time we provide enough nutrition to support strong growth. We then make a decision - the executives of the company - about the next process in the supply chain and where the animals go from there.'

I was taken aback by the amount of information I had been offered by Tom and, surprisingly, it wasn't delivered with the normal dose of sarcasm or cynicism and appeared instead to reflect his genuine interest in the cattle industry.

The last hour or so was spent with the workers at the cattle yard. The smell of eucalyptus drifted slowly through the air as gum leaves crackled and burned in the campfire. Stockmen gathered around, preparing for a good old-fashioned afternoon tea. Damper and billy tea made on open coals, accompanied by a pot of mulberry jam, probably the fruit of the very same old tree at the back of the homestead.

They were a friendly lot who loved a joke or two, and watching them throughout the day had also demonstrated to me just how skilled they were at handling the cattle. The high level of commitment and dedication to the industry was well and truly reflected throughout the day. I took some shots of everyone standing around the campfire, with the billy boiling, steam wafting up into the clear sky. During the break there was much joking and laughter among the men; the camaraderie in this group was clear to see. Someone brought a guitar out and played a few country and western melodies. It took me right back to my childhood when we would visit my mum's brother, who loved to play the guitar around the campfire.

I couldn't help but notice many of the men avoided talking directly to Tom. He was obviously not popular in the cattle yards. A look that I was now becoming increasingly familiar with - disagreeable, face down and drawn - seemed to suddenly emerge from nowhere. I took another glance in his direction. He had a pannikin of tea in his hands and was just standing there, looking down Old Mine Road.

Eventually Shaun, battered Akubra in hand perhaps

prompted by Tom, asked if I would like a lift back to the homestead. It was a relief not to have Tom dropping me back. Just as I was leaving, Mack Summers caught up with me again.

'By the way Sarah, we've got a helicopter muster happening tomorrow, and it's okay with the McCallums if you'd would like to come up for the day to see how we work from the air?'

'I would love that, Mack, thanks! What time?'

'Well, if you can be ready to roll by six, that would be good,' Mack said with a big grin.

Mack had obviously arranged with Tom to have me accompany him earlier, and it was a relief to know that I would probably not see either of the McCallums the following day.

Shaun was a proven old hand, not only had he grown up on a cattle station in the Northern Territory, but his father and grandfather had both been stockmen for one of the biggest cattle stations in the Territory.

He chatted easily on the way back to the homestead about his memories and the way of life working in the yards. Even in early childhood, he could remember helping his Dad in the mustering season, running barefoot through the dust with the cattle dogs until he was exhausted, and munching on beef and mustard sandwiches for smoko.

I ate dinner in the kitchen with May that night; a simple meal that she had cooked earlier. The housekeeper was on leave for the day and Tom would get his own dinner when he returned home. May allowed me to photograph her taking her bread out of the oven. I shared the photos of Joe, she looked delighted. May was so proud of her eldest grandson, and I could see that he was a big part of her life. We talked about her family; she was keen to tell me a story about her mother. On the day she was born, May's mother had chosen a special place in the creek bed, and with the help of her close family, had given birth to her first child. May said when she returned to her country she would visit this special spot with her family.

May had so many vivid memories from her childhood and the early days. Growing up with her family, the young May would go on daily treks through the scrub with her mother and aunties to look for wild honey and yams. Sometimes they would pick fruit from the wild peach trees and find plump lizards to cook on the open fires. May's mother taught her many skills, including how to survive on country by finding enough water and food, even if she was on her own.

A couple of hours passed quickly, and I could soon tell from her slow body movements how tired May was from another long day of chores.

'I really loved hearing your stories, May, but it's late. I'm sorry I have kept you up.'

May gave a raspy laugh, saying that at her age she wasn't used to going to bed late, she was such an early riser. Hands lightly touching, we bid each other goodnight.

'See you in the morning, May.'

'See you in the morning my girl, you're good company for me you know.'

Still covered in red dust from my day's outing, I decided a bath was what I needed. I also had notes to complete from the day's work that would form part of my story.

Despite my earlier misgivings about the owners, I was genuinely impressed with the way they had set up their cattle ready for the markets. Even while facing ongoing issues including the drought and other natural disasters, the station was still striving to achieve the best outcomes.

There were, though, still unanswered questions remaining about certain aspects of the business. Unlike his father, Tom would only talk to me about the marketing side of the business. I was disappointed too, in John McCallum's untimely absence.

Next morning I was up bright and early, and after a quick breakfast of tea and toast I saw Mack Summers through the screen door, pulling up out the front in the old battered station jeep. I grabbed my backpack, checked I had my camera and binoculars, and raced out the door.

Mack met the ground crew down at the cattle yards. I took snaps of the crew gathered around a map, deciding where they would be located for the day and which cattle would be targeted.

This meeting took about twenty minutes. Before I knew it, I was experiencing the exhilarating feeling of being up in the air. Although still early, the morning promised another sweltering day. Long golden shadows were cast by the trees and shrubs; a soft dawn light touched everything on the ground far below. Almost immediately Mack pointed out a mob of feral camels grazing the dry grass near the hills; they bolted into the distance as soon as they heard the helicopter engine. I already had my camera out, taking pictures of a smiling Mack in the cockpit as well as the scene below.

We scoured the land for over an hour, but apart from the odd kangaroo there was no trace of the herd. Mack said sometimes you find cattle based on a hunch about where they might be hanging out - usually not too far away from water troughs, especially at this time of year. With water such a precious commodity up this way it can narrow down the options grazing cattle might take.

Mack was suddenly circling back over a big creek and yelled out, 'There below us, see the herd?' I squinted my eyes against the glaring sun, eventually yelling out, 'Yes, I see them! Down amongst those trees!'

Their brown and white hides stood out clearly in that soft morning light, as they raced through the creek bed. Mack yelled, 'There could be nearly twenty in that herd, can you count them?' I grabbed the binoculars - the count was about sixteen, including two calves.

We passed quite low over the cattle again. 'Yep, sixteen in this herd,' I confirmed.

Mack took the chopper in at an angle and managed to turn the cattle in the other direction, making it easier for the ground crew to find them. Then he flew at a higher altitude, allowing the cattle to follow the new track.

Mack was already on the radio, telling the head stockman of the find and exact location. The small herd was located only about twenty kilometres from the homestead, so it didn't take long for the stockman to arrive. Fine red dust flew high into the air as they sped along the rough dirt tracks on their quad bikes. Finally, they spotted the herd ahead.

Now came the challenge to bring them around. It was a matter of keeping the stock calm during this time and ensuring they didn't panic and bolt. The cattle dogs jumped off the bikes at their master's command, quickly rounding up stragglers with a sly nip here and there. Mack landed the helicopter on the rough bush track and we walked over just as they were making their way back.

There were plenty of amazing photo opportunities, workers and their talented dogs all happy to oblige. We stopped for smoko, the cattle corralled now in a section of the creek bed.

Finally someone shouted, 'Okay guys, let's get this show on the road,' and everyone jumped into action. Man, beasts and bikes headed slowly and noisily back in the direction of the yards.

Later that afternoon we were back in the air. This trip was more of a wild goose chase, Mack told me, as we flew due south. One of the stockmen had reported spotting an injured cow with a young calf. As the cow may need treatment for her injury, Mack explained a special trailer would be brought in once the pair are found, to take them back to the station.

Eventually we spotted the cow and her calf seeking shade from the searing afternoon heat underneath some spindly ghost gums, and Mack reported back to base. We hovered in the distance, keeping an eye on the pair while being careful not to get too close in case the cow decided to do a runner and further damage her leg. Eventually help arrived; a couple of stockmen on horses and another worker towing a large trailer behind a four-wheel drive. The ground team cautiously approached the red cow and her calf. The men were obviously used to dealing with such situations - or perhaps this was just a lucky break - because they managed to quickly coax the pair into the trailer and the group set off back to Mirna Springs. Mack and I also headed home. It had been a long day.

'You've been a great help today Sarah, my usual passenger is not nearly so friendly and willing to assist as you.'

I was curious to know who his usual passenger was.

'Well, you may have already noticed that many of the stockmen find Tom McCallum quite difficult to work with.' I guessed Mack was alluding to his regular passenger being Tom McCallum.

'To be honest I have, it must be a challenge to keep Tom happy sometimes.'

'You've hit the nail on the head there, Sarah, this guy is so difficult to communicate with that many good stockmen have left the station and moved on. We have talked to John about Tom's ongoing antagonistic and behavioural issues but ultimately it doesn't change anything.

'I know you are only here for a short while, but just be careful of this guy, Sarah. I don't want to scare you, but you do need to know that he definitely has a sinister side, which reveals itself from time to time.' Mack glanced at me sideways with a look and I caught the friendly concern on his face.

'Thanks Mack. I will definitely heed your warning, but he's not even dining with me in the evenings now, so I rarely see him.'

'That's good, perhaps that's the way to go then. It's just that there are things that have happened out here ...' Mack stopped mid-sentence, and an awkward few seconds silence followed. No amount of prompting would get him to open up about what was really concerning him. He left me to try and interpret what he was about to say - presumably about Tom, or was it someone else? If so, I had no idea who that might be. Mack quickly diverted the conversation and his next enquiry also heightened my interest.

'On a different subject altogether, you probably know that a guy called Chad Dimitri disappeared out this way?'

'Yes, I had heard that. But what has that got to do with the McCallums?'

'Well, probably nothing, but I was flying that day on a neighbouring station and I did see a car that fitted the description of Dimitri's car heading towards Mirna Springs Station.'

'Did you tell the police?'

'Yes', he said, with a quick head nod, 'the police know, but there are no further leads that can point them in the right direction as far as I know.' Looking directly at Mack, I suddenly plucked up the courage to ask the question that had been eating away at me for a couple of days.

'What do you think is going on out here, Mack?'

Mack just shook his head. 'If I knew the answer to that one Sarah, I would have already told the cops.' Mack appeared to have no further insight into the disappearance of Chad, and even if he did, he chose not to divulge anything further to me.

There was a certain heaviness about his movements now. Mack was done with this conversation, and I got the impression he was ready to go home and chill out. I had learned so much about the cattle muster, but also a new snippet of information about the missing man. Perhaps he was lost on Mirna Springs Station after all? I thanked Mack profusely, and we bid each other goodnight.

Chapter Seven

Typing away madly, yawning at the late hour, the outline of the Mirna Springs article was finally starting to take shape. I hoped Callie would be impressed with my progress. My phone rang in that minute - probably my mother.

'Hello, it's Sarah.' I was taken aback when Constable Jamie Landers from the Dillalong police answered, asking very politely how my stay at Mirna was going.

The call was friendly, but I picked up an edge of controlled courtesy throughout our conversation. I figured it was probably Jamie's designated duty, and he'd been instructed to make the call. He casually asked then how I was going and if everything was okay with me.

It suddenly occurred to me that I had told Dillalong police I would call them when I arrived, to let them know I was safe and well. I felt an instant sting of shame and started to apologise profusely for not making contact earlier. Jamie reassured me all was okay, he just wanted to know if I was going alright?

After replying - rather too cheerily I thought - that all was going well, there was the slightest hesitation. Was he looking for further information from me?

'Well, I have two more days out here before I pass back

through Dillalong. I'd still like to catch up early Monday for our trip to Yingali Station. I've checked it out with my boss and she seems okay with me tagging along to write the story.'

Jamie seemed pleased I would still be making the journey. 'Okay, that's great news. Stay in touch then, and we'll definitely catch up with you Monday .'

After he hung up I contemplated for a second whether the police regularly provided courtesy calls to people travelling in the outback, but thought no more of it at the time.

But in the days to come I reflected on Jamie's call - more from a personal point of view though. Did I imagine there was some magical connection between us on the night of the Dillalong celebrations? What was I thinking? I'd only just come out of a long-term relationship six months ago, so I was definitely not on the rebound or seeking to find anyone special in my life right now.

That night, my focus was on writing my story. Many hours later I checked my watch, I decided to call it a night and had just switched the light off and climbed into bed when I heard a car in the distance. Minutes later it pulled up very close to the homestead.

Hearing voices near my bedroom, I climbed out of bed, gingerly opened the creaky French doors and tiptoed along the flagstone verandah to eavesdrop on the conversation. I stood listening for some time. In that incredibly still night air I could clearly recognise the voice of Tom McCallum, but couldn't pick the voice of the other person.

The visitor had arrived near midnight. I could see like outline of a ute parked near the front homestead gate. Judging by the noise, the car probably had a broken muffler and more than likely woken up half the camp. Importantly, I didn't think this blow-in had come from the direction of the road into Mirna Springs. He had arrived from a different track. But where?

I could hear the aggressive tone that Tom McCallum regularly took on – that was nothing out of the ordinary.

'The old boy told you not to come up to the homestead under any circumstances – are you looking for trouble?' McCallum really sounded in a foul mood. I didn't envy the guy who faced him.

I heard the stranger apologising - a hint of foreign accent, perhaps European, voice low and gravelly.

'A couple of important things have come up and we thought you needed to know.

There's competition in the market now and threats have been made over the past few days.'

'Who by?' Tom McCallum's voice, still aggressive, now with a touch of cynicism.

The visitor mumbled something, but I caught the gist of it.

'A second syndicate had been formed by a group from interstate and they're targeting this area.'

I wondered what interest there could be in an area like

this. How did this person gain the information, and what was the group competing for?

Crouching low, my first focus was on a few kamikaze moths intent on dive-bombing the light bulb on the front verandah, their soft downy fuzz floating away in the hot night air. I moved closer so that I could hear the conversation more clearly. Feeling more intrigued than shocked I listened intently as the newcomer continued to speak in a hushed tone.

'The team have managed to target an extra three hundred and seven cattle to be loaded off to Mirna Springs early tomorrow.'

Tom whistled softly. 'Wow that's quite a haul. The old man will be pleased about that.' He was sounding less aggressive now, more cooperative. He told his counterpart how careful they would need to be while transporting the cattle to Mirna Springs.

'Locals are looking out for their stock now because they've heard about other thefts in the area that are being reported to the police.'

Then he hissed, 'And we can't rely on Tim Grant to keep protecting us all the time, eventually even he will start to ask more questions. Make sure there are no mistakes this time and the truck takes the back road early.'

Moving any closer to get a better look would have risked me being discovered, so I stayed close to the French doors and remained out of sight. The two continued muttering in low tones for some time, and I didn't quite catch the end of the conversation.

The secretive exchange had pricked my interest though and I didn't sleep well that night. So if my interpretation of that clandestine meeting was in fact correct, the McCallums were involved in another cattle enterprise. Would that be the business of stealing and selling other people's stock? How could they manage to do this without other people finding out?

Was this why Tom was so aggressive and sullen towards me, through fear of me finding out the truth while I was out here? I was also intrigued to learn that there might be a 'back road' leading directly to the Old Mine Road.

This incident could have related to almost any business dealings on the property, but anyone hearing this conversation might conclude that this was an operation involving the local owners, perhaps with some help from outside interests. The journalist in me decided this was worth exploring further.

I heard them get in the station truck together and drive down in the direction of Old Mine Road. I was still awake and looked at my watch when they returned two hours later. They were obviously following up on unfinished business in preparation for the arrival in the morning.

If ever there was a time that I would live to regret what

decisions I made during my stay it was that third night. I wondered what could be happening down there. That was what I needed to know about.

*   *   *

Although still early, the air was already stifling. Flies buzzed around my head with unbelievable ferocity. My hat with the net was a godsend on that day.

I felt watched wherever I went. I wandered down to the cattle sheds to see if I could find Tom, to ask him more about the history of the place. Something made me look over my shoulder. A shadow moved at the entrance to the old washhouse. Eyes peered at me through the slats in the ancient wooden wall.

'Is anyone there?' I strode back towards the door. Ronda the housekeeper, wearing her usual scowl, hurriedly strutted off, basket in hand, without answer.

I wondered again if this woman had been given orders to watch me closely. I looked around for May but could see no sign of her. Perhaps she was in the kitchen.

It was my final day at Mirna Springs Station. I couldn't believe that the five days were nearly over. I hadn't covered all of the questions I needed to know, but reassured myself I had covered much of what I needed to pull the story together.

I decided to go for a long walk. Tom McCallum had warned me that if I wanted to walk around anywhere outside of the homestead grounds, I needed to be accompanied by either himself or one of the station hands at all times - non-negotiable.

'You can get lost in this country very easily and we don't want visitors losing their way out here, so stay close at hand if you don't mind.'

In my defence, I had looked for Tom but couldn't find him. I decided I knew the lay of the land enough to take a walk by myself. In some ways, this suited me perfectly; I needed to have time to work out a plan for the day.

Squinting into the morning light I could see something was happening down in the cattle yards; loud voices, the bellowing of cattle and yipping of the cattle dogs were echoing through the creeks. Every now and again there was the crash of a metal gate and more yelling. Perhaps they were tagging today? I assumed most of the station workers would be down at the cattle yard, including Tom.

There was something else in the air that morning, it almost hovered over me like a visible sign. Calling to me, wanting action. My attention was drawn to the Old Mine Road - perhaps it was a flash of metal in the far distance. Could it be some sort of building, or maybe a car? Whatever it was I estimated it was some miles away, but I knew that I needed to go and have a look.

Grabbing my binoculars and camera, which I shoved into my backpack along with a two-litre bottle of water, I set off walking carefully around the side of the house. I didn't want to be seen. Ducking below the acacia bushes, half crouching, I made my way down the rocky slope until I reached the bottom. Looking back, the homestead was no longer visible.

Now headed towards the primitive road that I had seen from the homestead. Months of dry heat had rendered all but the sturdiest of scrubs that grew by the roadside to a dried brown-yellow.

This track had been well used over time. Deep tyre ruts imprinted in places, the road must have been used through past winters, probably bogging some vehicles in the mud. Now, it was mostly just fine red dust. Occasionally it deviated around a rocky outcrop, avoiding a bumpy ride.

There were no footprints on the road apart from the ones I was making. Suddenly I could see the madness in walking on this road; my tracks were now on the road for all to see. Cursing, I jumped into the scrub and continued my trek following the road, but next to it.

It was clear why it was called Old Mine Road. Long-discarded items of rusty machinery now scattered haphazardly in the tall yellow grass, even a couple of old wooden wheels, spokes still intact: equipment left to rot in the grass one day when it was decided the mine was no longer viable. The area was filled with mine shafts and remains of an ancient well, sunk as the small mining settlement developed.

This area had a rich history dating back to the 1840s when

it was mined for its copper, a precious commodity at the time. In fact, the area was mined well before it became a cattle station.

The men working the mine would have been given short notice of the closure, and would have had to search for new jobs to help put food on the table for their families. I made a mental note to ask the McCallums about the history of this particular mine and how long ago it was operating – that was, if I got the opportunity.

For thirty minutes I walked quickly through the dense scrub, the dozens of small bush flies stuck to my back and arms and came along for the ride. Getting nearer, the distinct sound of humming motors, from where I was it sounded like generator engines, but I couldn't be sure. One thing I was sure of though, was that I was moving closer to some sort of activity.

Such was my haste, walking with my head down, I nearly lunged straight into a huge wire fence directly in front of me. Disbelieving, I crept back to the road and saw a massive security fence, over three metres tall, with a double gate to allow large vehicles through.

Unlike the entrance to Mirna Springs, this gate bore no signage. It had a large, new-looking padlock, and three rows of barbed wire threaded along the top of the fence. The fence snaked off into the scrub to my right; I couldn't see how far it went or where it ended.

To my left the fence trailed through the scrub and all the way up to the rocky ridge. I took out my binoculars and could see the fence did indeed end near the top of the small hill.

Whoever made the fence planned for it to be impossible to get around in a vehicle of any sort. They probably also figured it would be highly unlikely anyone would be walking in this area; they would have to get past the homestead to do that. Presumably the McCallums had the fence made – it was on their land - and they had gone to great pains ensuring nobody would enter this area unless they were accompanied by the station owners or their workers.

I should have turned back then, but despite the old saying, "curiosity killed the cat", I felt the urge to keep going, not even bothering to weigh up the risks at that point.

I made my way slowly up a rocky ridge, my heavy backpack impeding my progress somewhat. I realised time was of the essence, they would start to look for me back at the homestead if I was gone for too long. Clumps of yakkas and small foliage provided a good cover as I made my way up towards the top of the ridge, where I bypassed the fence in seconds and walked on.

A small hill was directly overlooking the area I wanted to focus on. Much of the higher section of the hill was covered in loose shale, and I had to be careful not to slip, or a small avalanche of rock could be set off that might then be overheard by anybody working in the shed, which was directly below. Getting near enough to a lot of the activity going on I could hear cattle bellowing and men's voices carrying through the still air.

'Nah, this way.'

'All yours, Ben',

'Watch this one.'

As I reached the top of the ridge I crawled on my hands and knees. Lodged tightly between two giant yakkas and a granite rock, heart beating fast, I took my binoculars out and quickly scanned the area.

The shed was a large building, probably about sixty metres long. There were openings on one end, and a large sliding door and louvre windows down one side. Even from a distance people were clearly visible as they went about their work. Unlike the old sheds that surrounded the station, this huge shed was obviously a new addition; shiny sheets of metal a dead giveaway. A windmill had been installed nearby to supply water for whatever was happening in the shed.

The hum of engines now loud, but not noisy enough to drown out the bellowing cries of cattle, many sounded as though they were in distress.

Shocked at the scene below me, I lowered my binoculars. What was I expecting to see? Something as ordinary as a second shed for the cattle at the station, or more equipment? But I already knew that wouldn't be the case, based on the conversation I had heard the night before.

This looked like an incredibly well-executed operation. A couple of tough-looking guys stood guard outside the entrance to the shed. Even from this distance they looked menacing: shotguns slung loosely over their shoulders, black jeans, shaved heads and tats. Every now and then they wandered from one side of the building to the other, keeping watch on the whole area.

What on earth could be so important to have armed guards on the doors? These were a completely different group of men to those I had seen during my time on the station.

It was a hive of activity in the shed; people were moving around with great haste. None of the station hands appeared to work down here. Where would these people sleep? The shed must also accommodate people while they are on the property. To gain a better view I decided to climb up even further onto a small rocky hill overlooking the large shed.

Even from this distance, I could smell the unmistakable odour of blood and guts; the foul smell permeated the still air and filled my nostrils. The taste of death in my mouth was tangible, and contributed to the sudden edginess and distinct sense of danger I felt I was in, sitting high on top of the hill.

It seemed that the rumours circulating in the community about illegal activities on Mirna Springs Station might have some truth after all. My large camera lens was on and I was clicking away. I managed to get some pictures that looked right into the shed, capturing the action as it happened.

This was a full-blown operation. The stolen cattle were brought here under cover of darkness, slaughtered and butchered, then taken in freezer trucks to a predetermined market. This black market operation would potentially be worth hundreds of thousands of dollars. The high value of rural livestock, particularly since the drought and bushfires, has increased the rate of "duffing" in regional Australia. Cattle and sheep are the main targets and transportation has been taken to a new level, with stolen stock even being transported in caravans and other vehicles to allay suspicion.

I could see the area where the cattle were being taken to be slaughtered. A chain of people worked to ensure the carcasses were dealt with efficiently and then placed in cold storage. I took pictures of the cold storage semis that were parked for convenience near the loading bay.

The group were utilising an alternate route in order to avoid detection. The well-used road snaked around the edge of the ranges before disappearing out of sight. I wondered where the road led and how they managed to ensure nobody accidently stumbled across that road.

Something caught my eye in the distance; a vehicle speeding down the back road near the ranges was sending up a swirl of dust. I wondered if this was a lost tourist or a pre-arranged visit to the sheds by members of the group.

With great anticipation I focused the binoculars on a dark grey Lexus four-wheel-drive. It slowed as it approached the shed, then stopped, sending more dust swirling. Two characters, neither of whom I recognised, made their way into the building. They were obviously known to the two guards outside, greeting them casually. The guards began looking around more carefully now, scanning the area, pacing up and down the sides of the building. I ducked my head down low and waited for a while before cautiously peeking around the granite rock again. All had settled down; the guards were smoking and chatting.

Madly taking photos, trying to make sure the vehicle registration plate was included, I also managed to get pictures of some of the unfortunate beasts that were brought in on the trucks. This could help to identify the real owners.

The new arrivals were no doubt an important part of the operation, they remained in the shed for some time. They were checking each station, and many of the workers were stopping work to talk to them. When they finally stepped outside, they were followed by a small group, by the look of hands waving in the air and fingers pointing down the road, some intense discussions were taking place.

The two visitors appeared well dressed - a standout, especially out here in the bush. Both were clean shaven, one wore aviator sunglasses and the other had tats around his clean shaven head and neck. Their shiny, pale brown leather shoes – probably handmade – set them aside from the rest of the workers. No doubt they were city slickers.

I had a sixth sense to get out of there without delay.

I had seen enough and didn't have to guess the rest. I slowly and deliberately started to climb down from the ridge, trying to make sure I didn't disturb the loose rocks in case the noise drew attention to the hill. My heart skipped a beat as I had a momentary glimpse of my fate, recognising the danger I put myself in just by being a witness to the activities in the shed.

My backpack, loaded down with a camera, binoculars and other items, made the descent increasingly awkward. After only a few short metres I found myself crawling along and hoping the protruding pack was not visible from below.

Halfway down I peeked over a rock. My heart skipped a beat. *Oh, hell!* Someone was pointing up at me and others were coming out to see what was happening.

The hairs on my neck bristled with fear. A gunshot rang out across the gorge and I almost collapsed in fright. A bullet hit a nearby rocky outcrop and sent shards of granite rock spraying up into the air, landing back down on my pack and my head. The sound of the shot reverberated, sending out ear-splitting echoes that bounced back and forth through the ranges.

Chapter Eight

The air was heavy with voices yelling the alert to others in the shed. Cursing and swearing to myself, I made a speedy retreat, still on my hands and knees. My heart sank as I got closer to the bottom of the hill. I was in deep trouble, no matter which way I ran. I got up off my knees and ran clumsily down the final few metres of the hill, figuring that if they had spotted me, haste was the key. I started running - fast.

My heart was beating in my mouth, and the fact my legs had turned almost to jelly made it harder to run, but I used my arms to spur myself on. I had a feeling this was a life and death moment, and any wrong decision could cost me my life. I would have to find a way to escape from this place. But how?

Once I hit the scrub I ran like hell. It was my only chance to evade capture; soon they'd have men scouring the whole area. I remembered the kangaroo track I found earlier and just kept moving. I charged through the scrub, branches scratching at my face and arms, but I was oblivious to anything other than escaping what felt like immediate danger.

My backpack bounced awkwardly from side to side. I silently cursed the load that slowed me down, but I couldn't release it because once they found it, they'd be able to locate me - with all of evidence recorded on my camera.

My mouth was dry from fear, and I had to stop momentarily. At first, all I could hear was my own heart hammering inside my chest, but then I heard another sound - the soft buzz of what sounded like a drone. Sure enough, I spied it in the distance. Ominously, it didn't come from the direction of the shed but along the road from the other direction. This drone must have been launched from the homestead! A chill ran down my spine as I quickly hid under a low clump of acacia bushes until I heard the noise moving off in the opposite direction.

I started running again. The drone cruised slowly along Old Mine Road, deviating occasionally and buzzing off into the scrub, but heading south. This didn't bode well for me. As well as having a dozen or so angry men charging after me I had no doubt that Tom McCallum was now looking for me, too.

I heard a vehicle coming from the direction of the sheds. It cruised slowly along the road only a hundred metres from where I was on the path. Luckily, the scrub was thick in this area and I was safe for that moment. The car windows were down, and I heard several loud voices arguing about which direction they should look next.

For some reason, the car did a U-turn and headed back the other way. Perhaps they decided I had moved in a different direction. Within seconds of the car driving off, I heard the high-pitched whine of a trail bike moving with speed down the road. The dense smell of petrol fumes hit me before I glimpsed the bike, which moved off the road and crashed through the thick scrub, very near to where I was running.

Looking around I could only see one place to hide in a hurry - a rocky outcrop near the track. It had a ridge on one side and I jumped, with what felt like superhuman agility, onto the rocks, clinging to the ridge and pressing my body against the outcrop. I was on the opposite side of the track, and hoped that whoever was on the bike would not stop to look for me there.

The bike slowed down very close to me and stopped. Fear rose in my chest as I clung to the rock, hoping again that my backpack was not protruding out far enough to be seen. There was a terrifying quietness, and in that moment the world seemed to stand still. I tried not to breathe. Loud footsteps crashed through the undergrowth, searching and cursing loudly. Surely I would be discovered any minute.

After what seemed like an hour but was probably only a few seconds, I heard the bike start up and move off again, heading down the track with great haste. Poking my head around the edge of the rocks, I got a fleeting glimpse of the back of the rider; all that I noticed in that split second were the guy's black boots, which were splattered with blood. He was obviously one of the slaughtermen from the shed. A chill went through my body and I found myself shaking in spite of the intense heat of the day.

I hadn't been discovered. With this thought forefront in my mind, I realised I had only minutes to get to the other side of the road and head back up to the homestead again. I had no idea what to expect when I got there; I would have to plan this out as I went. What I did know was - I was in big trouble.

Even though it was potentially taking me straight back into real danger, I took the same path up the hill as I had coming down, past some low-lying acacia, myrtle bushes, a tank and the homestead windmill. If you crouched low you could not be seen from any angle, and I crawled along with as much haste as I could manage. At the top of the hill, still hidden by bushes, I waited and listened. My fear level was so high that my legs and arms were trembling, my heart was racing, and a stress headache thumping at my temples.

I edged closer to the homestead, still on my hands and knees. My heart froze. I could hear Tom McCallum yelling uncontrollably, presumably on the phone to the search party.

'Find the fucking bitch, and when you do, bring her up here. She's gonna be one sorry lady when we catch her, I'll personally see to it that she never causes anyone trouble ever again.'

Fear and panic threatened to take over, but I told myself to be calm. If I was going to survive I needed to have a level head to work out how to escape and get help. McCallum's tone of voice changed, and I guessed he was now on the phone to his father, who still hadn't returned from his visit to town.

'That journo bitch has been poking around where she was told not to go; she's taken herself down to the operation on Old Mine Road. Yeah, this morning, yeah, well we are looking for her now. No, don't worry, by the time you get home it will have been dealt with, if you get my meaning.'

How the hell did all of this happen, I asked myself. I already knew the answer – he was right, I had overstepped the mark, gone where I was told not to go, and in doing so, found out the McCallum's darkest secrets. Now they would act quickly to catch me, and I sensed without a doubt that they would kill me. I had to get to my phone; I needed to alert someone that I was in trouble. I had left it in the bedroom. I thought about escaping in my car, but it would be a huge risk. I was well aware of what would happen if they managed to capture me.

My heart skipped several beats again as I heard the distant buzz of the drone. I squeezed myself in under a bush and waited in fear.

Five minutes later, I watched Tom bring his drone back to the homestead. Swearing and cursing, rifle in hand, he jumped into the four-wheel-drive, motor revving loudly in the still air, and skidded down the road driving like a madman. He was headed along Old Mine Road.

This was my opportunity. I wasted no time crawling up to the flagstone verandah, looking right and left. I made a dash to the kitchen door and managed to get the old screen open without it squeaking too much. Thankfully, neither May nor Ronda were there. I peeked through the kitchen window and saw them standing on the front verandah, scanning the area. They were looking along the Old Mine Road for signs of me.

I could swear that old May glanced back at the kitchen window for a brief second; if she did she would have certainly seen me standing there. I crept down the passage and into my room. I had to get my car keys and get out of this place. I would have at least fifteen minutes head start if I left now. It was now or never.

I stuffed my coat in the backpack, and reached for the car keys that I'd left sitting on the dressing table this morning. To my horror they were no longer there. My phone and laptop were also missing. My hopes of alerting someone I was in deep trouble faded immediately. Tom McCallum had made sure I wasn't going anywhere.

I was devastated but only for a moment. I had to go, and now. Every second counted towards me getting out of this place alive. So I made a split-second decision. I would try my luck on May's track to her homeland. I had very little detail on how to find her community, but nonetheless, this is where I would head. I could see little other option.

Surprising even myself with the amount of courage I managed to pluck up, I detoured back through the kitchen and out the other side. I hurriedly threw slices of May's bread, apples, cheese and a pocket knife from the cutlery drawer into my backpack, along with the two-litre bottle of water I'd packed earlier in the day. Even though I had already consumed some of it, I couldn't stay here even one minute longer.

The only way I could get out of here again was to follow the same path that I had taken up to the house. I sneaked back through the kitchen door, looking back to check where May and Ronda were. They were both standing out on the verandah. Still looking for any signs of me, I guessed.

Chapter Nine

Within minutes I was heading down the slope again, past the tiny overgrown graveyard, crawling back through the acacia bushes and down towards the windmill. The mechanical clank and heave of the windmill, driven by the fresh breeze, suddenly seemed deafeningly loud, drowning out the sound of my heartbeat racing in my chest. I finally arrived back at the bottom of the hill, reminding myself this was the only area on the whole property where you can move without being seen.

I paused for a moment to get my bearings, looking nervously in all directions to see if I had been discovered. If they launched the drone again I would surely be found, so, using all the courage that I could muster, I headed into the thick scrub, crouching as I ran, heading due west.

In the far distance, I could pick up the faint sounds of car and motor bike engines. There were a lot of people searching every inch of the land for me; they had probably even stopped work at the slaughter shed and called the men out to help in the search. The risk of being found was very high. I had to move fast now, or be caught.

The engine noise was getting louder and louder. I was running as fast as I could, with no cover in sight and nowhere to hide, in any direction. Just keep running. At one stage I glanced back to see someone on a quad bike heading straight for me. He had definitely seen me. My heart skipped several beats in the fear of finally being caught.

I decided to run up the slope, as my best hope of escape was to get amongst the scrub I could see on the other side of the creek. I spotted a large, dense swathe of tea tree bushes to my right, and crawled into the middle of the thicket, hoping it would hide me. Minutes ticked by. The motor bike sped up; the roar of the engine told me the rider was heading up the bank of the creek towards me. I slid in deeper under the bushes, my backpack again getting in the way of a smooth hideaway. I lay down as flat as I could, pressing my head and body firmly into the ground. I told myself if I stayed here long enough he might give up and move on, knowing all the while it was highly unlikely. This guy was not going to leave until he found me.

The bike circled around and around before coming to a halt. While the bike idled, the rider talked to somebody on a two-way radio, or maybe a phone. I could clearly hear what he was saying.

'Yeah boss, she's hiding in the scrub up near the Woorinya Creek. I'm on the bike, can you send some help up here and we can get her into the vehicle.'

This information made me want to run again, but I knew if I did I would have been captured almost immediately. I waited.

The bike engine fired up, the rider now driving meticulously through the bushes, scouring each area as he went. I got a glimpse as he drew closer and even more fear and panic set in, if that were possible. The guy looked as though he was almost as wide as he was tall. He had a long wispy plait down his back and tats on each hairy arm. He looked like he had stepped out of some horror gangster movie.

Suddenly, without warning, he crashed through the bush on foot, using his bare arms and his legs to kick and crush anything in his way. The putrid stink of body odour and unwashed clothes hit me.

'Come here you bloody bitch, you're gonna pay for all the trouble you've caused.'

I was grabbed by the scruff of the neck and dragged through the bushes. I managed to get one quick kick in and my foot landed squarely on the guy's knee cap. Disappointingly, there was not so much as even a grunt forthcoming from this tenacious bulldog as he continued to pull me headfirst through the scrub. Once out in the open I was shoved on the ground and instructed by the bulldog that if I moved I would be killed. He then lunged forward with a huge filthy hand and landed a forceful whack squarely on my jaw and ear. Momentarily dazed, my eardrum singing, I had trouble hearing for a few moments. I lay quietly after this, recognising that any further movement might provoke another assault. If I was injured in any serious way, I would definitely not going to be able to try another escape.

Something clicked into place for me right then. I recognised that strange gravelly voice from some previous encounter. Of course, that voice was one and the same; I overheard him talking that night on the front verandah of the homestead. So this was the guy who had the inside information on the stolen cattle and the plans for the following morning. Whoever he was, there was a connection to the operation running on the Old Mine Road.

Minutes later a four -wheel-drive arrived in the clearing, after making slow progress up the rough road, Two men were on board: one was a smirking Tom McCallum. He made his way over to us while the driver remained in the car. The bulldog pulled me roughly to my feet and dragged me forcefully towards McCallum, who was carrying a rifle - the same gun he had used to shoot crows with a couple of nights ago. He barely glanced in my direction, but when I did catch a brief stare I gave off an involuntary shudder. Looking into those cold blue eyes I not only saw the glimmer of hostility aimed my way, but I also recognised my fate laid out before me.

I spat blood out of my injured mouth and started to

protest.

'What's this all about, Tom? Why am I being treated like this? I'll tell your father when he returns home!'

He sees the joke in this comment, and answered me in a sarcastic tone. 'Well, will you now, and what if Dad already knows what you've been up to today, sniffing around where you were told not to go. You've only got yourself to blame for the predicament you've put yourself in.'

I could see that reasoning was not going to get me anywhere. I stayed silent as they dragged me to the car and shoved me in the back.

'Where are you taking me? I insist that you let me go, so that I can get my car and leave.'

'You are not going anywhere lady, just so you know, it's too late for that now.' Tom McCallum almost spat the words out.

My hands were shaking and I was wondering if they were going to kill me as soon as they stopped the car again. I thought about jumping out of the car, but the bulldog was on his motorcycle travelling right alongside the car, keeping a wary eye on me at all times. There was no chance of escape.

While we were driving, I was still intent on getting my bearings, in case there would be an opportunity for escape later. Something told me to keep my mouth shut now or they may make it worse for me. I was guessing we were about ten kilometres from the homestead; we were travelling due north.

The bulldog suddenly started to accelerate ahead. The terrain was extremely rough, there was no road to speak of where we were headed, and yet the men seemed to know where they were going.

A feeling of dread overwhelmed me. Perhaps they just intended to kill me and leave my body in the scrub. The car bounced from side to side, and I slid across the seat as we hit potholes and rolled over large granite rocks, climbing up the side of a hill. I looked out the window, but there was nothing on either side to indicate where we were, or even where we were going. Suddenly the driver hit the brakes, and my head jerked forward with the force of the sudden stop.

Chapter Ten

At first, I could see nothing unusual, but then, to the left of the car among the dense growth of native pine trees, I could see it. A small wooden hut, almost hidden from view from all angles, probably even from the air.. It was cleverly camouflaged, mostly by the natural scrub surrounding it, but also by the sharp rise on three sides that ensured it remained hidden from view. Whoever built this hut really knew the terrain, and how little chance there would be of anyone else discovering it.

The car pulled up next to the hut and I was dragged by the bulldog and the driver and shoved inside. They offered no explanation, they were not interested in communicating with me in any way. The door shut abruptly and was bolted behind me. I was left standing inside wondering what would happen next; my first reaction was relief that they hadn't decided to harm me - not yet anyway.

I stood by the door and listened. Tom spoke quietly, but loud enough for me to hear, 'Let's get things ready, I want you to clear a spot if you know what I mean, and have it ready for first thing in the morning. I'll meet you here at five am - bring her car down here too.'

'Down near the other one, boss?'

'Yeah, same place.'

A shadow passed just outside; peering through the crack in the door, I saw someone place a large padlock through the bolt in the door.

I heard footsteps, but no more talking. Then the sound of the bike and the car start up and leave at the same time. Eventually, I couldn't even hear the motors anymore. As I stood there in the silence I tried to pull myself together by rationalising what had happened earlier.

I pondered Tom's remarks. Why would they want to bring my car down here? My guess was that they would hide it here - it would be pretty difficult to find in this terrain. One thing was for certain though - they were planning my execution, and how and when they would kill me. It was a surreal moment, standing in that dingy hut contemplating the how, why and when of my imminent demise at the hands of these people.

It felt like the worst dream but no, this was really happening. I'd been cornered and trapped, just like the unfortunate cattle that found themselves down in the cattle pens awaiting their fate; locked in some sort of human holding pen. The hut, if you could call it that, was just a small room that contained … absolutely nothing. Probably built years ago as some sort of storage room. No bed, no water, just a bare room with a dirt floor and pine log walls. There was a stale, musty smell in the air. Rumpled hessian bags lay strewn on the floor, almost as though someone else has slept here previously and used them as a mattress. The dirt floor was scuffed, as if there had been some sort of struggle in here.

What or who has used this room is probably something that I would never know - perhaps I didn't want to know, either. There was a window but the glass was so filthy I could barely see through it. It was covered with heavy bars. Yes, this room had certainly been purpose-built to house a 'guest' or two by the McCallums and their associates.

It was late in the day, and night would set in quickly. I started to think about how I could get out of this place. My face ached and my head was still fuzzy from the earlier assault, but now was not the time to focus on anything other than finding an escape route out of here. My very life hung in the balance; a sobering enough thought to keep me motivated to devise some sort of escape plan.

I tried to keep my cool, walking from wall to wall, inspecting and rubbing my hands firmly along the wood. Built for strength, there would be no way these walls would yield to anyone kicking them in, the native pine from around here remained strong years after building. The hut had clearly been there for some time; spider webs laced the walls and the ceiling, which was also built of the same timber. Round and round I went, trying to see any chinks or holes in the wood that might allow an escape. There were none.

On one wall, down low, I noticed a scratching on the wood. I knelt down for a closer inspection. It was a name, clearly scratched using a metal object, perhaps thin wire or a nail. *Chad Dimitri.* A pulse of intense terror went through me. Was Chad also kept a prisoner in this room? Did he meet his fate at the hands of the McCallums and their associates?

I was spurred on to find a way out of here. If finding Chad's name wasn't a strong enough message for what was now intended for me, I didn't know what was. I went around in circles again, searching, desperately looking before dark set in. I went over and looked more closely at the old bags that lay among the dirt.

I thought I could see what looked like very old dried blood on a couple of them. I wondered then, if this is where Chad Dimitri lay. Was he already badly injured when he was brought in here? If so, he wouldn't have had the ability, let alone the chance to escape.

It was a dark thought, and I shivered with a mixture of fear about what fate may have befallen Chad, and concern for my own survival. It was at this moment that I took out my camera, taking a close up of the name scratched in the wood. I also took photos of the bags that lay on the floor.

Then I moved to the door and started pushing with as much force as I could muster, using both my arms and my body. The door was constructed out of just six or seven pine logs nailed together, but extremely thick and well built. Kicks and hard body shoves would have no impact on this door. I knew they had not only bolted the door from the outside, but also padlocked the crack between the wall and the door. *Nothing.*

In the distance, a faint sound of machinery, perhaps a tractor or a grader. What would they be doing out here that would need big machinery?

I tried the window again. This would be where anyone might look first as the most likely escape route. The bars across the window looked as though they were put in more recently. They were set across the inside of the window, incredibly thick and strong. There was no way I could saw or cut through these bars. On closer inspection I could see that holes had been painstakingly drilled through the timber beams and the bars cemented into place.

I sank to the ground and huddled in the dirt. A deep sense of desperation started to bite, but I tried to keep my mind busy thinking about how I could get out of this hellhole alive. What about digging underneath the walls – could it be possible? What would I dig with anyway? I searched through my backpack, which they hadn't even bothered to check. They were obviously very confident that I would remain their prisoner.

I had no tools apart from a small pocketknife, and this would not help me here. There was no way that I was giving up. I began to search for any holes or weak spots along the dirt floor, but there were none that I could see.

Then I glimpsed something laying among the bags on the floor. I crawled over on my knees and picked it up. It was an old metal lid that looked as though it was part of a Thermos, somebody's drinking cup while they were imprisoned in this dirty hole. I inspected the valuable find more closely. I turned it over a few times. Would it be strong enough? It had to be; it would take me hours to get a decent hole dug in the dirt that would eventually become, I hoped, my escape route.

I had to move with haste. It might take all night to dig a hole big enough for me to squeeze through. There was still some daylight left, so I carefully chose a spot where I would dig. If someone checked during the night they might see a hole if I dug at the front, so I started pushing dirt away at the back of the shack.

At first I used my hands and it was hard work. Once I removed the surface dirt, the soil underneath was hard. I felt driven to get out, my life was at stake, and they were coming back early in the morning. Using the heels of my boots, I kicked and shoved to break down the hard soil to make it easier to dig.

The last rays of late afternoon sun gleamed brightly through the cracks in the pine walls, catching the dust specks in flight; a spiral that travelled high in the still air and disappeared into the dark of the timber ceiling. I looked at my watch - I had been digging and scooping now for four hours.

I had worked out a plan. If I excavated the earth as I went, I could push it to one side, and eventually get to the bottom of the logs. Then I could dig a hole right underneath. I had peered through the window at the back of the hut some hours earlier and could see no obstacles in my way, just flat ground on the outside of the hut.

Darkness had set in and without checking my watch I figured it was about nine o'clock. I would have to work through the night and with any luck, be close to getting out of here before sunup. I would have to be; if they decided to come earlier than the arranged time of five am they would still find me inside.

Fear and panic took hold of me again and I started to scoop frantically with the metal lid. I didn't feel I was making much headway and in the dark, it was hard to tell how much further I needed to go. I ran my hands along the logs to feel if I had finally reached the last log. It felt like I had. Twenty more minutes of mad scooping and I was rewarded with being able to feel underneath the log. It was pitch black now, with no moon lighting the room, so I decided to make use of my camera.

Using the flash, I took photos of the hole and worked out what areas I needed to concentrate on. The flash of light also gave me an idea of how much progress I was making. For another four hours I dug without a break, using the camera on several occasions to get my bearings. Then the metal cup hit something really huge and hard. 'No, please, not a big rock!' I cried out loud - but yes, this rock was big and would not be easily moved.

I had no idea how deep down the rock went, or whether I would be able to get it out. Would I have to start digging in another area? It was too late for that, I would never get out in time. After using the camera and assessing the size of the rock, I decided to either dig it out or go around it, even though it would be questionable as to whether I would be able to squeeze underneath it at all.

I checked my watch again. Two am. Time was running out. I was madly digging now, using all the strength that I had left. The next camera shot told me I should be able to lift the rock out and if I could, it would just be a matter of scooping dirt away from the log on the outside of the building so that I could squeeze my body through.

Three-fifteen am. It was now taking all of my strength to pull the rock upwards and roll it to one side. At one stage I realised with a sinking feeling that I may not be able to move it, but, huffing and puffing furiously, I managed to lever the rock by using my legs and feet to push it to one side. I was totally exhausted with the effort but only allowed myself a few minutes to recover. By three-thirty I was digging through to the outside of the hut.

I tried several times to squeeze through, but realised it was going to require a lot more digging. In my darkest hour, my gut told me time was running out for me. My hands were swollen and bloody, one holding the metal cup, the other scratching through the soil and pushing it to one side. Dirt in my nostrils, my eyes and my throat. I wheezed, coughed and choked with the sheer effort of my bid for freedom. The last bid, I figured. I assumed my killing was imminent; it had already been scheduled, supposedly, in less than one hour's time.

Four fifteen am. I squeezed, pushed and shoved my body through the very tight hole. I jammed my backpack through first, then finally, covered from head to toe in fine dirt that clung to my skin like clammy glue, I was at last standing outside, breathing in the fresh morning air and taking in the total silence.

The chilled air was sharp, my lungs took the shock as I breathed out, exhaling steam once, twice, three times. I breathed deeply, smelling the sweet, sweet air. As my bleary eyes adjusted to the approaching dawn, I checked my surroundings. A deep shiver ran up my spine with the realisation of what could have been – and still might - be my ultimate fate.

I had given myself another chance to survive, however slim it might seem. There was no time to appreciate my newly found freedom; I needed to start running, and fast. I didn't want to get caught again, so I had to make sure they didn't know in which direction I was headed.

Luckily, there was no way they would know that I had talked to May about the track that she used to take all those years ago. Instinct told me that May would tell them nothing; if I was right, this might give me a good head start.

Dawn was just far away enough to still see the star-studded sky. Where was the Southern Cross? I got my bearings and started stumbling down the hill heading west. It was a long shot, but I would try to find my way based on my memory of May's map, hastily drawn in the dirt the day we talked at the homestead.

Moving fast through the creek now, trying to make some sort of headway before Tom McCallum and his stooges discovered I had escaped. By my estimation, I would only have about forty-five minutes head start on the search party - at most. They would set out in all directions looking for me, but hopefully they would assume that the only road I was aware of was the one that led into Mirna Springs Station, and that I would head in that direction.

I suddenly realised I was unbearably thirsty; I hadn't had a drink of water since yesterday. Still running, I removed my backpack, took out my water bottle and guzzled fast. A few precious drops spilled down my filthy face. Water was going to be a big problem. I couldn't think of this now though, I needed to be on the move without a stop for the rest of the day.

Chapter Eleven

Survival, Day One

I thought about my escape route as I ran. It was almost an hour now since I sprinted down that hill to freedom. The men would have already been to the hut and found me gone. They would be scouting the area for me, travelling up and down the dirt roads in a constant search. Even as I retreated down into the next creek bed, I could hear the distant sound of engines, and even imagined at one stage I heard a shout. I recalled hearing the devious housekeeper Ronda smugly discussing the situation with May as they stood together outside the homestead.

'They have her car keys, so she's not going to get far at all.' This woman was obviously right in the thick of the McCallum's fraudulent activities - she had been so easy to read right from the start.

But I still had that strong feeling May would not disclose our conversation to her.

My fear of being caught again was so great that my legs almost collapsed at times as I made my way through the dense scrub. My heart was beating fast; I had the jitters as I crashed into bushes, my backpack catching on branches, and my hat bouncing erratically on my back, the string cutting into my neck. My panic and exhaustion overwhelming, I was no longer thinking clearly. I kept looking back, half expecting someone to be on my trail already. There was no one there. I told myself to calm down; they would expect me to go back along the road towards the highway, because they believed this was the only escape route that I knew.

Minutes were replaced by hours. Over time running turned into a trot, then a plodding walk. Not because my fear levels had diminished, but because the heat of the day was so overwhelming it forced me to slow my pace right down. Looking at my watch, I was surprised to see the morning had long gone, it was now mid-afternoon. How much ground I had covered I didn't know, but I knew that in the following days I wouldn't have the energy to move so fast and quite so far. Fear continued to drive me though; I had a vision of them all out hunting for me, and was determined to put as much distance between us as possible.

I stopped to rest. As my heartbeat slowed, I looked around, but the beauty of the terrain was lost on me. I was confused and still in shock. I couldn't fathom where I was heading. All that I tried to remember were May's words, was it turn right and follow the creek bed for many miles, but did I turn right in the beginning? I simply couldn't remember. The situation seemed so surreal - from being assigned to write a story about a family business one day, the following day a fugitive on the run, simply because I knew too much now to be kept alive.

I knew I had to keep moving. I was fit – I'd been long distance running for years - but in spite of this, couldn't take another step. The heat was overwhelming. Thoughts of escape turned to thoughts of survival. Escaping from one danger replaced with another - that of dying from physical exhaustion or thirst in the outback. I decided to try and stay under the canopy of the creek gums to rest during the heat of the day. My biggest regret was not having my phone. I assumed it had been taken and probably destroyed by Tom. It could have been my way out of here, one call was all that I needed to make. I had matches, but too scared to light a fire for fear of being found. A pocketknife, a couple of slices of May's bread, a two-litre bottle of water – more than half now consumed - four apples and a small packet of cheese. These few items would have to do for the whole journey. However long that journey would be.

Thankfully, strong walking shoes, a coat which would do for a blanket at night. My trusty camera wrapped up carefully in the bottom of the backpack. Water my biggest issue from here on. Oblivious to the heat right up until now, but as the shock of my departure wore off, I felt increasingly overwhelmed by the oppressive dry heat. I would need to really dig deep to survive.

The distinct sound of a motor startled me. It sounded like the station helicopter. I peered across the horizon, shading my eyes to spot it, but it must have been some distance away, as the noise gradually faded. I reassured myself that they would have decided the only route I knew would be the road into Mirna Springs; hopefully, it might take them another half day to realise I had gone in the opposite direction. By then, I would have covered a lot of ground and be harder to find. Without stopping, I grabbed the water bottle out of my backpack and took a long slug. Checking the contents, I instantly regretted it - I couldn't do that again, not if I wanted to survive.

The sun finally disappeared behind a gloomy mountainous ridge. In the cool of the evening, I sat chewing slowly on a large chunk of May's bread and slice of cheese. I found my binoculars in the bottom of the backpack and cursed the fact I'd been carrying that extra weight all day. I was starting to realise the burden of carrying extra items would slow me down, and I needed to get rid of anything that wouldn't aid my survival. I carefully hid them in the middle of a big acacia bush - hopefully, anyone passing wouldn't find them.

I knew I wouldn't sleep well in the open, somewhere there must be a spot in the creek bed where I might be hidden from view. After a short while, a lucky find - shining in the last of the evening light, a large gum on the edge of the creek bed. A flood had washed away some of the roots, exposing a small hole on the downside of the creek. I crawled into the hollow and felt the cool of the dirt on my back. Overcome with a deep sense of fatigue, I dozed off quickly but slept lightly, waking with a nervous start throughout the night. Each time I peered into the darkness, I still expected to see men charging through the bush ready to capture me again. To try to walk on in the dark would be foolhardy; I wouldn't be able to get my bearings as easily, even with the stars. There were certain landmarks May described that I might only find in the daylight.

A full blood moon appeared, hanging in the black sky like a giant medallion and casting eerie shadows along the creek. I crept deeper into the tree hollow and continued to doze fitfully, waking every half hour or so, listening for sounds. The only noise I picked up was the grunt of a big buck kangaroo out scavenging grass in the cool night air. Eventually, the soft light of early dawn appeared. I felt a sense of relief that I was still safe, but the gravity of my situation was now quite evident. I would have to head off as early as possible if I wanted to give myself a chance.

Chapter Twelve

Survival, Day Two

Freezing nights and unbearably hot days – that's the Australian bush for you. The extreme conditions can wear you down quickly. It was five am and I was already up and walking, having spent a cold night in the creek bed, even now still hesitant to use the matches to light a fire.

There was a mist in the air as the leftover chill evaporated into the early sunlight. Over the next rocky ridge, a beautiful and unexpected sight; a group of kangaroos, young joeys standing near their mothers for safety, grazing on a rare grassy spot. They sniffed the air, sensing I was near them, the joeys climbed quickly into their mothers' pouches. They were gone in a flash, soon just a speck on the horizon. I pulled out my camera, taking a few shots of the little group bounding away into the distance.

Standing on the top of the ridge I experienced a moment of fear, coupled with a feeling of immense loneliness. What lay ahead? I considered my plight. Flies were already buzzing around my face, and I put on my fly net and hat. I paused briefly, listening for any threatening sounds, but heard nothing apart from some noisy crows in the gums above me.

I moved on.

I hadn't told May I had planned to walk on her country; it might have endangered her life. In fact, I left in such a hurry I didn't even have a chance to say goodbye to her. She was the only friendly face at Mirna Springs. But I had a feeling she might have an inkling as to where I might be heading. I was sure May had seen me when I returned to the homestead, but she wouldn't have said anything to either Tom or the housekeeper. An image of her kind old face crept into my head and almost heard her voice encouraging me to find the way.

Come on my girl, you can do this, I know you can.

It's strange what goes through your mind when you are in crisis. I knew I was lost now. As time passed, any immediate danger became less of a worry, the prospect of being found diminished. But I had to face the realisation I was in the middle of nowhere with little water and scant knowledge of where I was headed.

I admonished myself. *You should have got May to draw the map on paper, you talked to her often enough.* Panic set in. Loud sobs come out of nowhere, sounds that echoed eerily through the creek. Wiping the tears off my face, I tried to pull myself together by talking out loud. 'Think, focus on what you are doing now. You are still alive, and you are going to get through this, no matter what.'

As I walked, I got thinking about why I wanted to be a

journalist in the first place, and the fact that I have felt like a failure in the past. This wasn't the first time I had stuffed up. I remembered one event I was assigned to cover, a high society tea-party, a charity fundraiser. I arrived late, drank too many glasses of champagne and ended up interviewing the wrong person. The organiser of the party was scathing of my behaviour. She reported me to the editor of the paper I was working for, who lectured me for twenty minutes about the merits of a good journalist. She obviously did not think I was one. Yes, I was a new graduate finding my way, but it was a lesson well learnt about how to improve my performance, and how I needed to work on some of my own issues. So why *did* I want to be a journalist? As I contemplated this, a thought ran through my head. What is authenticity anyway? *What and who do I value?*

Here I was, in a dangerous predicament and yet reflecting on my flaws and imperfections. *Why now?* Could it be that when faced with the real possibility of dying we take stock of our lives and how we have lived?

I continued my slow trek through endless creek beds towards the majestic purple ranges I had gazed at from the homestead only a couple of days ago. Appearances can be deceiving, they didn't look the same as I drew nearer. They were still beautiful, but instead of the misty blue and purple mountains that were so mysterious and unreachable when gazing from afar, I could see the distinct outlines of silvery gums and olive yakkas that grew out of the side of rock formations and through the gorges that ran down each towering hillside.

I realised how easily deluded you could be out here in the bush, seeing a range that looked so near but in reality, was so far away, perhaps close to a good day's walk.

The question arose in my head again. What and who do you value? A vengeful anger started to build inside of me, driving me forward. I had a strong desire to ensure the Dillalong community learned the truth about their lost stock and shrinking water supplies. I knew about the McCallums now, and what they stood for. I needed to tell my story to ensure some level of justice was carried out.

It struck me in that minute how absurd it was clinging onto old fears for so long. In the past, my own harsh interpretation of my work got in the way, always trying too hard to meet the expectations of others. May's philosophical but timely message to me came back in that instant. *You will make your own path by walking.*

In what I could only describe then as a deepening of my inner wisdom,

I stepped forward with even more strength and stronger intent, over the jagged rocks towards my destination.

I decided to climb to the top of the range to get a better sense of direction. The steep ascent revealed a small kangaroo track, up through the slippery shale rocks and hard, smooth granite areas. Clumps of small plants were dotted around, a few of them flowering - unusual, given the harsh conditions, the drought and the sharp wind that cut a swathe through the masses of dry grass growing from the cracks in the rocks. A few spindly gums had survived by spreading their roots into the crevices of the hillside. Further up was a thicket of tall native pines, with the occasional she-oak growing on the side of the steep slope.

The hours passed, I persevered with the exhaustive climb to the top. The rocks jutted out at odd angles, making it almost impossible to get over or around. At one time I took a tumble on the slippery shale and toppled over, rolling further back down the hill until a large rock stopped me from falling even further. I felt pain as a sharp rock sliced through my forearm. I sat there feeling sorry for myself for some minutes then told myself to snap out of it – move on! I searched my backpack for anything I could wrap around the wound but found nothing. Blood streamed down my arm and was covered almost immediately in a layer of flies feasting greedily on the liquid. Thankfully, the blood soon dried in the heat, but I would have to be careful with this arm from now on; infection was the last thing I needed. I checked my watch; it was already past four o'clock.

I heard a sudden movement on the rocks. A small group

of feral goats were watching me carefully, pieces of long grass hanging from their mouths. They were quite beautiful, with their long grey, white and brown tufts of hair that blended in with the rock. I had heard about the feral goats in these ranges - people from the city paid to come and shoot them to help the environment. *Good luck with that.* These goats were incredibly quick and agile and disappeared in seconds.

Finally, I reached the summit. I didn't know what I expected but despite the exhaustive climb and overwhelming tiredness, felt deeply moved by the rugged, yet ethereal beauty of this eight-hundred-million year old mountain range. I literally felt as though I was standing on top of the world, looking down at spectacular deep gorges, remote wilderness, and misty blue ranges that seemed to stretch on forever.

In the distance Wilpena Pound, a stunning natural amphitheatre seventeen kilometres long formed by a ring of ancient mountains in the heart of the north Flinders Ranges. The area a giant syncline, or fold in sedimentary rock, full of fossilised coral skeletons from the time in the world's history the area was a vast inland sea.

This was May's people's country. I was walking along a path few white people would have trodden. But May's people would know this area well. I took out my camera, sensing that one day I would look back in awe on this scene - that is, if I was lucky enough to survive.

I sat for a while in a daze, taking in the view and wondering where to go from here. Again, reflecting on May's words - perhaps there was some way to pass through this area, but all that could be seen stretching for hundreds of kilometres against the evening sky were more high ranges.

A slight breeze had picked up below in the creeks, but up here it was blowing a gale and it was hard to keep balance. The wind was icy and I knew I had to make a decision about what to do; it might be the difference between surviving or perishing.

Down in the valley huge river red gums stretching as far as the eye could see through the endless creek beds that snake through the land. Some of these gums hundreds of years old. Generation upon generation of people have walked this land and still these trees survive.

Way out on the plains a large whirly wind, dust whipping high up into the air, along with bushes, grass and anything else light enough to be carried off the ground by that force of nature. The wind reminded me of the intense dryness and bleakness of this barren land. The severity of the drought showed no signs of breaking any time soon.

I was desperately thirsty, and guzzled almost all of my remaining water, conserving a tiny proportion for the next day. I felt I had missed something, somewhere. But what?

I remembered a story told to me by my grandmother of a child lost in the Flinders Ranges, Nicholas Bannon. Nicholas was nine years old and became separated from his family while walking to the summit of St Mary's Peak in the Wilpena Pound in the 1950s. My grandmother remembered the headlines in many of the national papers read, "Search continues for Lost Boy."

Over the ensuing days, the population of Adelaide and wider Australia tuned in, chatted and argued over back fences as they followed the frantic search for Nicholas. The little boy's parents enlisted the help of black trackers, police and many volunteers from local towns, but despite a huge search, Nicholas was not found alive. Years later, hikers found his remains on the edge of the Pound.

Recalling this story, I considered my own potential demise if I couldn't find my way to help. My biggest fear was that if I didn't make it, my body would never be found out here in the wilderness. I decided then and there that the best hope was to climb back down and look for an opening further down in the valley.

By the time I reached the foot of the ranges again darkness had set in. Exhausted, I curled up under the nearest tree and fell asleep almost immediately.

Unlike the previous night, when I had carefully sourced a good hiding place to feel safe, I was too tired to even contemplate being found this time. The last thing I remembered before I fell into a deep sleep was a vision of May's old face. I felt her presence, and this gave me comfort.

Chapter Thirteen

Survival, Day Three

I woke with a start. Somewhere in the distance, the sound of an engine. I scanned the sky trying to find out where the sound was coming from. Towards the east, the glint of a red helicopter, bright against the early morning sky. It must be the station helicopter, headed towards the ranges, covering distance quicker than I could have imagined. It was headed my way.

Could they be looking for me? I felt certain they would be. Desperately looking for a quick hiding place, I took shelter under a large granite outcrop. I slid underneath and waited, heart beating fast, too afraid to move. I listened as the whirr of propellers and deafening engine noise closed in. They were obviously looking carefully. Minutes passed, eventually the sound became more distant and then faded. That was a close call; if I had slept up on the ridge last night they would almost certainly have found me.

I was thankful I hadn't risked a fire, the smoke in the morning air would certainly have alerted them to my whereabouts. I decided after that incident, not to light a fire at all, the risk of being found was too great. I wondered what story they'd invented when they talked to Mack Summers, the pilot. He would certainly have been concerned for my wellbeing if he knew what happened to me in the lead-up to my fleeing the station. Even though I guessed Mack had some knowledge about the McCallums and what they were up to, he would be shocked if he knew the whole truth.

I had to turn back to the edge of the range and search for an alternate track. I felt so despondent. It was too late now, but of course I started to wish I had asked May for more detailed directions to her country. I knelt down and drew a map again in the dirt. Remembering the finer details was already a challenge.

'So, she said turn right, it can only mean she meant before you get to the ranges – you skirt around the edge and then come out the other side and look for the marker rock.' I found talking to myself comforting and re-drawing the map gave me some hope that I might find my way through.

Perhaps I would find water along the way. I was hopeful. Downing the last bit of water, around a quarter of a cup and one of the last apples that morning gave me renewed energy. I told myself I needed to put in a good day's walking.

By midday, I guessed it was already over forty degrees. I was really struggling to keep walking; the searing heat even made air hard to inhale. The birds and kangaroos have much better survival skills than humans, they would already be hiding away somewhere in the scrub conserving their energy in the heat.

I looked up. Large, puffy desert clouds, so beautiful against the clear azure sky, drifted by and soon seared away. There was no moisture to speak of, just a brief respite from the blasting heat when the sun was blocked for a short while.

Another whirly wind swept across the plain, picking up lumps of grass and dust as it went, finally, just a small spot on the far distant landscape. I trudged on, telling myself to use every bit of energy by walking for as long as possible today, making the distance between me and my assailants ever greater.

Through my haze of exhaustion, I spotted what looked like a small building on the side of the creek bed. Momentarily full of hope, I broke into a run. The first thought was finding help. Getting closer, I soon realised the true size of the tiny metal structure, disappointment hit. It was just a long abandoned shack, probably used by shepherds tending sheep or cattle long ago.

No door, just rusty old tin sheets put together in haste to provide a rough shelter. Old bits of wire and nails protruded from the walls, the roof was covered in piles of leaves and branch debris, weeds grew in and around the door.

My great-grandfather once told us how he had lived in a shepherds hut on his father's sheep station as a twelve-year-old boy. He would stay there for weeks at a time, and rations of tea, sugar, flour were brought out from the homestead.

He was put to work as a shepherd in the ranges after losing a leg trying to stop a runaway horse and buggy. His leg was caught in the spokes of the wheels and later amputated. He would wander through the creeks and gorges on crutches.

Each shepherd was responsible to protect the sheep or cattle from dingoes or other predators, and ensure they had enough water to survive. The shepherds huts were made of pine and pug and sometimes had a stone chimney, as this one did. There was also a square stone fence that would have been built as a holding pen for cattle or sheep by some lonely shepherd who worked out here perhaps more than a hundred years ago.

Despite my own desperate situation, I couldn't help but marvel at the effort gone into gathering the heavy rocks from the creek bed and heaving them up the side of the bank.

I walked into the derelict old hut. There was nothing of interest apart from a dented kettle, singed black and minus its lid, long abandoned and lying on the dirt floor. I imagined boiling the black kettle and making a cuppa. I tried to put the idea of having water and quenching my thirst out of my head, but it stayed with me. I also wondered who this land belonged to. Fear started to rise inside me again. Could it be I was still on McCallum's land, even though I had walked so far? I hoped like hell that wasn't the case. After three days of solid walking, surely I must be clear of their property and well on the way to May's community.

I camped next to what was left of the tin shelter for some time, first sitting down and then lying down in the dirt to rest. I needed companionship, the comfort of being able to let someone know I was lost out here. That strange old humpy did provide some sort of familiar comfort, though. I took out my camera, clicking away at what was left of the building and surrounds, suddenly overcome with a deep sense of fatigue, I found it hard to keep my eyes open.

Waking from a heavy slumber, I realised with some dismay I had overslept. I needed to move while I still had energy. I would continue to follow the creek bed, keeping the ranges on my left to be sure I was headed due northwest. I ate the last remaining apple as I left the hut. The moisture really helped with my thirst.

Half an hour further along the creek bed, an invisible force seemed to stop me in my tracks. I looked up, spellbound. To my left, a gigantic boulder sat high up on the creek bed, looming like a messenger, as though it had been placed there deliberately hundreds, or even thousands of years ago. It looked unlike any other rock I had seen, dominating the skyline with its unusual shape and colouring. Then I noticed something else - a hole went right through the middle of it. In that moment, I knew I had found the May's marker rock.

*　　　*　　　*

A massive sense of relief flooded over me. I must be heading in the right direction. I was so grateful, I knelt in the creek bed then and there, offering a silent thank you to May and the Traditional Owners of this beautiful land. This area would have been a central meeting place for many people, and countless ceremonies unique to this country would have been held here through the ages. I could almost hear the sounds of ancient voices and song.

I glanced around, feeling a sense of reverence for all the people that had walked along this creek bed long before me, on their own journey. I felt so honoured to have found this special place, the sacred domain of May's country. For the first time I allowed myself a small grain of hope that I might actually survive.

Chapter Fourteen

Survival, Day Four

The pastel turquoise sky promised another scorching day. The urge for water was overwhelming as I searched through my bag – but already knew the answer to that one.

A flock of noisy corellas landed in a dead river red gum growing near the creek bank next to me. They looked down at me with curiosity; perhaps they had never seen a human before. Quite likely - after all, I was deep in the outback of Australia. These majestic birds live for up to eighty years, so the search for the perfect hollow in which to rear their young would be never-ending and, no doubt, highly competitive among the bird population. But the corellas are incredibly wise, and would know where to look to find food, water and shelter. They know all there is to know about these ranges. In that moment, their presence touched me deeply ... the spirits of this country.

The chill rapidly left the morning air, I slung on my backpack and set off through the gorge. Beautiful wattles and small slender gums dotted the way, forming a dense thicket.

Gigantic granite rocks resembling tall castles lined the creek bed. Some of the boulders were almost perfectly square and arranged with such precision that I stopped and stared; it was as if some giant hand had carefully considered the placement and shape of each rock. The wonders of nature.

The morning wore on and the need for water was increasingly overwhelming. It would be another forty-degree day. My energy levels were low and the intense heat was not helping. Hundreds of flies buzzed around my face and neck, which were by now covered in perspiration. I felt thankful for one small mercy: I still had my fly net hat. The coat had been long abandoned - I would regret this at night, but the burden of carrying an extra item was too much to cope with.

A strong, hot northerly wind sprang up, burning through my skin. Looking due north, I felt instant unease - a massive dust front was moving towards me across the parched land, and judging by the distance it had already covered, it looked to be moving fast. I knew these dust storms could be severe, and I figured the best place to shelter would be in the creek bed. Within a few minutes, clouds of gritty red dust had swept across the plains, ahead of a powerful wind that barrelled down the creek bed. Tiny fragments of red dust stung my face and arms as the wind blasted everything in its path.

I shut my eyes against the force of the wind, struggling to breathe as my lungs filled with the fine dirt. The sensation was claustrophobic. I huddled even closer into a small enclave in the side of the creek bed, covering my face as best

I could until the worst had blown through. Vision was limited - I could barely see a metre in front of me, everything beyond was just a dusty blur. The wind howled and squealed, eerie whistles and screams rushed and echoed through the trees and around the creek beds. Huddling in desperation, hoping the storm would pass quickly, I tried to recall happier days in the bush. The days I normally chose to remember were the good days, but there were also lots of sad days. Our family moved to the city to get the best treatment for my brother Josh, who had been diagnosed with Acute Lymphoblastic Leukaemia. He was only thirteen years old when he took on a battle with the deadliest of diseases. Months of chemotherapy, radiotherapy and ongoing medical treatments took their toll on our beautiful Josh. He never complained though, and his courage in facing the disease became his legacy.

My dearest brother enjoyed every moment when he was well. Josh loved life, after all he was a thirteen-year-old kid, hanging out with his mates. Everyone who knew him said he lit up the room when he walked in, always a smile on his face and a cheeky sense of humour. Two years younger than me, Josh would have been turning twenty-one this year, getting ready to celebrate his big birthday with us. If only he was still with us now - he was my main man. *My world is an emptier place without you, beautiful brother.*

Two hours later the dust had all but disappeared, and a strong, cooler wind blew in. In a twist of savage mercy, my heart lifted when a few grey storm clouds gathered and large drops of rain fell on my face, leaving huge splosh marks on my skin as they mixed with the thick red dust. Far in the distance, lightning flashed over the ranges. The rainstorm lasted for all of a minute, and the precious water had disappeared by the time I crawled out of my hiding place. I felt distraught, I didn't even get an opportunity to drink any of the precious drops as they fell.

My eyes still gritty, I wiped my face with the bottom of my t-shirt as I got up and made my way gingerly back along the rocky creek bed. My mouth was so dry I could no longer swallow properly, and my lips were sunburned and cracked. The desire for water was now so strong I felt delirious and jittery.

I lifted my head and felt the cool breeze on my skin; a brief respite from the intense heat. It was a cruel blow, the sweet smell of rain swept across the land, the last remnants of the storm clouds disappearing. The cool air chilled my skin; somehow this small gift giving me the will to keep going.

Stumbling painfully along the rocky creek beds, something grabbed my attention. Intrigued, I moved closer. A group of small finches lurking near crevices in the giant rocks, but something else; a deep velvet mark seeping from the rock - the dark shadow of moisture. How to get the energy to climb. Slowly and laboriously I reached the area I'd seen from below. After sitting and resting from the physical effort, I crawled towards the shadow. As hard as I tried, I couldn't seem to reach the higher part of the granite rock, but eventually located a small gouge in the cliff face and, using the last of my energy, I hauled myself up to the next level, pushing both hands into the hollowed-out rock.

Creeping along the narrow ledge, I discovered some visible water seepage; perhaps it had come from some distant water vein following the brief rain. I was so thirsty that I licked and slurped at the rocks wherever I could see moisture. Searching earnestly for any other signs of water, I used my pocket knife to dig down into a soft spongy area where moss was growing. I felt moisture in the dirt, then, eventually, a tiny amount of water. I had no cup to get the water out, so used the plastic lid from my empty water bottle to scoop tiny amounts of dirty water up and gulp them down my parched throat. Despite the mud, the taste was beyond glorious. Using the lid to pour the remaining liquid into my plastic bottle, I scooped and scooped until there was nothing left. I had collected nearly half a litre of water.

Further inspection told me I'd had just a lucky break. There didn't appear to be any other areas along the ridge with damp spots or mossy areas; most of the granite walls looked dry and impenetrable. Maybe these precious drops of muddy water would save my life. My energy levels were still so low, the effort to climb up in the oppressive heat and dig was exhausting. Even climbing back down from the side of the cliff face now required much effort. My watch marked the hour. Already well past midday, I found a grassy area in the gravel of the creek bed and, after the sheer effort of the precarious climb, fell asleep immediately.

It was the galahs that woke me. A large flock, screeching, squawking and bickering amongst themselves, they decided to camp in the tree above me. The young galahs entertained me with their upside-down antics, practicing hanging onto branches with just one leg as they constantly hijacked their parents for food. The noise in the creek became louder, the babies making a "whaaka whaaka" sound, followed by a guttural "whuk whuk whuka" when their parents spared them a bit of food.

It was after three, time to move on. I couldn't believe I slept for so long. Thirst hit me again with a vengeance; my mouth and throat dry, my eyes gritty and sore. I drank half of the water that I had collected in one massive gulp.

A glimmer of hope hit me when I suddenly remembered I had told Jamie I would be back at Dillalong on Monday. It must be well past Monday now. Would they respond to me not checking in? Travellers to the outback must get delayed regularly for one reason or another; more often than not a false alarm.

The authorities would probably have no inkling of the

devious operations on the station. In her own way, May did try to warn me that I needed to be careful. She had obviously seen and heard a lot, but her one real reason to stay out there was to protect her beloved grandson, Joe.

I remembered the phone call from Jamie on the third night following my arrival. I had the impression that he was checking on me - hopefully, he would remember when I was due back. But I was lost deep in the land, it would be nearly impossible to track me. The path I had taken was hit and miss; I had loosely followed May's mud map but clearly taken some wrong turns. The chances of someone finding me, I realised with deep dread, were very slim.

Another dusk approached. This time, the usual evening siren song of the cicadas suddenly, eerily, became quiet. The bush seemed emptied of all living creatures other than me. A soft hush settled into the hills and creeks. Again, I was gripped by an acute sense of loneliness. Fighting for my survival now, the rest of the water I had found already gone. I had to stay strong. Somehow I had to get through this.

Josh had passed away suddenly following an infection that finally beat him. Try as we might, whenever we got together as a family for Christmas and other special events there was always a missing link in our lives that we could never seem to fix. I think we held our grief in, not talking about it and hoping it would get better as time passed. But it never did.

I imagined Josh ahead of me now, smiling, his beautiful face looking back at me. My dearest brother, he was with me on this journey. I talked to him, telling him what had befallen me at Mirna Springs and how I was walking to May's community to get help. All of that day I felt his presence, reassuring me, giving me hope.

Chapter Fifteen

Survival, Day Five

Not much sleep all night. A cold snap set in, causing a heavy dew. The water supply long finished, I made a desperate attempt to collect small drops of condensation off the backpack, turning to nearby bushes in search of any remaining moisture. The dew was short lived however - even in the early morning light, the heat was oppressive and any hope of quenching my intense thirst quickly gone.

I didn't think I could cover much ground. I felt confused and disorientated. The days were falling into each other; I couldn't remember what day or date it was, despite reflecting on this for some time. My rational thinking was all over the place. My arms and face were badly sunburned, the gash on my arm infected. Every movement I made now was torture. I had read stories about survival in the bush and knew that without water, my days were now numbered.

My sixth sense told me they were no longer looking for me at Mirna Springs. They probably figured I would be dead by now, given the heat and lack of water. I imagined the McCallums feeling smug, knowing they wouldn't have to deal with the nosy journo bitch from the city - she walked right out into her own grave!

But I had lost the will to even care.

A bunch of noisy crows were flying high in the clear sky above me. Their harsh caws and croaks communicated secret messages to one another via the still morning air. A scary thought occurred to me - perhaps the crows were aware of my predicament and waiting for my final day.

I saw a far-off glint, high in the sky, and the sound of an engine, distant but distinct in the quiet of the bush. It made me think of a small silver fish, shining in the pale blue morning light. Could this be a search party? Or was it the McCallums looking for signs of life? I didn't have to worry for long - the plane didn't even circle, it was headed west on its own mission.

Disappointment bit deep. I sat down heavily and started to sob. My voice had long gone, just a strange croak was all I could manage. Anybody hearing it might have been scared out of their wits, thinking it was some unknown creature lurking in the bush. For a very long time I sat frozen on the rock, desperately asking myself the same question over and over: *what am I to do?*

*   *   *

I wandered through the creek beds and ridges, at times stopping to get my bearings, looking at the sun to make sure

I was heading in what I hoped was the right direction. May said once you are past the ranges, you need to be walking west.

An old campfire, stones still scorched, in the heart of the creek bed. Rocks neatly built in a circle, probably many years ago. I leaned forward to touch the dull grey coals covered in tiny spiderwebs. People had wandered this creek bed, just like me. Who might they have been? Was I near to any of them now? Apart from finding the old hut – and by now I couldn't even remember which day that was - I hadn't seen any other evidence of human presence in this vast wilderness.

For days, I had walked through the creek beds, the terrain had barely changed, but looking up across the horizon now I stopped dead in my tracks. As far as the eye could see, wide open plains stretched for miles on either side of the creek. The flat, red earth, dotted with low clumps of grey saltbush, seemed to stretch on forever. I was momentarily transfixed. I was no longer in high granite country. Even the surrounding hills no longer loomed above the creek, they were low and flat. The swathes of native pine and she-oak on either side of the creek had disappeared. Now, just the occasional small spindly gum grew, the beautiful, almost luminous white trunks contrasting with the red dirt. The effort used precious energy, but I pulled the camera out and take pictures of this beautiful red country - this might be the final record of my journey. My thoughts were not so positive anymore.

Heavy weariness overtaking my body once again, I dropped to my knees under the nearby gum tree, camera lying by my side. I wasn't even bothering to find a soft spot now, I just lay down on top of the large rocks in the creek bed. Each time I did lie down, I found it more and more difficult to get up again. Each time I rested, I wondered if I would wake again. Would this be my last day on this earth? I was breathing heavily now, and I recognised the signs. My body was shutting down. Strangely, I was beyond feeling fear. I asked Josh if he was still with me; I couldn't visualise his face but felt his presence. I told him how much I missed him. I told him I might be with him soon.

I woke from a heavy sleep to find small black ants crawling over my body, biting me on my arms and hands. They could probably smell the dried blood. Some had marched up onto my face and I could feel their tiny legs crawling through my scalp. I jumped up with a start, screaming soundlessly and using precious energy to try to brush off any of the little critters who wanted a piece of me. Then, after such a burst of activity, all I wanted to do was lie under a tree and go back to sleep again. I tried to estimate how much ground I'd covered today. It was all just a blur.

It was dusk when I woke. I must have slept for several hours.

My body felt stiff and sore, my mouth dry, my heart was beating loudly in my chest with the forceful effort of rising. A soft warm breeze caressed my face, and as I looked up I could see the big river red gum branches move ever so slightly. This was a narrow part of the creek, where the trees grew close together, forming a dense canopy that almost blocked the evening light out altogether. My hand brushed against what felt like a strong piece of sticky string. It seemed to be attached to an enormous rope like spider web, and I looked up to see hundreds of gold spider webs stretched between the gums, shimmering in the evening light. High up in the air were dozens of huge Golden Orb spiders, barely moving in their webs despite the evening breeze. Some of the spiders, probably females, were the biggest spiders I have ever seen.

I knew these spiders were common in northern parts of Australia. Their bite was venomous to small birds and other creatures but regarded as harmless to humans. I was momentarily fascinated with the long glistening lines containing victims that had met their fate after being entangled in the powerful traps; legs and wings of various creatures wrapped partially in spider silk - insects and the occasional small bird.

I could see egg casings in some of the webs. The young Golden Orb spiders would emerge from their egg case and, as young spiderlings, drift on the wind and land hundreds of miles away to take up residence in their new home.

I touched some of the lower pieces of golden silk. I hadn't seen such a large grouping of spiders in one area in the bush before, and the effect sent chills down my spine. I pictured myself walking through this area in the darkness and quickly decided to move on. Ahead of me, the last minutes of an amber sky lit up the distant horizon, reassuring me I was still headed west. I stumbled slowly; I had developed a strange gait, my steps no longer had purpose as I wandered on and on.

Despair, combined with extreme fatigue and exhaustion, hit again, along with hysteria, but I didn't even have the energy to break down. I was well past that. *Perhaps this is the place where my life will end after all.* No tears came, I was too tired and dehydrated to produce any. My resting place for the night was chosen haphazardly. I crawled into a small hollow in the side of the creek, turned feebly on my side, and fell into a deep sleep within minutes.

Chapter Sixteen

Survival, Day Six

The mid-morning heat struck my face with vengeance. As soon as I woke I felt pain and intense thirst. It took an immense effort just to turn and get to my feet. I had slept in a precarious position, on top of a bank under a huge gum by the side of the creek. I couldn't remember how I came to be here; no longer able to recollect which direction I came from or how far I had walked yesterday.

I sat myself up by rolling over sideways and propping myself up against the tree. My trusty backpack beside me. I considered leaving it where it was because of the amount of exertion it took just to pick it up and sling it on my back, not to mention the weight I had to carry. I sat for some time contemplating what I should do. Even though I had just woken I found myself falling asleep. Each time I woke, I told myself to *get up now, get up,* but again and again, I drifted back into a deep sleep.

I must have slept all morning; the sun was now high in the sky, the heat had well and truly set in. Sitting, scanning the sky, hoping for a miracle, perhaps a plane might spot me. But the silence of the bush rang loudly in my ears.

The white cockatoos were back again. Inquisitive by nature, this time they landed right above me, taking it in turns flying to the lower branches of the tree to look at me. Their piercing black eyes seemed to remember me from some distant past; it was as though they were looking deep into my soul. In that moment of silence, despite my pain and torment, I felt a profound sense of peace.

Finally, back on my feet for what was perhaps my final burst. Back pack abandoned - why did I even bring the damned thing with me anyway? Wandering in a daze along the creek bank, a drunken crazy gait, each movement pronounced, each step much harder to take than the last. Vision contorted, I seemed to be seeing double of everything. That's when I noticed the pile of rocks - not the smooth, rounded rocks of the creek bed, but a dark granite. It must have been carried here from the distant ranges. But why and by whom? I scanned the creek bed looking for clues, desperate for anything that would help me. Nothing. I stumbled on.

Then, in the distance … something shiny. I squinted. It looked many miles away, but it stood out like a beacon in this vast empty land. I stood still, staring at the glinting object through the oppressive wave of heat until I had to shut my eyes against the glare.

*   *   *

I had woken in a strange stupor. Nothing seemed real

anymore. It felt as though I was hallucinating, I couldn't think rationally about where I was and what I needed to do. How could I cover distance to find this thing when I was so weak? I looked up again at the shiny thing in the distance. Heat was coming off it in shimmering waves, but I decided it wasn't real. It must be a mirage.

Totally disorientated, I staggered and lurched aimlessly on. One minute I was leaning forward looking down into the creek bed, the next a sensation of falling down, almost like flying.

The pain was excruciating when I landed. I told myself I must be sleep walking. I slept again for a very long time.

*   *   *

Loud eruptions of laughter reverberated along the ancient creek bed, echoing off the rocky cliffs on either side of me. The sounds of pure joy, children's happy voices carried through the still air. They were the most beautiful sounds I had ever heard. Was I hallucinating? The sounds seemed to be getting closer. I tried to turn my head in the direction of the voices, but I didn't have the energy to move my head or my body.

I looked up to see small faces staring at me with wonder and puzzlement. They were speaking a language I did not understand. I looked down at my sunburned hands and arms. They were caked with dirt, scratches, deep cuts and dried blood. My lips were so cracked and swollen that speaking was too difficult; my voice just a strange croak. I couldn't seem to communicate. What must they make of me? They looked puzzled, as though they were trying to figure out who this strange human being was and where she had come from. Despite the obvious excitement, I drifted off ...

*   *   *

'Hello, Sarah. My name is Libby, I'm the community clinic nurse. Do you know where you are and what has happened to you?' She answered for me. 'You are on Aboriginal lands. Some of the children found you in the creek bed about a kilometre from here. They sounded the alarm when they couldn't wake you up. You are very lucky to be alive, I think we managed to find you just in time.'

I nodded weakly in reply.

'You were reported missing when you left Mirna Springs Station six days ago. It's nothing short of amazing that you have trekked through such harsh country and found the community. You have broken your arm probably from a fall, and your other arm is infected. You have some bad sunburn and were extremely dehydrated when you came into the clinic. We've popped a drip on you to help with hydration, and we've notified the RFDS, who will probably fly you out tomorrow.'

I looked over at a second set of concerned eyes and recognised a familiar face - Jamie Landers, the police officer from Dillalong. I tried to manage a smile, but my mouth didn't feel like part of me anymore. In the next instant, everything started to rush back again and I jolted forward almost involuntarily in an effort to get up. The nurse eased me back into bed, saying moving right now was not a good idea.

'The McCallums are after me, they want to kill me.' I uttered the words with a raspy voice; my normal voice had disappeared without a trace. Even when I tried to emphasise the word "kill" it came out as not much more than a whisper.

Jamie leaned in towards me, took my hand and spoke quietly. 'We don't want you to worry about that right now, they no longer have the ability to harm you, or anybody else for that matter.'

'Why?' I whispered.

'The property had been under surveillance for some time. We have been gathering evidence over many months, waiting for the right time to go in and make arrests. That all happened, after you left.'

I could see the concern on Jamie's face. I wanted to know more about what had happened out there at Mirna Springs, but I could also see that he didn't want to disclose much more at this point.

I struggled to get the words out. 'But are they back at the station now?'

'No, they have both been detained.'

The nurse came back, and Jamie retreated to the chair.

'How long have I been in this room?'

The answer shocked me. Three days. Jamie said they had been searching the area for me and if I'd been out there for too many more hours I probably wouldn't have survived. The local children who had found me in the creek bed had gone back to get help. I was so dehydrated that my body was going into shock by the time they got me back to the clinic. They were very concerned about me and sought specialist advice from Telehealth, who advised them to stabilise me before flying me out.

Over the coming hours I drifted in and out of consciousness. At one stage I could hear singing and the sound of clap sticks. The singing seemed to go for hours, and I asked the nurse what was happening. She told me the people who live here were singing for joy; one of their old people had returned home and the whole community had come out to welcome her back to her country. I wondered who this very much-loved Elder could be, and how long she had lived away from her people.

A strong breeze picked up pace, swirling through the leaves of the giant silver gums outside my window. Just beyond, pale grey smoke billowed upwards through the trees in the creek bed, travelling high up into the sky. I had a moment of total awareness then, an understanding of what had happened to me. I noted that my heart was still beating in my chest, and I was very much still alive and kicking. I was conscious enough, and even well enough, to feel something that was beyond appreciation and gratitude. I felt a total sense of euphoria, and if I hadn't been bed-bound I might have jumped out of bed in that instant and leapt around the room to celebrate my survival.

Through the window I had glimpses of the local people coming together, the bright colours, the singing and dancing and the dust from moving feet swirling up carried upwards by the wind. I wished I could go out and join them. Tears streamed down my face and I found myself laughing out loud at the same time.

'I made it, Josh. I made it.'

*   *   *

Old May was looking intently down at me. I thought I must be dreaming, until she spoke.

'Hey girl, you found my country. I'm very proud of you my girl. I had to come, you know, check, make sure you were okay.'

Emotion took hold of me as I looked at that weathered face, the face that had endured so much, the deep knowledge in those brown eyes. She had led me here. I knew that.

'I wanted to make it here May, so you would know I really listened to you that day.' I laughed as tears fell. Her thin hand held mine, and in that moment, I felt so blessed that I knew this special Elder, this extraordinary woman.

May couldn't hide her excitement and deep elation. I had

never seen her face so animated as she told me she had returned to her mother's country for good. She said she would never go back to Mirna Springs again now. May, a much-loved and revered Elder, had returned home, much to the joy of her family and her people. Every man, woman and child had turned out for the celebrations. She was home.

May told me more of what happened after my speedy departure from Mirna Springs.

'I seen you my girl Sarah, when you came back to the homestead, you took some of my bread before you left,' she said, chuckling. Then on a more serious note, 'Yeah, I knew where you might be walking but I told no one back there.' 'But May, did you think I had set off to find your community on your old track?'

'Yeah, I thought about you travelling every day, wondered where you were. Hoped you would make it eh, if anyone could make it, it will be Sarah.' May touched her heart as she spoke. 'I think, Sarah, she is strong, has a big heart, so special this girl, she will make it through.'

There was a deep silence. We were both too emotional to speak in that minute.

'Tom and John, they've both gone away now, maybe they won't come back anymore to Mirna.'

'So you aren't worried about Joe anymore, May?'

'No, not now.' May gave a huge sigh and I could see that

a weight had been lifted from her shoulders. She finally felt free to live the rest of her life happily here among her friends and family in her community, the people she loved the most, for the remainder of her life.

Later that day, after waking from another deep slumber, there were more visitors - the six children who found me in the creek were all gathered around my bed. They had big beaming smiles as they recalled how one of the boys, Dax, spotted my hat blowing along the creek. They had been on a lizard hunting expedition, and had a competition going to see who could spot the most lizards in the creek. Apparently they had these competitions many times a week, each child wanting to lay claim to being the champion. When they noticed what looked like someone lying on the rocks they ran over to investigate. They shook me several times to wake me up but when they couldn't, realised I must be very unwell.

'You were real sick,' one of them said with concern, 'but we got help.'

My voice still barely a croak, I thanked them all and told them how lucky I was that they had their competitions in the creek that day, because otherwise, I might not have made it here safely. I promised them when I was well, I would visit them on their land again. Some gave me a hug, and they all said, 'Bye Sarah, come back and see us, yeah.' I shook each little hand in turn, and as they left they looked back at me with cheeky smiles on their faces.

I could see them through the window, running and jumping as they headed back down to the creek where the singing and celebrations were happening. Many of these children were born here on their lands. Like their parents and grandparents before them, they knew the area like the backs of their hands. I would be forever grateful and thankful to these little people who saved my life.

Chapter Seventeen

The clinic staff were preparing to fly me out when I heard the Flying Doctor plane circling. I was suddenly overcome with emotion, and felt scared to be leaving this safe haven. I needed surgery to set my arm properly, they were still concerned about my electrolytes and vital organs, and I needed further tests and monitoring to ascertain if I had sustained any long-term damage, so I was being transported to the Royal Adelaide Hospital. Decisions were being made on my behalf, and I needed to trust their judgement. I knew I would get the best of care, but still felt reluctant to leave the place where I had been given a second chance at life. In retrospect, my anxiety was probably not unusual, given my recent trauma.

The new arrivals walked through the door, and I felt overwhelmed once again. 'Hi Sarah, how are you going? My name is Dr Alder from the RFDS, we've come to take you back to Adelaide for further care.' He had a flashing smile, a short grey beard, twinkly blue eyes behind steel-rimmed glasses and was dressed casually in jeans and t-shirt. I offered a weak smile and in return received a reassuring smile and a pat on the arm from someone keen to get the show rolling.

Along with Doctor Alder, Nurse Camden would be taking care of me onto Adelaide.

'We hear you have had quite the adventure out here!'

'We've been really looking forward to meeting you, you are quite the legend!'

I forced a warped but painful smile; I didn't feel like a legend.

'Most people thought there was no way you could survive without water for such a long period of time.'

'The heat has been intense out here, it's a been phenomenal weather pattern for weeks now, with no end in sight.'

I listened to their chatter as they prepared me for the flight, drifting in and out of sleep. They did tell me my backpack and camera had been located, and were loaded on the flight with me.

Jamie was there to say goodbye. I wondered again if perhaps we had had some sort of connection back then, but I didn't have the energy to think too much about it. He had apparently stayed on the lands for the first two nights after I was found - Libby said he'd been hanging around to make sure I was going to be okay.

Kneeling by my bed, Jamie reassured me I was in good hands, and that when he visited next I would be fit and well. I hoped he was right.

I found myself asking, 'When will I see you again?' He said he was due for leave and would be coming down to Adelaide soon.

As they wheeled me out to the plane I looked back, trying to see his face. I felt overwhelmed again and tried unsuccessfully to stop the tears from falling. The crew reassured me all was okay, I would be in Adelaide before I knew it and my family and friends were awaiting my arrival.

We took off quickly. Now I was in that tiny silver fish, flying high over the same ranges I had walked through over the past six days. I forced my head up and looked out at the clear sky. The first thing I noticed was a flock of white corellas, flying low across the arid lands. Then those eternally majestic purple ranges, encircling the silver fish. An amphitheatre of green and grey shadows in the gorges far below. Flashes of brilliant colour; a snapshot of earth from above in all of its glory. I was still alive to see it all.

Sleep must have overwhelmed me within seconds, to this day, I can't remember much else about the flight. Within an hour and a half, we had landed on the tarmac, an ambulance waiting to take me to hospital.

The rest is a blur. I spent the majority of my time in a deep sleep. They told me later this was quite normal for someone suffering severe dehydration; the body has started to shut down. I'd had a close brush with death - but it wasn't to be my last.

Mum and Dad were by my bedside within an hour of me being admitted to hospital. To my surprise Mum's reaction when she saw me was to gasp and then break down and cry; I don't think I had yet grasped the full reality of what had happened up there. Family were unable to hug me on that first day, but they held my hands and gave me much comfort and reassurance as I focused on healing and reclaiming my life.

The medical staff and my family told me repeatedly how I was lucky to be alive, having beaten the odds lost in the bush in the heat of summer with little water. There are stories of others like me who were fortunate enough to walk out of the bush to tell their survival tale, but also some tragic endings for those not able to get to help in time.

Those first days in hospital I would wake early and an hour or two later fall asleep again. My energy levels were all but gone, and I started to wonder if I would ever return to being my old self again. As each day passed though, there were small but significant improvements, and eventually, I was able to walk with ease.

One thing that had not been talked about openly yet was the reason I had run from Mirna Springs in the first place.

Chapter Eighteen

On my third day in hospital the police visited me. After checking on me that morning, the duty doctor mentioned the police were keen to speak to me to get a statement as soon as possible, so arrangements were made.

I was propped up in the armchair for the visit, still wearing my hospital gown. I knew I looked pretty scary: a drip in one scratched and bruised arm, plaster on the other, horrendous sunburn, hair unwashed, tangled and dishevelled. I drew on all my strength and courage to make sure the police heard my story, so that the pieces of a very large puzzle could finally be pieced together. With any luck, some of the mystery could be solved with the new information that I was able to share.

Two detectives introduced themselves as Marcia Strand and Harry Denning. Both worked out of Central Office in Adelaide. They started the session off by providing an overview of information that the police already knew. I assumed they had already read reports about my escape from Mirna Springs Station and my six-day trek through the bush.

Harry mentioned they were gathering evidence to assist them in finally charging, and hopefully convicting, a known group of criminals thought to be responsible for multiple crimes in South Australia as well as other states. Harry said the group in the spotlight was a syndicate of well-organised individuals who police believed were involved in organised rackets including stock stealing, extortion - and possibly murder.

In my confusion and medicated stupor, I asked, 'Who might have been murdered at Mirna Springs Station whilst I was there?'

Harry shook his head. 'We don't believe a murder took place at the station whilst you were present.'

Confusion still reigned. I couldn't seem to get my head around what they were trying to tell me.

Harry asked if I was okay with having the interview recorded, and I agreed. After fiddling with his audio equipment for a minute, we started with small talk: I was asked to give my name, date of birth, address and phone number, where I work and my role.

Marcia then posed the first critical question. 'So, Sarah, can you tell us why you happened to be staying on Mirna Springs Station between the dates February twelfth and fifteenth of this year, and what activities you were involved in while you were staying there?'

I explained to them both, providing detail but not going into the specifics - that my employer *The New Times* had made arrangements for me to travel to Mirna Springs Station to write a story that included a synopsis of the owners of the station.

'My story was scheduled to be published in the lift-out magazine in the "Australian Life" section,' I said with some regret. It was doubtful whether this story would ever be published now. The detectives asked questions about what activities I had been involved in during my stay. I gave an overview of the people I had talked to and my movements each day.

Harry asked, 'So, Sarah, can you tell us what happened in the lead-up to your escape from Mirna Springs and the attempt to find the Aboriginal community settlement?'

My thoughts raced back to that day: the heavy heat, the walk along Old Mine Road and what I discovered once I got past that new fence - the long shed and what was happening there.

I described as best I could my intention to find out what down that road. It was partly triggered because something of interest caught my eye that final morning and of course, a level of curiosity, not having been down that road before. I also explained an incident the previous night that left me wanting to seek further answers, based on a conversation I overheard between Tom McCallum and the unknown person who arrived at the homestead.

They produced a photo of the guy I had aptly nicknamed "the bulldog". The distinctive tats, the hair and the size of the man, a dead giveaway. The detectives identified him as Tony

Gazzedi, a well-known criminal with the nickname, "rabbit".

This was the man who visited the homestead and discussed plans with Tom McCallum to dispose of stolen cattle at the shed the next day. I was able to identify this man as the night visitor simply because of his distinctive accent and gravel-toned voice.

He was also the guy who found me in the scrub and locked me in the hut. I knew this information would be critical to the prosecution's case, so when shown the photo I felt confident it was the same man involved in the illegal operation on Mirna Springs.

It struck me as comical that the "bulldog" had another nickname, "rabbit". My mind started to work overtime as to how and why this guy was given such an amusing title. I decided there were many things I didn't know about this insidious character - and that also pleased me, because I really didn't want to know.

An hour and a half quickly passed. The whole story had started to spill out of me. They listened intently, enquiring every now and then about the details, teasing out certain things I noticed or heard. They were particularly interested in my description of what I found on Old Mine Road.

They were obviously briefed about how I came to be now sitting in the hospital. The main interest now, filling in the gaps, learning what transpired in the lead-up to me setting off through the scrub in a bid to find an escape route. They heard the story in my words, but were expert at gathering the information they required. As a journalist, I knew I'd be a star witness in any prosecution trial. They were interested in crucial key dates and times that would provide further evidence. Some dates were very clear in my mind, others, particularly once I was out in the scrub, were not as clear to me. I relived the escape and the crawl down the hill, I described to them the moment that I looked back, hearing the sound of motors, knowing I was being chased.

Suddenly feeling overwhelmed, I started to shake and needed to stop. Nursing staff, who had been hovering, called an end to the interview. 'She's due for her meds now. Sorry, but we need to get her back to bed.'

'I'm fine, truly,' I argued, but I could see Marcia and Harry stopping the tape. In some ways, I was relieved the interview was called to a halt. Harry and Marcia arranged to call again, and I was back in bed and asleep within ten minutes of them leaving.

They returned two days later and we continued the taped interview. Time was of the essence - some of these people still needed to be apprehended and charged.

One thing that did stick in my mind afterwards was Marcia asking me if I had met, or heard of, a man called Chad Dimitri while staying at Mirna Springs. I was shown a photo and given a description of Chad's car. I recognised Chad from the photo on the wall at Dillalong police station.

'Yes, I visited the police in Dillalong and saw the poster, so I was aware Chad had been reported as missing.

'But no, I didn't hear of, or see anyone matching his description during my stay up there. However, I did make a chance discovery in the hut where I was imprisoned.'

'Go on.'

'Well, it was entirely accidental. I was down on my hands and knees searching for a way out and noticed a scratching on the log cabin wall. It said "Chad Dimitri".'

Marcia and Harry suddenly sat up straight. They drew a diagram of the hut and asked me to mark the side of the wall where I had discovered Chad's name. I told them about the blood-stained hessian bags on the floor.

The reality of the situation, and the knowledge these men had probably murdered an innocent person, was overwhelming in that minute. I had to stop for a while to regain my composure. The detectives remained patient, though, and after a brief pause the interview was reconvened.

Still pursuing this line of enquiry, Harry asked if I had heard any conversations that included information about Chad or his whereabouts. Despite my brain still experiencing some post-trauma confusion, I sensed the importance of my disclosure regarding Chad Dimitri's name being left on the wall of the hut. Chad had now been missing for an extended period of time and his family, friends and of course the police were all looking for answers.

'This is pretty important information, Sarah, and could be vital to solving this case. You said you took some photos, would it be possible to see the pictures you took inside the hut?'

Marcia carried my backpack over from the hospital cupboard. I felt very protective of the photos - after all, they told the story of my survival and I wasn't keen to let the camera out of my sight until I had viewed all the photos myself.

After some discussion I agreed that the police would take the camera, on the promise it would be returned to me as soon as practical. We charged up the camera, which by then had a flat battery, and connected it to Harry's laptop.

They gathered around me and flicked through the photos. Harry stopped at one of the shots taken inside the hut, the one that clearly showed Chad Dimitri's name on the logs. Despite knowing these photos could solve the baffling case of a missing man, I was overwhelmed again with the realisation my own fate had almost been sealed that day. I felt eternally grateful I was still alive and able to relay my story to others.

I overhead Harry on the phone to his superiors. 'This could be the breakthrough that we'd hoped to find.'

I wasn't surprised when he returned to ask if I'd be happy to talk to his superiors about my discovery, and two hours later my room was filled to capacity with visitors. This new group of people included the superintendent, who had called to specifically ask for much more detail in relation to my earlier statement. They thanked me before they left, reassuring me this information was not going to be released to the public just yet. The police would confirm the information and work with local authorities. It was also pointed out what I already knew - I happened to be the only witness to the contents of the hut and what happened at Mirna Springs. The authorities considered it imperative I receive full protection in the lead-up to court proceedings.

Full protection? This was not something I had contemplated at all. Surely these people would not be interested in coming for me? I had a visit from Mum and Dad later that day, and they encouraged me to call my lawyer, Ed Curren, for advice.

It was only when I finished the final interview detectives filled me in on what had been happening at Mirna Springs Station since the day of my escape.

From that first day it was obvious the McCallums didn't want me at the property, authorities believed my presence complicated matters for them. But because Callie, my editor, had already made arrangements, it might have seemed suspicious and alerted the McCallums if the interview and accommodation arrangements had suddenly been cancelled.

Although I was not aware at the time, contingency plans

were in place to keep me safe in case anything went pear-shaped - which in the end, of course, it did anyway.

Hours after I fled, authorities swooped in and made multiple arrests. Ironically, they hadn't anticipated I would suddenly disappear without a trace the day before I was due to leave, and instigated a massive search. My whereabouts unknown, it was feared I had already been disposed of by Tom McCallum and his associates. Police searched the area on the road that led into Mirna Springs Station, thinking I may have taken this route. My car had been located, and my mobile phone and laptop recovered, but they offered no clues. The McCallums told police I had been warned not to wander away from the homestead, but I 'just took off into the scrub for no reason and probably got lost.' At no time did they admit that they were looking for me as well - with the intention to make sure I never left Mirna Springs Station alive.

The Star Force, a tactical group of highly trained personnel who supported police in crime control, had been involved in the sting, and because the syndicate might have been operating in other states, Federal Police had become involved as well. The reason behind the secrecy and last-minute action was because the authorities were hoping to catch some "big fish".

The men I had observed arriving at the shed in the Lexus were big operators, the brains behind some of the major stock thieving across several states, and they were now in custody. I wasn't surprised to learn there had been a shootout when the police special forces, who came in by air, landed and overran the area. A police officer was wounded and one of the guards, presumably from the hidden shed, had also been wounded. Both were expected to make a full recovery. John McCallum wasn't on the station that day but was later located in Dillalong. Both John and Tom McCallum were arrested and were facing multiple charges. They were not granted bail.

On the second day of my disappearance the police questioned other employees on the property. Harry said they had spoken to May, who offered the most detailed information. May believed I might be walking to her community, and described the track to police. Her information had been helpful; she told them I was 'running away from the bad people.'

Given the weather conditions, and the fact I hadn't taken much water, I was not expected to survive the walk. May assisted police and the search party by drawing a map of the route she walked to get to her people's country. A party of twenty police and volunteers started searching for me, following May's information.

The red helicopter I had spotted on the second day was piloted by Mack Summers, who had been assisting the police in the search. The silver plane I had seen on day five of my trek was a search and rescue plane; on board was a team who had been informed of the direction I was headed in. They had painstakingly searched the area.

If I hadn't been found alive, my camera would have provided a powerful testimony; a record of what had happened to make me want to begin the treacherous journey across the country in the first place. It also contained information vital to solving the mystery of the disappearance of an innocent man, Chad Dimitri.

*　　*　　*

That last day in hospital I had a visit from my ex-boyfriend, Taj. He heard what happened during my time at Mirna Springs via mutual friends. Taj and I were together for nearly three years. The relationship wasn't to be. We cared deeply for one another, but Taj and I had opposing ideas about too many things. In fact, as time wore on, we actually shared very few common interests.

The last time I'd seen Taj was that final day I packed my gear and announced I was leaving for good. The memory of the arguments and the late nights sitting up waiting for him to come home still hadn't faded from my memory. It was the old Taj that I remembered from years ago though who sat down next to my bed that day and tightly squeezed my hand.

Chapter Nineteen

Finally, I was home. It seemed as though I had been gone for years. I walked from room to room, touching the furniture, looking through the window at my small garden. I had missed the place so much. Despite my daily shower in hospital, the first thing I did was have a long, hot shower. I had a little laugh later though, when I thought about the red dust being washed off my skin, but not out of my heart.

Callie had given me a month off to recuperate. The wound on my arm was almost healed, the plaster removed from my broken arm. Because of the severe sunburn I had lost a few layers of skin and still had pink spots on my face and arms.

Sometimes I found myself just sitting for hours, not moving a muscle. Reliving what happened to me seemed to take up a lot of my waking hours. Some days were good, others bad. I was traumatised, and needed to give myself time to heal. I was young and I knew I would make a good physical recovery; it was my mental health I needed to take time on.

My heart skipped a beat following a phone call on my third day home. It was Jamie.

'Hi, how are you feeling, I heard you were released from

hospital. I'm coming down to the city in a couple of days and wondered if you are up for a visit at some stage?' Jamie sounded almost nervous - perhaps I was too. I think we both recognised we'd developed some sort of undeniable connection, but as to what would happen from here was anyone's guess.

I recalled the last words I had spoken to Jamie as they were about to fly me out - I had asked when I would see him again – a little smile broke out on my face. I kept the conversation lighthearted; I was feeling so happy to be home again and to be honest, I was delighted just to be talking to him.

'I would love a visit. How long will you be staying for?'

The national newspapers were starting to provide daily reports in relation to a breakthrough in the case of the missing man, Chad Dimitri. I opened the newspaper to a double-page spread, the story written by one of my counterparts at *The New Times*, police reporter Kat Allen. Part of the story included details of the discovery of Chad's name scratched on the hut wall. Police alleged the victim was held prisoner for an unknown period of time before being murdered on the property. Blood-soaked hessian bags had been checked for DNA and found to be a match with Chad's older brother, Daniel.

It seemed unbelievable, but the people responsible for his murder had not only buried this unfortunate man's body, along with his mobile phone, they had dug a hole large enough to bury his Pajero four-wheel-drive as well. Both the car and his remains had been recovered after a massive police effort. Following the latest evidence, two men had been charged with murder, and more arrests were expected in relation to the killing.

The paper reported that Chad's body was located on a property named Mirna Springs Station. Owner John McCallum and his son Tom were charged with murder and remain in custody in Adelaide goal. The McCallums were facing a number of other serious charges in relation to cattle stealing, and threats to people and property. Police were investigating the possibility of accomplices from an interstate syndicate being involved.

The men I witnessed arriving on the back road that morning were part of an elaborate national network, also known as the syndicate. No doubt some of the men working in the shed as slaughtermen were also part of the group.

Kat's summary included a section about the victim's family and friends. The murdered man, Chad Dimitri, was an amateur historian who loved collecting information about early settlers in the far north of the state. He had often travelled to remote areas to interview families and document his findings and was hoping to write a book, according to his wife Maria. She was travelling interstate when Chad disappeared. They were normally in touch every day or so, but Maria didn't think it odd when she didn't hear from Chad for six or seven days, because she believed his phone was out of range.

She reported Chad missing to police after trying for seven days without contact. She initially believed he might have become lost in a remote location, or perhaps his car may have broken down. The alert was raised, a huge search party failed to find any trace of Chad. The search included members of his own family, including his father and brother who travelled from Sydney. Maria Dimitri also stayed in the area for several weeks to help assist in the search. Search and rescue planes scoured the ranges for signs of life. Some volunteers and close relatives kept searching even after the official search was called off.

As the weeks passed, Maria Dimitri's worry turned to grief. She had a sixth sense Chad had died, either by the hands of others or by accident somewhere out in the bush. The couple's two young children were also grieving for their father.

Photographs included the recovered vehicle and a map of the area in which it was found. Looking carefully at the map now, it wasn't surprising to notice the burial site was located near Old Mine Road. A more precise inspection of the map revealed the site being just half a kilometre north of the road. The conversation I overheard outside of the hut sprung to mind, when my car was asked for. I suddenly realised Chad's burial site must have been near the hut and this is where they had also intended to bury me - probably along with my car!

I shuddered as I realised that my fate could have been similar to Chad's; missing without a trace, the McCallums claiming I had left the property of my own accord.

According to records from Chad's recovered phone, he had travelled to the area in February the year before. After spending some time at another property in the area, he told the owners he was heading for Mirna Springs Station to interview the McCallum family. Police believe Dimitri had travelled to Mirna Springs Station without first arranging a visit, had stumbled unwittingly upon the illegal operation being run on the property. This had ultimately cost him his life.

Chapter Twenty

Whenever Jamie could take time off, he would come down to the city to visit me. We'd been seeing each other regularly for a couple of months. There was no denying the strong spark of attraction between us, but it went much deeper than mere attraction. Jamie had been part of the search party scouring the countryside after I fled Mirna Springs Station. He was there in those early days during my recovery. His support through those difficult times was unconditional. I was still living through a crisis, but Jamie never shied away; he still wanted to be there for me, that meant a lot.

Sitting opposite Jamie in my garden, I smiled inwardly, realising how relaxed and comfortable we were with each other. I found Jamie Landers unlike anyone else I had ever met - amusing, engaging, caring, but also deliciously romantic; he was all of those things and more rolled into one. Recently, though, there had been a subtle change in our relationship; the bond had deepened. Out of curiosity and a burning desire to know where I stood, I asked Jamie if he was single. I knew he had been with a local girl, Jess, but he finally told me that it hadn't worked out, and she had moved on about a year ago. Jamie couldn't stop grinning when he observed the look on my face. How did I feel about this disclosure? Well, certainly interested! As if sensing this, Jamie reached out and grabbed my hand. That's when I thought it was time to tell Jamie about Taj. I explained that Taj and I were an item for close to three years and had only just broken off our relationship before my trip to Mirna Springs. I didn't go into too much detail, just that Taj and I were two very different people, and although we had talked about marriage, I was never willing to take that step. As I talked Jamie nodded, and I noticed he couldn't stop grinning. Talking about Jess and Taj seemed to have removed a final barrier between us, and we could both declare how we really felt.

'Right from the minute you walked through the door of the Dillalong Police Station I thought, 'Wow, who is this amazing girl, no chance could she be single!' Jamie had a twinkle in his eye as he spoke. 'When we talked later that evening I was concerned though about you travelling out to Mirna, knowing what we already thought might be happening out there, but also thinking that I had no way of telling you what was suspected at the time. '

The memory reminded me of how complicated the turn of events had all been. 'The biggest challenge I faced was trying to get a couple of characters like Tom and John to talk to me, the unwanted visitor; they were hiding some pretty dark secrets, and I learned pretty quickly that I was the unwanted visitor.'

'It still blows me away when I think about the incredible courage and strength that you had to muster once your cover was blown,' said Jamie. 'They were out to get you, no matter what.'

'To be honest, if Tom had treated me as a normal person would, and not warned me to go wandering around, I would probably never have gone down Old Mine Road in the first place.'

'Yeah, your curiosity was what helped crack this case wide open, but it nearly cost you your life.' We were both silent for a few minutes as we contemplated what might have been.

*   *   *

With the court case coming up, I decided to contact Maria Dimitri and her family. Now that Chad's body had been recovered, they were able to organise a funeral for him, I felt the time was right. I called explaining who I was; when I initially fled Mirna Springs Station they captured and imprisoned me in the same place Chad may have spent his final days. I felt an immediate bond between us. Maria had so many unanswered questions about what really happened to her husband, she asked if we could catch up and talk. Her family were seeking answers, and while I didn't know if my recollections would help them, I agreed. I suspected she was needing closure so that she could move on - if that would ever be possible.

We met Maria Dimitri and Chad's brother Daniel on a cold rainy morning in a city café. My friend Rosie came with me for support. The minute I set eyes on Maria I felt utter sadness for her and her family. She was pale and withdrawn, the unmistakable signs of immense grief shadowed across her face and soft brown eyes. Maria said not knowing what Chad had gone through before he died had made her and the family determined to attend the court case. Maria's brother-in-law reiterated the family's wishes. Although Chad's parents were devastated, they wanted to attend as support for Maria. I explained the strong spiritual connection I felt with Chad as a result of what happened to both of us. It had felt as though he messaged me from the dead in that room, to make sure he was finally found and his killers brought to justice. If Chad was indeed looking on from afar, I wanted him to know I would follow this through to the end. I believed this is what he would want. So I would be at the trial, making sure my story was told. Above all else, I wanted to see justice carried out for Chad and his family.

As we walked away, Rosie squeezed my hand. 'Are you alright, Sarah?'

'I'll be okay Rose. If anything, meeting Maria today made me feel stronger and more resilient in the fight against these people.'

Ever the good friend, Rosie just nodded her head in agreement.

We were driving across the city to see my parents. They had invited Jamie and I for dinner. Glancing across, I was surprised to notice what looked like uncertainty, perhaps even some trepidation, on that sweet face. Holding back a smile, I squeezed Jamie's arm reassuringly.

'Are we on the right street now?' I gave a quick nod. 'Okay, let's do this.' Jamie was meeting my parents for the first time and I had sensed some nervousness on his part all week.

'You will love my parents, Jamie, they are really the nicest people. They'll put you at ease straight away.'

Jamie gave a small grin. 'Your dad sounds like a character. I love the fishing story you told me, so I'll bet he will have some pretty funny stories to tell about his weekends out on the water.'

Jamie's parents both died years ago. They were killed in a car accident when Jamie was just eighteen years of age and his brother David sixteen. He and David have a special bond, and catch up when his brother visits. Following their parents' death, many sad years followed. Living with their paternal grandparents they finished school and secured jobs. Both grandparents died recently. We shared a common thread, having been through indescribable despair following the loss of close family. Despite this, we were still surviving, living our lives as best we could.

From our very first conversation I considered Jamie to be a natural at putting people at ease, so I wasn't surprised when the dinner with Mum and Dad went really well. I noticed with amusement Jamie's initial fears melting away within minutes of arriving. He managed to secure a place in Mum's heart by not only helping set the table, but by his general exuberance when insisting on washing the dishes after dinner.

As we settled in the lounge for coffee after dinner, I couldn't help but marvel at Jamie. He had managed to put everyone at ease. My parents have worried about me over the years, certainly more so recently when they found out about my adventures in the far north. Luckily, they had no inkling I was lost out there until after I was found. With Josh already gone, the fear of losing their remaining child would be too much to bear. Dad gave me a hug and a big wink as I jumped into the car, and they were both still waving and blowing kisses as we drove off.

Chapter Twenty One

Three months later

The story of Connor and Jane Edwards plight aired on Chanel Seven and featured in all the major papers. Following the couple's personal account, all hell broke loose, and authorities were pressured to intervene. An enquiry was ordered into how the family were threatened and, in the process, lost their livelihood. The town and surrounding districts were up in arms about the water restrictions due to the mining exploits. Further protests were held, Tim Grant resigned as the local MP, and a Royal Commission would look into activities in the area. This was the best outcome anybody could have hoped for.

Callie called me into the office to pass on her congratulations.

'Well, Sarah, the board has agreed that your reporting resulted in a major breakthrough in crime-related exploits in the far north.'

I was genuinely surprised to learn I had been nominated for a special award for proactive investigative journalism.

'I always believed in you, Sarah, and you've proved me right,' she said with a kindly smile. 'It has just taken you a long time to believe in yourself.'

Yeah, I told myself, *it actually took a near death experience for me to realise that.*

I didn't have time to reflect too much on that last comment as several staff members, including Callie, gathered around, many diving in for giant bear hugs. Such was the excitement we ended up holding hands and dancing like crazy people around the office. Others wanting a piece of the action joined in, then someone popped a champagne cork and I heard the clink of glasses.

Days later, more good news. Dillalong had formed a committee with Connor Edwards as Chair. The new committee were supported by the towns people. Issues identified as urgent would be taken directly to the government to ensure appropriate action was taken immediately. The townspeople wanted movement in relation to the crucial water supplies – the lifeblood of the town. It was a great outcome for the locals, I felt more confident now that Connor and Jane could survive this crisis and remain on their property.

Jamie told me that the photographs taken of activities at the shed on Old Mine Road would ultimately be regarded as crucial evidence in court. My camera survived the trek, despite it bouncing around in the bottom of my backpack for six long, harrowing days. How I didn't decide to ditch the camera in my more confused moments I will never know. Even my laptop, containing all of my notes, which I was sure would have been destroyed, was retrieved by police, along with my mobile phone. This meant I wouldn't have to rely entirely on memory to recollect some of the conversations I had throughout my stay.

Confirming what had been reported in the papers, my newly appointed lawyer, Ed Curren informed me the men working in the second shed on Old Mine Road were not locals, as was suspected, but blow-ins connected with the infamous gang from Sydney. The McCallums held a long association with them; they were hardened criminals with far-reaching contacts, able to rally a team of people at short notice to engage in illegal activities throughout the country.

Ed reminded me again that I had escaped a critically dangerous situation. These people had wanted me dead. I took flight from one situation only to be faced with a life-or-death situation after getting lost in the bush for six days. The fierce country I grew to love as a child almost took my life.

Friends often rang and asked how I was going, I found myself reassuring them that I was fine. I even told my parents all was well. Being truthful about how I was really coping, however, was another matter, and at some stage I started having nightmares … being chased through the scrub, being shot at and even dying, looking down at my own dead body. My nights, instead of being peaceful, continually sleepless, my thoughts swirling through my past ordeal.

I was struggling to get my head around what really happened, and how I actually managed to survive. I knew a traumatic event could affect anyone weeks, months, even years after an event. I had to talk to someone; my coping skills seemed diminished. Eventually upon the urging of Callie, I took the step of contacting a local psychologist. I stood outside her office, wondering if I had made the right decision; after everything I had been through, wouldn't it be normal now to be having some bad dreams? My inner self was firm. *Yes, you are doing the right thing, bite the bullet and just go and get help.*

This was the start of my weekly sessions with Dr Milly, and soon I found myself looking forward to these appointments. Over the months we covered a lot of ground, but for me the most important and significant part of the sessions was telling myself that I was now safe. Milly convinced me that I could begin to believe that I had survived my ordeal and, knowing that, could finally start to move on with my life. But it turned out that I wasn't really safe at all and I was blissfully unaware of this fact.

Chapter Twenty Two

The phone woke me from a deep sleep. I looked at my alarm clock - for God's sake, it was one o'clock in the morning! I grabbed my mobile from the bedside table and answered with a croaky 'hello'.

There was no answer, just heavy breathing. Not intimidated, I hung up abruptly. It would be either a wrong number or some deranged individual who gets off on ringing people in the middle of the night hoping for a response.

Still, I wondered who it could be. I didn't give my number out freely, and it wasn't listed. Over the next couple of weeks I received several similar calls - silence, then deep breathing. Eventually, I started switching my phone off when I went to bed. I needed my sleep. I didn't mention the calls to anyone, not even Jamie, who usually rang every night. I was hoping the person would move on and forget about me. How wrong was I.

*　　*　　*

The weeks since my return to the city and "normal life" had passed quickly. I got up at the same time each morning, jogged along the boardwalk with my old school friend Rosie, and then afterwards we would sit in one of the coffee shops having a quick catch-up chat with coffee and warm croissants.

I found these everyday activities were important for me. I was able to talk to Rosie about almost anything; she seemed to accept that since my almost fatal adventure in the far north I was in some ways a different person. Rosie took it all in her stride, such was her ability to understand me. I caught up with friends I was comfortable with, and that allowed me to gradually pick apart my experience in a safe environment. For that, I was thankful.

It was during one of these ordinary days when Rosie and I were sitting in the sunshine, coffee in hand, that I noticed a guy in the distance who seemed to be lurking around and was - I wasn't sure, but perhaps - listening to us. I took note of his face. I was sure I hadn't seen him before.

I didn't mention my observation to Rosie - perhaps I was imagining the whole thing. In fact, I wondered afterwards whether I had developed some sort of paranoia because of the trauma I had been through. I made a mental note to discuss this with Milly.

Days went by and I thought no more about the strange guy until I saw him standing on the corner near my office when I finished work. Again, I thought that after everything that had happened to me, I was probably being paranoid, but all the same, I took a photo of him. He turned around and walked away in the opposite direction.

When I arrived home, I focused on the picture and tried to

figure out if I knew this man. The photo was blurred, but I could tell he had a medium but powerful build, tats on one arm and a shaved head. He was dressed casually, but the clothing looked expensive.

I showed the picture to Callie next day, asking her if she knew the man's identity, but he wasn't familiar to her either. Callie was concerned though, and I took her advice literally.

'Sarah, this is serious. You need to contact your lawyer immediately and tell him what you've just told me, he can accompany you to the Police station. In fact, I am going to ring his office now and we are going to get an urgent appointment for you.'

'No, hold off on that for now, Callie.'

'What do you mean hold off, it's either that or contact the police. Which would you prefer, Sarah?'

'Oh well, if you put it like that – okay, I guess I could have a chat to Ed about this guy.'

*   *   *

Despite the mental chaos in my life, I was resolving another issue that had been at the forefront of my mind for more than a year. I had agreed to meet Taj again. We had broken up a long time ago, but big things had happened in the meantime for both of us.

He and I were sitting in one of the lounge seats in the Sunup Cafe. The meeting seemed a little stilted at first; I found it hard to get the words out that I needed to say, and perhaps, judging by the look on Taj's face, so did he.

Looking across the table at the familiar face, the tousled brown hair and cheeky but nervous grin, I was reminded of what attracted me to this very sweet guy in the first place. It seemed like a lifetime ago now, but when we first met, it was an instant attraction.

Taj wanted to know if I was truly okay after my ordeal. His concern for me was obvious. Always the caring person, that's how I remembered Taj. I reassured him I was on the road to recovery. I picked up a high level of guilt on Taj's part, but this may have had more to do with what happened in the past than the present.

'I said, I've really missed you, Sarah,' Taj repeated. I had been thinking about our previous life and completely missed the remark.

'Oh, sorry, I'm off with the fairies today. I've missed you too, Taj, it's been a long time since we caught up.' Suddenly, his eyes bright with excitement, he grabbed my hand. 'Sarah, there's something I wanted to share with you.' Whilst I was interested in what he was about to say, I also knew there would be no going back in this relationship; it was truly over for me. Taj had been on a very long journey to recovery trying find himself again following a serious accident in which he almost killed his best mate while drink driving. His addiction to booze had almost killed him as well. He lost his job, and was hospitalised after a mental health breakdown following our breakup. He had been to hell and back. As he spoke about his own survival, there was recognition; I started to think about the abyss that I had also fallen into.

'Sarah, I've started to get my life back on track. I haven't had a drink now for over three months, I've been going to AA every week and so far, so good.'

Taj paused, wanting to say so much more but not knowing where to start. 'I just wanted to say I'm sorry for all the hurt I caused you, and I wanted to tell you that face to face. It means a lot to me that I can tell you that now.'

'Thanks Taj, for having the courage to meet with me today and saying sorry. It means a lot to me as well.'

We both laughed together then, probably for the fact we had shared so much in the past but also realising those days were over now, and we were moving on with our lives.

'I wondered if we could stay friends in the future, you know, be able to give each other a friendly wave or catch up for the occasional coffee or whatever. What do you think?'

When we said goodbye we both knew there were no ill feelings between us, we had finally put all of that aside. Much of the hurt and pain we had experienced together was able to be resolved with that friendly catch-up.

*   *   *

Around the same time I became aware of the mystery stalker, I found a weird letter in my mailbox, addressed to me in large print letters. Inside the envelope was a single page with the same large print.

"Sarah Wills, we know where you live and where you work. If you value your life you will keep your mouth shut in court. Any disclosure by you about what you witnessed during your trip to Mirna Springs Station will ensure you have signed your own death warrant."

It finished with: "By the way, don't even think about going to the police because we will find out and will show you no mercy."

Next day at work I couldn't concentrate, all I could think about was the threatening note. I felt anxious and confused about what to do. It finally hit me like a ton of bricks - I had been in denial about my situation, burying my head in the sand. Of course they had been looking for me all along, they would never give up on finding me. They had too much to lose.

I thought about the pending court case. I had been subpoenaed to appear as a witness, already briefed by my lawyer. Other than the occasional request to cover a court hearing for the paper, I had no personal experience dealing with the court system. I had known for some time I needed to prepare myself for the hearing, but shelved thoughts about it because my priority was my sense of self-preservation and recovery.

If these people wanted to me to feel rattled though, they

had succeeded. I needed to be a step ahead of them but what should my next move be?

Chapter Twenty Three

I decided to err on the side of caution, making sure I had someone with me when I finished work and walked to my car each day. No one could get into my building; I was assured my apartment was burglar-proof. Of course, criminals can break into anything if they have the will. Rather foolishly, I decided not to go to the police. I was to regret that, though. A few days later, I finished work early and stopped off at the supermarket on my way home to buy a few groceries. The outdoor car park was busy; there were lots of people around. I felt safe, even though I was alone. As I walked to my car, carrying a bag of groceries, the usual hustle and bustle around me gave me a false sense of security, and my guard was down. I had just reached my car when, out of the corner of my eye, I glimpsed a man walking quickly across the car park towards me. Still, I was not on full alert, not believing anybody in their right mind would attack someone in a car park in daylight with security cameras all around and people about. Wrong again.

Just as I was opening the car boot, someone grabbed me from behind. Startled, the groceries fell to the ground and the bag burst open - but this was the least of my worries. I tried to scream but a large hand was placed over my lower face. Fighting back, I almost wriggled free, but it was a losing battle. The man was much larger than me, and was using his legs as well as arms to wrap around me in a tight squeeze.

I realised he was attempting to drag me over to a black van parked close to mine. I still didn't know who I was grappling with; the man stayed behind me, with one arm around my waist and the other arm up, his hand held tightly over my mouth.

Whoever this creep was, he was extremely strong. I couldn't break free; elbowing him hard in the chest, repeatedly, didn't have any impact at all. I managed to turn my head sideways and he lost his grip over my mouth.

I screamed for help as loudly as I could, and his hold loosened slightly.

I was able to twist now, and got a clear glimpse of him. It was definitely the same person I had noticed outside the cafe weeks ago. He was wearing a hoodie that was pulled down to cover his face, so from a security camera point of view he would be hard to identify.

'You're coming with me, bitch.' His voice was low, menacing.

'That's what you think.' My knee connected with his groin, and he fell back slightly, allowing me to twist away. For a split second I was out of his grasp, but he was too quick, grabbing my arm and dragging me again towards the back of his van.

He was an incredibly powerful guy intent on taking me away. I resisted with all the strength that I could muster, using my legs to kick and my arms to push, attempting to twist back and forth out of his intense grip. As I started screaming again, at the top of my lungs, I saw two men running across the car park towards us.

As they neared, I was shoved forward onto the ground. The fight was over. The assailant ran back to his vehicle, but not before he'd spat out the threat: 'We'll be back to get you, bitch.' He jumped in the van, looking at me long and hard, then pointing to me with a finger, put two fingers to the side of his head – yes, I get it, *you want to put a bullet through my head*. He sped off quickly, car threading quickly through the throng of traffic, out of sight within seconds.

The security guard and a customer approached me. 'Are you alright, love?'

'Yes, I think so,' I replied shakily. 'He tried to drag me into his car.'

'We saw it all,' said the guard. 'I've phoned the police, they'll be here in a minute. Let's go inside and wait. Did you know this guy?'

I shook my head. 'No, never seen him before in my life.' *Actually I do know this guy, he's been following me for weeks now.* It was obvious somebody was very keen to ensure I would never attend that court hearing.

The police arrived to take a statement. How on earth could I start to explain what had been happening to me?

As I tried to describe the past few months, I realised the seriousness of the situation. How many times had I dodged a bullet? Talking about it took me right back to the hut in the ranges; the fear was potent. I recognised the guy who attacked me as the one who has been stalking me, and gave a full description to the police, including the grainy photo that I had taken on my mobile. I told them he had been following me for some time now, turning up at my usual haunts and at my workplace. The police said they would review security footage from the car park, to see if they could track the black van and put a name to the offender, warning me that the van may have been stolen.

They then insisted I go to the station with them; one of them would accompany me in my car in case I was followed again. I asked the police officer accompanying me if she would mind if I visited my lawyer on the way, and she agreed.

If only Jamie was here with me now, he would know what to do. But he was hundreds of kilometres away and couldn't get leave again for another month.

I rang Ed Curren's office and asked for an immediate appointment, and somehow they managed to squeeze me in between appointments. The police officer delivered me to Ed 's office and then left.

While I waited for Ed, I had a few minutes to contemplate my situation. A big part of me wanted to be able to have my say in court. I wanted to see justice done and these people put in prison where they belonged. Another part of me, though, was very aware they were without a doubt an insidious bunch of crims who didn't care who they hurt; they would intimidate and threaten until they got what they wanted. I had been warned not to go to the police - but who else could I turn to right now?

I was desperate to have some firm guidance as to what I needed to do next. I had a copy of the threatening letter, along with an enlarged printout of the guy who had been stalking me - and finally, attempting to abduct me.

Ed finally stepped out of his office, apologising for keeping me waiting. He was wearing a grey pinstripe suit with a natty bow tie and had the classic brisk manner of a courtroom lawyer, always thinking ahead even when listening, ready to offer an immediate answer or solution.

He smiled at me as he guided me to a seat opposite his big desk. 'It's been a while, Sarah. What brings you here today?"

'Ed, I needed to speak to you urgently. Things have gotten totally out of hand this last few weeks.'

Hands clasped together in front of him, he listened intently as I summarised recent events, including being watched and stalked by the unknown stranger, the threatening note and the late night phone calls. I felt surprisingly composed as I described the attempted abduction that had taken place just a couple of hours ago. Perhaps I was still in shock.

Ed looked concerned, sitting up and leaning forward in his armchair as I painted a picture of those recent months. His reaction was stronger than I had anticipated.

'I'm not going to beat about the bush, Sarah, these people are hardened criminals and your life could be in danger as we speak. I suggest we head straight down to the police station and see what solutions they can offer you. Under the current circumstances I think you need immediate protection.'

My heart skipped a beat and fear started to rise again in my belly. I knew I was overreacting, but I just wanted my old life back.

'No Ed, that won't work. They have threatened if I go to the police they will make a move against me straight away. There has to be some other way to deal with this.'

Ed drummed his fingers on the desk. He appeared impatient with me. 'Sarah, they are not just threatening anymore, they've attempted to abduct you! The danger you talk about is already present. I'm afraid I am not who you should be talking to about this. I will help you to get the right advice, but we really do need to get the ball rolling on some kind of help, possibly witness protection.'

Feeling overwhelmed, I argued, 'Ed, I'm not so sure. I've heard about people who were in these programs for years and they lost all their freedom and rights. I just don't want to be one of those people, I value my life but I don't want to live the rest of it always looking over my shoulder.'

'That said, Sarah, you still need to get the right advice and help. I wouldn't say it if I didn't think it was completely necessary. We'll take my car. I will ring the supervisor at the Macklin Street police station and we can have a confidential chat with him on the way.'

'Ed, please, they are probably outside the building right now and they will follow me to the police station, so no, the answer is still no.'

'We'll take the lift down to the basement carpark and exit on the next street, on the other side of this building. It wouldn't be the first time I've performed this little trick with a client.' Without waiting for an answer, he rang the police station and arranged the visit.

Driving through the streets with Ed, the whole situation felt surreal. Here I was, living back in the big city, surrounded by friends, family, fellow employees and other people whom I regarded as my close supports. Much of my life had started to return to some form of normality, with a predictable daily routine that didn't require a lot of planning or forethought. All of this also had the effect of cushioning my recovery. Familiar life and its predictable nature had become my safety zone. Now these men had managed to find me, intimidate me and threaten me. My old fears had returned with a vengeance.

Ed broke into my thoughts with a surprise confession.

'You probably need to know, Sarah, that I've been identified as your lawyer in this case. As you can imagine, it is a high profile case that has attracted a lot of attention from all the wrong quarters, if you know what I mean. I have to watch my back until the court hearing as well.'

I hadn't even thought of how this case might affect so many people. I worried for Ed, even though he assured me that he had defended many people in his long career and there was no way these people were going to have any impact on his decision making.

Before I knew it, I was walking into Macklin Street police station with Ed, having to think about what I really wanted. Some people might call me stubborn or obstinate, but I felt determined I didn't want to put my life on hold on account of a bunch of criminals. Although I was committed to attending court to give evidence, I was already weighing up how it might cost me the freedoms I took for granted.

Following a gruelling three-hour interview, the special agent told me his plan, to take effect immediately. I wasn't ready to take this so far - but did I have a choice anymore?

I could no longer go back home to my house; I was to stay in a hotel tonight. Someone would collect my car from the lawyer's office and I would be given another car to use in the meantime. I was advised once I re-located, I wasn't to return home until after the court hearing, and even then, it would be advisable for me to have someone accompany me.

They contacted my employer, and I had a conversation with Callie about working from home until after the court hearing. Callie, as always, was very supportive. She would talk to the board about how they could assist me during this time.

The following day, as instructed, I waited at the hotel until someone made contact to let me know what the next step would be. It was a nerve-wracking time. I hadn't prepared myself for this, never imagining I would have to leave what I had believed was the safe haven of my home.

Later that morning, I received a call on my new mobile phone from a police constable named Lena. She would be there in fifteen minutes to take me to my new accommodation. I didn't have the opportunity to ask further questions, the call was brief. I was having to place my trust in a team of people I didn't know, at least until this whole saga was over. I was already counting the days until the court case would begin.

Constable Lena picked me up, we drove for about twenty minutes to the outskirts of the city, pulling up at a small cottage in a quiet area. The garden looked neat and well kept. Lena told me this would be where I'd be located until further notice. They were taking no chances; someone would stay at the cottage with me day and night. I would be kept safe at all times - after all, I was the star witness.

The cottage was surprisingly spacious, a kitchen dinette and open lounge area, two regular size bedrooms. I was curious about who normally lived in this house, and if they had to leave on account of me. Lena assured me this was a rental property that was occasionally used by the department - no doubt to house people like me.

I knew I just had to get through this, one day at a time. I started by exploring each room and familiarising myself with my new surroundings. The garden was surely the best part of the property; the original owner of the house had planted a lot of trees and shrubs - a long time ago, by the look of them. A courtyard at the back had a large orange tree growing near a pergola, and I envisaged myself spending the majority of my time sitting outside in this cool shady spot.

Nights were the worst. I did get to know some of the people on duty, and we chatted for company, but it wasn't the same as being able to pick up the phone and talk to my family or my friends. I also wasn't able to receive mail or messages. During those times, I felt very alone. I felt cut off from the world and took to watching television for a few hours a day, taking a great interest in world matters and the weather map. I just hoped that I didn't have to resort to watching Days of Our Lives.

During the day I wandered around the garden. I had asked to be allowed to go for a jog through the paddock on the other side of the road, but was told that for my own safety, I had to remain at the house at all times. I played cards with some of the daily visitors who, like me, were trying to pass the time. I knew they were keeping a careful eye out for me at all times, and I trusted in their judgement, I tried not to think about the people who were attempting to discover where I was.

Someone turned on the ABC news and my attention was suddenly drawn to an announcement. The item discussed the pending court case regarding the murdered man, Chad Dimitri. The hearing was scheduled to take place in the coming weeks. The McCallums were named. They were still in prison, along with a few of their cohorts who were also facing murder charges. I moved closer to the screen. Footage of Tom McCallum was shown following his arrest and his first appearance in court. Even though in handcuffs and with a prison escort, his nature appeared unchanged; he stared directly at the camera, uttering abuse as he strutted into the courtroom.

Seeing that face again, I remembered Ed's solemn words. *These are dangerous and hardened criminals; they will stop at nothing to wheedle out of these charges.* I imagined them in court and found it hard to believe they might evade these serious charges with no conviction. I had to see this through; no matter what else happened, I was doing this for Chad Dimitri and his family.

*   *   *

I was pacing like a caged lion. I felt edgy, nervous. I couldn't go out in case I blew my cover. I hated being the star witness. I'd been living in alternate accommodation now for three weeks, and it was frustrating the crap out of me. I had rarely gone out of the door; someone delivered my groceries, and someone went and got my clothing and stuff from the house.

The days seemed to last forever. I was missing Jamie so much, I felt determined to make contact with him soon. I just needed to hear his voice again. I even missed my morning jog with Rosie - no coffee and croissant at the corner cafe for me anytime in the near future. I longed to get my life back and couldn't wait for this whole thing to be over - if ever it was going to be. My parents were briefed about the situation and were understanding of the need to lay low until the court case. Even then, I knew I would have to be escorted to and from the hearing each day and a guard would have to stay with me as long as I was under the police protection scheme. In some ways, I felt angry that these hardened criminals didn't care if they harmed other people to get what they wanted, that they were able to impact my life while they were under the investigation microscope. *Where's the logic in that?*

I could no longer use my old phone, and if I did contact my parents I needed to be extremely careful not to reveal my location to them. I knew the next two weeks would seem like years, and braced myself to get through it. My heart was breaking - my mother was very ill and I couldn't be there to support her. Life can be so unfair, and mine in particular sucked right now. I buried my head in my pillow, and the tears fell silently.

Next day, knew I needed to stop feeling sorry for myself. This wasn't all just about me. I sat in front of the computer and started to write, and didn't stop until late afternoon. I wrote about the events that led to my escape up north, in the ranges - until now, apart from the police and my lawyer, I had only told the people in my inner circle who meant the most to me what happened to me at Mirna Springs Station. Suddenly, there was this burning desire to write down my account of what happened, day by day. The whole exercise was really beneficial, it had a grounding effect, helping to clarify my experience while also making me think clearly about the testimony I would give in court. Something unexpected happened while I was writing. Initially, my focus was on writing an insightful story about a well-known family working in the cattle industry. My story today, however, was much more about the dark dealings of two undesirable characters who waded in so deep they would be forever stuck in the dirt of their own making.

*　　*　　*

Using the new phone, I was finally able to contact Jamie. He'd been worried about me, and warned me not to take any chances right now. He knew how dangerous these people had proven to be and wished that he was here to look out for me. I would give anything right now to see his face again, even for a few hours, but we both knew it wasn't possible.

As a crazy suggestion, I asked him, 'What about the trip that we planned to Yingali Station with the kids? Could we still arrange it?'

Jamie hesitated, obviously thinking about my proposal.

'They probably won't allow it, but leave it with me. I'll speak to Sarge and then he would have to talk to the people who are organising your protection. We'll see what we can come up with.'

'Okay. I really miss you, can't wait to see you again.'

'Me too.'

I held out little hope this venture would actually happen. I was sure that they didn't want me leaving my hideaway under any circumstances.

One visit to the lawyer was allowed. I arrived undercover at Ed Curren's office for a final briefing. Ed, his usual chatty self, expressed delight in confiding to me that McCallums were going to plead not guilty to all charges.

'But what does this mean for the hearing?'

'Well, if they had pleaded guilty, especially to the charge of first degree murder, it could lighten the sentence somewhat, but they would have been advised of that by their defence lawyer.'

'So you're saying that if found guilty by the jury they could face a lot longer prison term?'

'Yes, that's right, and believe you me, there is some pretty compelling evidence that Chad Dimitri was murdered and his body disposed of on their property.'

He added, 'The charge of attempted murder is also bound to stick. You are the star witness in all of this, there is no doubting that the testimony that you give will bring this case together and make it easier for the prosecution to prove each charge.'

'But surely they would realise all of that?'

'Well, they have one of the best criminal lawyers in the land and they seem confident that they are both going to be acquitted. They have dropped all of the blame for the murder, and even the cattle stealing, in the lap of their counterparts, and are now claiming that they were unaware of what was going on out there.'

Ed looked at me and said quite seriously, 'That's why your testimony about the conversation you overheard between Tom McCallum and the guy who came to the homestead is just as crucial as the testimony you give about what you witnessed when you ventured down Old Mine Road.'

Yes, I know all of that. I also knew that once I had testified in the witness box, the rest was up to the judge and jury to decide the fate of those involved. If only this could all be over and done with sooner!

Chapter Twenty-Four

There was a sense of urgency in the house. I had been woken before dawn and told I was leaving the cottage today.

'We've received new information that leads us to believe that you could be in danger again.' Lena was busily looking for my suitcase. Bleary eyed, I climbed out of bed. 'You mean they already know that I am out here?'

'Well, we don't know for sure but it's not worth taking the risk. We don't think they know which house you are staying at, but they may have some idea that you are now in a certain location. We didn't want to rattle you unnecessarily yesterday, but word is out they have their scouts actively searching for you day and night. We doubled up on the shift last night and a few of us stayed here just in case. Do you remember talking to Jamie about the trip to Yingali Station?'

'Okay yeah, but I didn't think that would be happening under the circumstances.'

'That's looking as though it's the best option right now. Arrangements have been made and they're expecting you up there later today. Let's get you packed and out of here as quickly as we can.'

It was four days since my last conversation with Jamie and somehow, it seemed my wish would come true after all and I really would be going on this journey to Yingali Station.

There wasn't even time to get excited. I packed quickly making sure I hadn't missed any vital pieces of equipment. My bags were lined up against the wall. Camera bag, walking gear, backpack, small bag of clothes. I was told my escort, Constable Rachel Steel, would be picking me up within the next fifteen minutes. I was wired up, full of nervous energy, ready to move on again.

How on earth had this visit been organised so close to the court case? I suspected authorities decided because I was the key witness in a murder trial, the safest place they could think of was out in the middle of nowhere at Yingali Station, a hundred kilometres over the border in the Northern Territory.

I was relieved to be out of the small cottage I'd been living in for weeks. There was little respite, strict instructions not to be left alone, even for a short while. A walk, even after hours, was out of the question. As Lena said, these people were actively looking for me.

The visit to Yingali would be as a guest, to learn more about the program that had received such critical acclaim. The scheme was born out of an idea by a group of concerned people to help troubled youth develop communication skills, self-confidence, and a strong work ethic. Daily duties involved working with stock, including animal handling and care. According to Jamie the program also had a strong element of team building skills, encouraging individuals to work together to achieve the best outcomes.

Success was attributed in part to the volunteers, but also to the strong sense of trust the kids developed, as they were encouraged to create a future for themselves.

This was the trip Jamie and I had planned many months ago, departure was on the day I didn't make it back to Dillalong. Completing this journey was not just about tying up loose ends from the past; it represented something much deeper and significant for me. I had asked myself if I would ever have the courage to return to the bush. But as nervous as I felt right now, I realised I had to go back, if for no other reason than to rediscover how to become a self-reliant and independent person again.

There was also another pressing issue that had been forefront of my mind for some time now. I had just come out of a major crisis - no, I was *still* in a crisis. I needed to be sure about my feelings for Jamie. The speed in which our relationship has developed had shocked even me. I was determined to be clear about how I was feeling and not have regrets later. But travelling halfway across Australia to prove a point - what was I thinking? In that fleeting moment, it felt as though my life was totally out of control. I had just started to recover from a major crisis, people were still out searching for me with nothing but bad intent, I was facing a major court case as the star witness, and here I was chasing across Australia on another mission. But then my rational side pulled me firmly back into line. Get real. You are being moved because your life is in danger. *You don't have a choice.*

I was smuggled out of the property in the half dark, nearing the crack of dawn, gear loaded for the week. Despite my nervousness, excited to be back on the road again. Even though it was just another part of the witness protection program there was that deeper and very alternate meaning for me for in taking on this journey.

Constable Rachel Steel would be with me the whole time to ensure that the week ran as smoothly as possible.

The journey was a long one. We stopped once along the way for a quick lunch break and a brief walk to stretch our legs. Rachel remained vigilant throughout the trip. She was both driver and escort, which seemed a bit unfair. I did offer to drive, but Rachel reassured me that she was okay, and that she was responsible for the government vehicle.

Any car that passed our way was scrutinised closely. I looked anxiously over my shoulder a few times throughout the trip. Rachel also kept tabs on the traffic. Halfway through the journey we noticed a four-wheel-drive with a lone driver that came very close to our vehicle. It was the way the car was being driven that gained our full attention; it would speed up to our car, then drop back again.

While Rachel's attention was firmly on the car behind us, she remained calm. 'There's a service station coming up in about five kilometres, we'll pull in there and just wait to see if the other car stops as well.'

It was a nervous wait. The vehicle behind us had stayed with us for some distance, and all the while, we were hoping it was just someone travelling the highway in a hurry to get from A to B. We pulled into the service station, turned off the engine and waited. A four-wheel-drive made the identical move, stopping abruptly near the café. We observed from a distance, both tense and on full alert, wondering if the occupant would dare to approach us here in this very public place. To our relief, the situation suddenly changed from a potential crisis to a comedy.

The car door opened and a young child rushed out holding his crotch, with his mother yelling, 'Quickly, you can make it, the toilet is over there.'

Noticing us, she grimaced. 'Kids, honestly, you just get on the road and all they want to do is go to the toilet every five minutes. This one is so fussy he will only go to a real toilet and not by the side of the road.' She laughed out loud. 'I'll be glad to get back to Alice Springs with this lot.'

We set off again and apart from the huge road trains regularly hurtling along the highway, passing vehicles became few and far between as we travelled further north. We were both confident now that we hadn't been followed, but we remained on full alert until we reached our destination.

As we cruised along the endless white line, Rachel revealed a bit about her decision to join the police force. She had an uncle in the force who always impressed her with his unselfish attitude to helping others. He lost his life some years ago following a major crash involving a truck, a stolen car and a police vehicle. Rachel said her uncle left a lasting impression and this had helped her to make the decision. She loved the diversity of the job, and was looking forward to the week at Yingali Station.

My thoughts turned to Jamie. How many weeks had it been since we had seen each other? Phone calls were never the same. In spite of everything else that was happening, all I wanted to do was to see his face again, and feel his arms around me, holding me tight.

In that moment, my new mobile rang.

'How's the journey going?'

'Jamie! How did you pull this one off?'

'Well, I'll tell you all about it when you get here. If you're making good time, you should arrive sometime this evening. I'm really looking forward to seeing you again, Sarah'.

'Me too, I can't wait'.

Some hours later, we crossed the border into the Northern Territory. Our anticipation heightened. After another hundred kilometres we turned off onto a dirt road, our GPS informing us Yingali Station was now just fifteen kilometres away.

Finally, we were driving over a cattle grid and through the large metal gates with wrought iron sign overhead: "Yingali Station, established 1896". The owners' names were painted in bold letters underneath: "Max & Lillian Sweeny".

Jamie said the property had been a dust bowl up until about two months ago. Rains had surged across the plains as a result of huge tropical low in the top of the Northern Territory. The area received almost all of its annual rain quota in just three days. Water - the essence of life itself – had transformed the arid desert into a colourful tapestry overnight. Despite being an arid outback area, beautiful wildflowers in bright pinks, blues and cream were sprinkled across the land, and a soft carpet of long green grasses transformed the paddocks. The red dirt formed an amazingly beautiful backdrop to this miracle of nature.

No doubt the owners would be revelling in the changes that had taken place in this raw and unforgiving landscape in such a short space of time. Along with many other land owners up this way, the Sweeny's made no secret of the fact that due to the extended drought the station was almost bankrupt and they had feared it going into receivership. Hopefully, the rain would change the owners' fortunes; introducing new stock to the area would replenish their bank accounts.

And there it was, Yingali Station homestead. It looked like the typical Australian farmhouse, a large square structure with a sweeping veranda and a pitched roof supported by four rows of internal posts painted in various shades of green. We climbed out of the car and stretched our weary bodies, taking in the scene in front of us.

Jamie was first out to greet us. He looked as though he was going to burst with happiness and to be honest, I felt the same way. As I felt his strong arms wrap tightly around me, I didn't want him to let me go.

Jamie did the rounds, introducing Rachel and I to the very friendly owners of the property, Max and Lil Sweeny, and then the staff who had travelled with the eight young men who were taking part in the program.

Finally, we got to meet the participants themselves. They had all arrived on the previous day and looked quite settled, bunked down at the shearers' quarters. A mixture of ages and backgrounds, the group had a couple of mentors who would stay with them throughout the two weeks.

We also met Jaripuka, an Aboriginal Elder, who lived in the local area. Jamie told me that Jaripuka would take the boys bush tomorrow, to reintroduce them to their land and their cultural practices.

There were also a couple of non-Aboriginal boys in the group. Jamie explained that they could choose to go with Jaripuka and the others or they could stay at the homestead with Dave, the other main mentor for the program who worked with all of the participants.

Everyone was provided with a list of daily chores including some designated tasks that group members could nominate for, either because they were interested in that area of work or because they wanted to learn the ropes, with the possibility of finding work down the track.

Max Sweeney's gruff behaviour gave the initial impression he was a tough old fella from the bush, but we quickly learned that underneath that exterior he was really a soft-hearted, generous man who looked out for everyone who happened to stay on his property.

Perhaps once a redhead, Max's hair - what was left of it - was silver-white, his skin wrinkled and creased from years spent in the burning sun. Dark motley freckles covered his legs, arms and thin bony hands. Long bushy eyebrows poked out awkwardly from under his felt hat, which was full of holes and sported what looked like a crow's feather slipped into the sideband. Now seventy, Max had worked with cattle for most of his life; he was born on the station and had rarely left since he was a boy. The property had been bought and developed by Max's great-grandparents in the late 1800s and remained in the family to this day. Max told us his schooling was via two way radio, or School of the Air. Many children and their families living on remote properties relied on this form of education. This was eventually replaced by internet and mobile phone technology.

When approached to take part in the youth program, Max didn't hesitate to get on board. He and Lil were not lucky enough to have children, and they wanted to make sure that there were others who could be trained to take over the station when Max could no longer cope with the work. The program had been running at Yingali now for nine years.

Lil was a softly spoken lady who went out of her way to make sure that we were all comfortable and well fed each day. She told us the story of how she came to live at Yingali as a young bride, and had rarely left the place since.

Lil said station life was the only life she knew, but she had no regrets, 'Probably 'cos I can't see myself living in the big smoke,' she joked. She showed us to our rooms. We were guests in the homestead and they made us feel very welcome.

I got talking to a young Aboriginal boy taking part in the program. Benjamin told me a bit about his birth family. His mum, Dulkna, lived in Darwin; he was unsure where his father, a white man named Barry, lived. He talked with love and pride about his baby sister, Lisa, who was six and lived with their maternal grandmother in Alice Springs. Benjamin had been living rough in Alice Springs and Adelaide. He said he had done a lot of "bad stuff" like stealing cars, pinching grog and cigarettes, and had recently been charged with robbery. He was only fifteen years old, and yet so much had happened in his short life. His mother Dulkna was jailed when Benjamin was ten years old. Benjamin said she had attacked an acquaintance with a knife after a heavy drinking binge, wounding him badly. Initially charged with attempted murder, the charge was later changed to causing grievous bodily harm, which bought her a three-year jail sentence.

Benjamin stayed with relatives in Alice Springs, but they were also drinking heavily and couldn't care for him. There was little food in the fridge and he didn't have a bed, often sleeping on the floor or outside on the lawn. Benjamin said he wandered the streets late at night with a group of boys. Most of these children were from broken homes and without any adults to out for them.

This was Benjamin's last chance to redeem himself. The Youth Justice Department put him under a protection order that would expire when he turns eighteen years of age.

Over the following days, I got to know Benjamin a little better. I noticed the special care that he lavished on the horses, he talked to each horse in turn, and always ensured they had adequate food and water for the day. There was a caring side to Benjamin, perhaps even the potential to put his skills to the test by getting employment on a station such as Yingali in the future.

During smoko, we sat quietly, both drinking the bitter, black billy tea out of metal pannikins. 'Hey Benjamin, I liked the way you handled the big mare today, she's a feisty one. I thought she might kick you at one stage, but you really calmed her down.'

Benjamin was thoughtful for a moment before answering.

'Yeah, my uncle used to say if you want a horse to do what you want it to, you have to build some trust first.'

'Well, whatever you did, that mare decided she trusts you alright, you even put a saddle on her and took her out into the paddock. Well done.'

Benjamin grinned, and one of the other boys gave him a nudge. 'How about showing me how you build that trust, Benjamin?' Another grin.

I sensed the time was right for me to make a move, so I left the boys to talk amongst themselves. They had already experienced so much broken trust in their short lives; hopefully this program would give them some element of trust - first of all in themselves, and in what they may be able to achieve, but also learning to trust others, maybe for the first time.

We set off early to beat the heat. Jamie driving the battered old Land Rover, me sitting alongside, Benjamin, Louie and Buck in the back. Following on behind, Dave and Jaripuka in the truck with the rest of the crew. We were headed out to the old cattle yards. It was a regular day, the boys tasked with cleaning up the yards and getting ready for the new cattle scheduled to arrive by truck later that afternoon. We all seemed to be falling into some kind of daily routine.

The cattle yards were located about a kilometre from the main homestead. A smaller house was located down near the yards, which presumably had housed the stockmen and their families over the years. It was in a state of disrepair, I decided to give the cottage a bit of a clean-up while Jamie and Jaripuka were overseeing the boys.

Once inside, I could see the house had been used more recently, it just hadn't had a good tidy up for some time. I found a broom and worked on each of the rooms, giving them a good sweep throwing out any rubbish. The old wood stove was soon lit and a kettle of fresh rainwater from the tank outside singing away on the burner. A flashy tablecloth, home baked scones and jam from Lil's kitchen, and a fresh pot of tea. Jamie was first in the door, looking around with a big grin, giving me a quick hug before the others arrived. Soon we were all crowded round in the small kitchen, everyone keen to try some of Lil's scones and jam. Amidst the joking and laughter, Jamie looked quietly happy, the program had kicked off to a good start.

Jamie encouraged one of the quieter boys, Dudley, to tell us how he went in the cattle yards. Dudley, the reserved member of the group found it hard to express himself. When he had no words, I handed him an extra scone and he took it with a shy smile. Jamie had told me that just being here was like opening another world up for the boys, some never knowing what it was like to have three square meals in their bellies, or where they would be sleeping the next night.

On the way back to the homestead, Benjamin talked about his day. He was riding the mare, circling the boundary in a practice run, preparing him for the real deal; herding the cattle. Benjamin says it was the best day he'd ever had. He wanted to become a cattle man like his cousin Joe, who works on Mirna Springs Station.

My ears pricked up hearing Joe's name along with Mirna Springs. It turned out Benjamin's cousin Joe was his Uncle Beaver's son. This meant Uncle Beaver was one of May Miller's children.

*　　*　　*

In the distance, a crease in the red dirt appeared, surrounded by large hills. As we travelled closer, I could hear excited shouts coming from the truck behind us. We were near the edge of a rare and beautiful oasis in the middle of arid Australia.

Sitting way below the overhanging rocks a large waterhole, ripples of deep green reflecting the sun's rays and scattering silver sparkles across the surface. Due to the recent rains, underground water had appeared out of nowhere, gushing through the giant red rocks and creating a waterfall that spilled into the pool below. Reeds and soft grasses waved in the desert breeze. A frightened wallaroo, disturbed following a peaceful drink at waters edge, bolted off into the distance, water still dripping from its mouth.

We just happened to be here at the right moment in time - the luxury of seeing this rare gift from nature in such a revered place that was known by so few. Young and old spilled out of the vehicles, an unlikely collection of people, but everyone overwhelmed with the wonder and excitement of that moment. This was the Jataru waterhole, named by the old people thousands of years ago. We had travelled off station country and were now on Jaripuka's mother's lands. Jaripuka told us he was born not far from the waterhole in a valley that ran between the steep ranges to the north. Although the spot was not a sacred place, it was still an important site, requiring Jaripuka to go ahead and talk to his ancestors, the past custodians of this land.

Jaripuka was one of those custodians now. I watched him go down slowly, stepping with purpose deep into the red gorge. He was alone when he spoke to the spirits of the land.

There was a hushed silence out of respect for the old man. In spite of these boys having so much trouble respecting other people's property, the law and their families, I was deeply touched by how much respect they were able to give to Jaripuka in that moment.

We heard chanting as he touched the overhanging cliffs on either side of the water hole. He then walked to the gleaming pool and again, invoked the spirits to talk to him.

Finally, happiness written all over his face, Jaripuka was calling us down, beckoning with both arms. Nobody needed a second telling. The boys raced down the small path leading to the waterhole, everyone wanting a swim in the cool, deep water.

Jamie looked at me, grinning cheekily. 'Going in for a swim?'

I didn't need to give an answer, he knew that I had been looking forward to this trip for days. Even Rachel raced to get to the water first, such was the enthusiasm that we all had for a cool dip that day.

Everyone was laughing and splashing in the water, yelling with joy when someone did a massive dive bomb, splashing all those around them. Rachel, Jamie and I headed to the other end of the waterhole. Long reeds lined the edges and smooth boulders created a natural staircase leading into the water. This was probably where the wildlife came in to drink. The three of us stepped across the smooth stones and took the plunge together, taking in a sharp breath on contact with the surprisingly cold water. We swam across to the middle in silence, overwhelmed at the tranquillity and peacefulness of the place. Jamie swam close and then disappeared underneath the water. I gave a small scream of surprise as I felt a quick tug on my feet. Jamie surfaced near me, a teasing grin on his face, streamlets of water forming silver beads that trickled tantalisingly over his hair and face.

For the next hour we laughed and chattered like children. The majestic red rocky hills surrounding us formed an amphitheatre that hid this oasis - perhaps the First Nation people viewed the hills as centurions, guarding the waterhole from above. We spent close to two hours at that special spot before time was called and we were on the road again, headed back to work.

Jamie was present in a professional capacity, his work with the group regarded as paramount to the success of the program. He was on duty twenty-four hours a day at Yingali. We were always aware of his responsibilities, but whenever we could, we snatched precious moments together, our mutual bliss shared in unspoken language.

Bini - invariably the observant one - caught up to us one day as we walked along the track. 'Hey, you two, you like each other, eh?'

'Yep, we like each other Bini,' Jamie answered with a grin. 'I like Sarah a lot, she's a special girl, she's come from a long way away to spend time with us up here.'

'Yeah, who's your people then? Where you from, Sarah?'

'My people live down in the big city Bini, but I grew up in the bush, so I like it up this way.'

'You gonna stay up here then? Maybe stay with him?' he said with a chuckle.

'Not sure, Bini, we don't know what the future holds yet.'

Day four. Dawn was not quite on the horizon yet when Max woke us up with a quick knock on our doors. We usually stirred at a similar time to Max and Lil, so I was guessing he needed to talk to us about something important.. I dressed hurriedly and made my way down to the kitchen. I was surprised to see Max, Lil, Jamie and Dave all assembled in the room already.

'We've lost one of the boys, Sarah, so we're asking everyone to join the search. It's Dudley. You might remember he said yesterday that he was missing his family and wanted to go home.'

I did recall that during the muster Dudley, the youngest of the group, had said he was unable to contact his mother and was worried about his little brothers, who had both been getting into a lot of trouble back in Alice Springs. The boys were all allowed to make a phone call to their family once a day. Mobile coverage out there was very hit and miss, but Max allowed everyone use of the landline when needed.

'It seems that a couple of the others noticed he was missing when they went to bed last night but they didn't think much of it until early this morning,' Jamie said.

After much discussion it was decided that we all needed to search the property first. Max asked that Rachel, Lil and I search the homestead and all of the outbuildings. Jamie and Dave would search the shearer's quarters and the old homestead nearby. We would meet back at the homestead in half an hour. In the meantime, Jaripuka would stay with the remaining group and they would carry on with their normal duties so as not to cause any further disruption to the boys' daily routines.

Thirty minutes later, we were all back in the kitchen. No sign of Dudley. This was cause for worry; Dudley was just fourteen, he didn't know the area well and nobody seemed to know which way he might be headed.

Jamie left to report Dudley as a missing person to his counterparts in the area, in case the boy might be headed for the highway and could potentially be found by a patrol car. He returned to tell us the authorities had asked that we provide hourly updates to the nearest police location.

Max didn't want to waste any time. He directed each driver onto the various roads and tracks around the property, including the main road that led back onto the highway.

I joined the search with Jamie and Dave, taking the track running behind the shearers' quarters. This track led back to the waterhole, and although an unlikely bet, Dudley could have headed out this way because he wanted another swim or to spend time alone. The track was a winding one, in some places rocky outcrops could hide a person who didn't want to be found, so we checked along the way.

We reached the waterhole and looked around, deciding quickly this was not the track Dudley had chosen to take.

We all met up again at the homestead. Max and the others

were looking at a map of the area on the kitchen table, and Max pointed out certain areas where someone on the run might be tempted to hide. The most likely was the track that led directly back to the main highway, but Max and Lil had travelled up as far as the highway without any luck.

Jamie was in touch with the local police, who had sent a patrol car out onto the highway in the hope they might locate Dudley. Seeing the worried look on Max's face, I reassured him that we would keep looking until we found Dudley, even though I had no idea where he could have gone.

Search parties were sent out again, this time in different directions, still no success. Now late afternoon; the other boys had finished work for the day and were asking about Dudley. Max and Jaripuka did their best to reassure them Dudley would be found - although nobody was really sure where or when.

Later, as we were preparing the evening meal, the phone rang. Max speedily picked up.

'Yes, yes, okay, where did you say? Oh, that's great news, we've all been pretty worried about him, but he's alright you say? Oh good, well tell him we're all thinking of him and the boys are missing him too. I'll get Constable Landers to ring you back, he's down with the others right now, but thanks for ringing, I'll let everyone know.'

Max hung up and gave a huge sigh of relief. Dudley had been found on the highway some hundred kilometres or so north of the station. He was hitching a ride up to Alice Springs to be with his family. He told the police that he liked being a worker on Yingali Station, he mentioned his new friends, Jaripuka and Jamie, but decided he missed his family so much he couldn't stay any longer.

The police took Dudley back to Alice Springs. We didn't know what would happen to him; any repercussions for absconding, and could this impact his current court order? We hoped he wouldn't be placed back into youth detention again for breach of his agreement.

Jaripuka walked down to see the others. We knew he had the skills and knowledge to walk them through what had happened. He spent several hours down at the shearers' quarters sitting around the fire, talking about the day and asking how the boys were all going, before expertly changing tact and asking them about what they wanted to achieve from the rest of their time at Yingali Station.

Later that night Jamie followed up with the local authorities. Dudley wouldn't be returning to Yingali Station. There was concern about the potential for further absconding - Dudley couldn't promise he wouldn't try to run away again. He was remanded and placed in youth detention until a magistrate could decide what action needed to be taken.

Next day was work as usual. There was no mention of

Dudley, even though I imagined the others were probably missing him. Perhaps they realised Dudley had chosen a different path from them, and for the time being, they were happy to continue in their roles.

I felt a sadness for Dudley, and for others like him. There were many complicated issues at play, none of which could be resolved overnight - but I did know that being locked up in the system was not the answer for these lost children.

Chapter Twenty-Five

That day was one of many that will remain etched in my memory forever. Jamie and I walked and talked for hours. We both relished the precious time that we were able to spend together, each day was better than the last. The uncertainty when we would be able to see each other again following this trip hung heavily though. As dusk descended, Jamie pointed out a colourful frillneck lizard keeping a cautious watch, his beady brown eyes observing us from a distance.

'Hey, Sarah, have a look at this, he's eying us off. I think he's as curious about us as we are about him!' Jamie kneeled down to point out the bright reptile. The lizard remained perfectly still as we admired his perfect camouflage. Then we laughed hysterically as the friendly frillneck suddenly ran up Jamie's leg and promptly latched onto his shirt.

The longer we lingered the more I realised the land had an unexpected beauty that calmed the soul. No expectations out there, just the silence and peace of the land itself. A tapestry of silver sprinkled throughout the galaxies was now vivid in the clear desert sky. We slept in our swags under a gum tree, the deep silence of the bush only punctuated by the occasional thumping of a passing kangaroo or the howl of a dingo.

Next morning we laughed and joked as we rolled up our swags and set off back for the homestead. In that moment, it felt as though neither of us had a care in the world. I wanted it to last forever. I glanced sideways at this amazing person, who was oblivious to my scrutiny. Tall, powerfully built, a gentle giant who had become one of the most significant people to set foot into my life. I found myself hoping nothing would ever break the connection I had with Jamie. It seemed nobody else on this earth could make me feel this secure and so completely happy - but that also scared me. Uncertainty also had a voice, setting off little negative swipes in the back of my head. *Would you feel this way if you weren't in such a huge pickle? Is this just a fling to get your mind off the more troubling issues in your life?*

'What are you thinking about? Penny for your thoughts.' Jamie had stopped in his tracks, turning in front of me to look deep into my eyes. He had caught me totally preoccupied with a bolt of self-doubt and misgivings about my decision making ability.

I was almost lost for words in that minute, but managed to reach out and hug him. 'I really enjoyed last night, I could stay out here forever. I feel so at peace right now and so happy that I'm up here with you.'

'Me too. You do realise how much you mean to me, don't you Sarah? I see you as part of my future now. I'm not going to let you go you know, and no matter how long this drama takes, I'll be waiting at the other end. We can get through this together.'

A second of silence followed. It was a poignant moment. I answered with difficulty, almost choking out my answer. 'I can't imagine life without you anymore.' The emotion spilled out of us, and we both shed tears as we held each other tight.

Finally, it was time to make a move, to face reality once again. We knew the others would be looking for us. We walked slowly back to the homestead, arm in arm.

*   *   *

While we were at Yingali, we heard on the grapevine that May Miller's grandson Joe was still working on Mirna Springs Station. Despite the fact that neither John nor Tom McCallum were ever likely to return to the land claimed by their forebears, Mirna Springs would continue to be run as a going concern until a decision could be made about its future. Joe had taken on the role of leading hand, responsible for both the hiring and overseeing of station workers. Following several conversations with Benjamin, Jaripuka and Jamie negotiated directly with Joe about the possibility of a job. I could see the excitement on Benjamin's face when it was decided he would be taken to meet Joe.

I was unable to travel to Mirna Springs Station due to the pending court case, but early next morning I was up with the flies, saying goodbye to Benjamin, Jamie and old Jaripuka, who was going along as a support for Benjamin. I had a feeling Joe would be impressed with Benjamin's riding skills and his strongly developed intuition with animals. I couldn't explain how it was meant to be, but I felt the power of it.

Chapter Twenty-Six

Cyclone Ellie, currently located off the coast of Darwin, was coming down through the centre travelling inland, headed our way. Max went down to the shearers quarters to let everyone know that the storm was expected to hit some time that morning. There was little time to warn Dave, the supervisor, and four of the boys who had gone out yesterday looking for stray cattle and had camped overnight near the creek.

It felt like the calm before the storm. As if sensing some apocalyptic event was about to overwhelm us, dozens of insects started to batter the windows, trying no doubt, to get into a safe haven before the chaos.

Within an hour, the storm hit. The Sweeneys had no luck in raising the alarm with Dave and the boys; they were out of range. It was now too late to travel out anywhere beyond the homestead.

'The real danger we're facing is the aftermath of the storm,' said Max gravely. 'The heavy rain could flood the creeks if it comes in from the north.'

I wished Jamie was still here; somehow his presence was

always reassuring to everyone.

In no time the wind was lashing through the gnarled old ghost gums and scrawny Cocos palms near the homestead. We all pitched in to help the Sweeneys, lashing down loose objects and locking up anything that might be blown away in the storm. As strong squalls of heavy rain began to fall, we huddled together in the kitchen. Lil had the kettle on and was busily making everyone a cuppa. I sensed she was trying to reassure us that storms like this have passed through before, and it was just a matter of waiting to weather it out.

Despite this, there was a palpable uneasiness creeping through the room, knowing Dave and the boys were stuck out there in the scrub. If the creeks flooded suddenly, they could be in real danger. These arid lands can be treacherous - dry and hot enough to perish in one day, but when flash floods come without warning, lives can be lost in the blink of an eye.

Hours passed. There was still no word from Dave or the boys. Max was having multiple conversations on the two-way radio. He had found out that the main creek, which passed through his property and ran all the way down into parts of South Australia, was now flooded. Even after the worst of the storm had passed, there was no way it would be possible to put out a search party. The wind was still very powerful, the rain coming down in sheets. Going out now would be too hazardous, a vehicle could become bogged - or worse. It became a waiting game. The phones were down, there was no chance to ring Jamie and let him know about the missing group.

By mid-afternoon, the storm was still raging outside. The rain hadn't let up. I thought about Jamie, wishing over and over that I could at least talk to him about what was happening. I wondered where he was, and if he had heard about the cyclone.

A decision was made. Max Sweeny would go down to the road nearest the creek crossing to see if there were any sign of Dave and the boys. He asked Rachel and I if we would go along to help, while Lil and the others would stay behind – someone needed to be close to the two-way radio to receive news or instructions about the floods.

Just getting outside and into the Land Rover was a challenge. The wind was howling, the rain heavy and drenching. As we headed towards the shed, we had to dodge an old fence, now just pieces of shredded grey wood threaded with rusty wire strewn across the ground, one end flung precariously over the rain-soaked scrub.

We made slow progress along the muddy road, which, in a short amount of time, had turned into a perilously dangerous slush. We were aware acutely aware of the risks trying to travel during such a massive storm, and knew that we could get bogged at any time - this was not the place or the time to be stranded out in the middle of nowhere.

Not a word was spoken. We were all anxious, focused on

getting to our destination without disaster - but also worried about what we might find when we got there.

Thankfully, the rain was easing by the time we arrived at the forked road that led directly to the big creek, the Worriana, which runs through hundreds of kilometres of land before transversing into South Australia.

Despite being warned the creek was in flood, none of us, not even Max, could comprehend the force that we were now witnessing. We could hear the mighty roar of the water even from a distance. The powerful deluge swept away everything in its path, a filthy brown swirl of mud and water creating small waves powerful enough to push a large dead tree along with it. We were all transfixed by the sight of mother nature at its most formidable. This water had the power to give life to the land and all its inhabitants, but just as quickly could snuff life from the unwary or the unlucky.

'I've seen some floods in my time, but this one takes the bloody cake.' Max regarded the water for some time, as if trying to decide what needed to be done next. Rachel and I waited for his instructions. He said we should all try to get down a bit closer to the banks of the creek. As we climbed out of the Land Rover he warned us. 'Be really careful, the banks will be slippery now and I don't want you falling in. We'll have a quick search down here and move on if there's no sign of them.' Heeding his words, we were careful to keep our distance from the surging water. The deafening roar was a constant reminder of the wild torrent raging by and how we were all vulnerable to that danger.

A scan along the banks proved fruitless, but Max knew where Dave and the boys might be camped so we drove on, a powerful mix of apprehension, fear and dread setting in. Everyone lost in their own thoughts. Past a short bend in the road ahead was a thicket of dense scrub. We had arrived at what would have been the campsite.

Finally, we spotted the boys huddled together under a tarp, however our initial elation disappeared when we approached them, it was immediately apparent to all of us, the head count was only three - Dave and Bini were missing.

Frightened and tearful, they told us what happened. Whilst packing up the camping gear by the edge of the creek Dave and Bini had spotted two stray cattle and decided to drive the jeep down the creek to round them up. They were in the middle of the creek when the water came down in a huge rush. There had been no chance to escape the speed and ferocity of the deluge. The huge wall of water washed Dave and Bini, along with the cattle, down the raging creek and out of sight. That was the last the boys had seen of them. They hadn't known what to do next, but knew they couldn't walk back to the homestead at the height of the storm. They were also reluctant to leave the area in case, by some chance, Bini and Dave escaped the water and came back looking for them.

The boys were obviously in shock, we threw a blanket over them as they huddled together in the back of the Land Rover.

After standing at the water's edge and calling out, Max decided that we needed to follow the road alongside the creek just in case Dave and Bini were still alive – which, he admitted, was not looking good for them right now. We drove slowly and laboriously along the rough track, sometimes sliding dangerously through the mud and sludge. Finally, a sighting of the upturned jeep. As we drew closer, the tragedy became very real. Taken by surprise, Dave and Bini would not have had a chance against a wall of water that was so powerful it could wash anything away in its path.

The rain had slowed to a drizzle, and we could see our surroundings more clearly now. 'Does anything catch your eye?' Max rasped desperately. He was looking ahead through binoculars and Rachel and I were scanning the banks and even up into the trees in case Dave or Bini had managed to scramble onto a branch. Nothing. We yelled and screamed their names, over and over, but could hear nothing above the roar of the water.

We were just about to move further down the creek, when Rachel spotted something moving on the side of the jeep. 'Left side, at the back!' She was pointing to the movement. Max focused the binoculars on the jeep. 'By god, you're right Rachel, someone is holding onto the wheel of the jeep, I can see their fingers moving.'

I felt overwhelmed with fear and trepidation. How could anyone manage to survive this long out there in this terrifying torrent? From this angle, we couldn't tell who was clinging to the jeep and even if they were trying to communicate, we wouldn't have been able to hear them above the roar of the water. What was even more frightening were the large branches rushing with great speed, with potential to dislodge the vehicle at any time, sweeping it - and the person clinging to it – even further down the creek. There was no time to lose, we needed to come up with a plan of action. As we tried to work out what to do, Rachel shouted, 'Look, it's Bini!' He'd managed to briefly raise himself up so that we could just see his face. Rachel took control. 'Max, it's bloody dangerous out there but we need to do something quickly. The jeep is in danger of being nudged out of its current position by floating debris. Have you got a boat? I know it's a long shot, but we could try to launch a boat upstream, tied to the shore with ropes, and use it to get to Bini.'

Max said he had used his boat before in floods, but never in these conditions. He was in a quandary about whether it would work, but we had to do something – and fast.

Driving back to the homestead was a slow slog sliding through the slimy red mud, Max and I finally reached the shed and started to load ropes, a small boat and two life jackets onto the top of the Land Rover. We worked in silence; we knew every minute now was critical. Could we really save

Bini - and would Dave be found alive.

The others were waiting anxiously in the homestead. Lil and Max had a brief but urgent discussion about what was happening down at the creek, and Lil managed to make contact with the authorities on the two-way radio. We were told the weather was still too wild to send out a rescue team with a helicopter, but they would send help once the wind dissipated.

Max and I set off again along the muddy track, nursing fears we might be too late. By the time we got back to the creek, nearly an hour had passed.

The rain had stopped, but the muddy torrent hadn't eased. It would be a delicate and extremely dangerous operation to even get the boat into the water, let alone get on board without it toppling over.

Without asking, Rachel assumed the role of rescuer, and was already donning a life jacket and placing the spare in the boat. Max seemed shocked Rachel had decided to take on such a dangerous role and yelled at her above the noise. 'Rachel, I think it might be best if I take control of the boat, it's too dangerous out there for you.' But Rachel wouldn't budge. 'It's going to be alright Max I've completed rescue training and I'm a strong swimmer.' Max seemed unconvinced and kept insisting he should take the boat out instead. The option of throwing a line to Bini and pulling him across the creek was also discussed, but it was just too risky.

Finally, they reached an agreement. Rachel needed someone on shore to direct everyone in their roles. She assessed the situation and made decisions based on the moving current, the available gear and the type of boat. She told us that each of us would have an important role during the operation.

The first stage - launching the boat – could potentially spiral into another crisis. As an added precaution, she tied a separate rope around her waist so that if she did fall out of the boat, she could be pulled back to shore.

Rachel was hoping Bini would be able to climb into the boat by himself; the recovery effort would be seriously hampered if he was injured. We were all so aware that this could go horribly wrong. As Rachel stepped into the boat she looked small and frail. 'Rachel, please be careful,' I yelled, but she could no longer hear me above the roar of the water. She was already focused on where she needed to head.

The three boys wanted to be part of the rescue operation and Max said the extra muscle power was definitely needed right now. Before the boat was launched we used a winch to secure the boat with steel rope around the base of a giant gum. Max also tied a long rope to the bow for added strength and what he hoped would be some sort of control over which direction the boat moved. We all held that second rope. Max said to listen carefully for his instructions - we might have to haul the boat back across the water ourselves.

Rachel needed to get the boat across the stream and navigate the boat between the jeep and the tree, before she could attempt the rescue. This itself was a challenge, she needed to constantly dodge fallen tree branches and logs in the muddy water.

Halfway across the creek, the boat came close to capsizing. Rachel had attempted to steer it past a broken branch but the boat was caught, veered sideways and almost tipped. She was pushed to one side and came close to slipping into the water - even from our vantage point we could see the fear on her face. We all held our breath until we could see she was safely back in the middle of the boat and steering it once again in the right direction.

Finally, she approached the swamped vehicle. By this time it had slid a little further down into the fast moving current. Rachel made the difficult manoeuvre between the capsized jeep and the tree, attempting to pull Bini up from the side. The first and second attempts failed, the boat lurched dangerously in the current. The sound of water surge still deafening, we could see Rachel's mouth moving as she shouted instructions to Bini. She used her hands and arms to coax Bini to hang onto the gunwale and swing one leg over the boat, pointing to the middle of the boat in case the extra weight risked the boat being swamped. We watched anxiously, barely breathing. After several gruelling heart-stopping minutes, Bini managed to haul himself into the boat. While battling to keep the boat balanced, Rachel was also trying to help Bini with his life jacket; he seemed to struggle to get it over his head. Unbalanced, the boat swung around again in a 360-degree turn. Water started to seep over the top. Max screamed from the bank. 'We'll pull you backwards, try not to move too much, stay still or it may tip again.'

For fifteen tense minutes there was little progress. Getting the boat into a safe position so it could be brought back to shore seemed impossible. The three boys and I crowded around the rope, waiting for instructions from Max and Rachel. Finally, a small lull in the swirling water, the move was made. We started pulling. But just as they were almost to shore, the boat tipped again. This time, water flooded into the bow, threatening to sink the boat entirely. There were only seconds to get Rachel and Bini back to safety, we all put everything we had into the effort. All five of us worked until our hands were raw. Just as they hit the edge of the embankment we pulled the boat up, using the winch and many strong hands. The boat hit the solid ground at the top and flipped upside down, dumping Rachel and Bini unceremoniously onto the muddy banks, where they lay, side by side, exhausted but definitely alive.

It was a surreal moment. They were encircled, everybody cheering loudly and hugging each of them in turn. Rachel had pulled off a miracle rescue; her courage and incredibly steady head had been paramount to the whole plan. Even when things looked bad and the boat nearly capsized, Rachel kept her cool. I helped her off with her life jacket and wrapped her in a rug. 'I am so thankful that you're both okay. I don't think anyone else could have pulled off a rescue like that - you are one amazing, incredibly courageous lady.'

'You are one hell of a woman. I could never have pulled that off.' Max was so overwhelmed with emotion he seemed lost for further words - which was not like Max at all.

The rescue had seemed to take hours, but looking at my watch, from the time the boat was launched until Bini was brought safely back to shore, it had taken a little over an hour.

The focus quickly turned to Bini. Although shivering and in shock, he had initially responded well to the hugs and well wishes, but had suddenly collapsed. He seemed to be having trouble breathing, he couldn't speak to us, and he was shaking violently. Foam was coming out of his mouth. We carefully lifted him into the back of the Land Rover and rushed back to the homestead, wrapping our arms around him to keep him as warm as possible. Max reminded us that there could potentially be near, or dry, drowning problems following such a rescue, Bini had been in the water for a long time. At the homestead, Lil was able to get medical advice via the radio. Bini was wrapped in blankets that Lil had warmed up, put to bed, and given warm drinks. We noticed with some relief that he started to respond well to the care, and his breathing was less laboured. He needed special attention that night, but he was well and truly alive. Max said he would live to tell the tale of his dramatic rescue for years to come.

The same couldn't be said for Dave. Through tears, Bini later told us that after being tossed out of the jeep, Dave had been swimming for his life but the current had quickly carried him away. A log rushing past in the torrent hit him hard, and he disappeared under the water and didn't re-surface.

Bini also related how he had managed to grab onto the back wheel of the jeep and how the swirling water had continually knocked him out of his position between the jeep and the gum tree. It was just by luck that he was able to grab the wheel and hang on each time he was washed under. Bini said his biggest fear had been that nobody would find him there and that eventually the flood would wash the car away and he would be drowned.

As the day wore on we found out the storm had wreaked havoc across the state and was now headed down through central South Australia. It caused big problems for people caught unaware, particularly those in low-lying areas, and Max said there were a number of urgent rescues carried out that day. The authorities called it a 'once in a hundred year' storm. After a couple of days, it moved on and lost much of its force. The creeks went down, the wind abated, and a search and rescue team were sent in to help locate Dave. However, it was now search and recovery; they were looking for a body. Dave had likely drowned in the first few hours following the flood.

Chapter Twenty-Seven

Jamie, Jaripuka and Benjamin returned to Yingali Station with an announcement that ordinarily would have been cause for celebration. They had managed to secure a job for Benjamin at Mirna Springs. He would start on probation and if all went well, he would be promoted to permanent hand, working with the cattle. Joe Miller would be his boss. Benjamin couldn't hide his excitement at landing the job.

The night before Benjamin was to leave for Mirna Springs, instead of the usual get together and farewell party there was a much quieter atmosphere. Everyone seemed to want to reflect on their time at Yingali Station. Lil and Max had cooked a feast and we all gathered around the long wooden table underneath the dark velvet desert sky.

It was Bini who organised a candlelight vigil in honour of Dave. Dave had led the boys with skill and empathy through both the good and the bad days. If one of the boys said they couldn't go on with the program, that they were finished, Dave would be the person who stayed with them, talking to them, encouraging them and showing them they could get through the bad days. Dave was remembered as a brave and courageous person, a powerful role model who didn't give up on anyone easily. His supportive presence rubbed off on many. Max said Dave would be thought of by both past and present participants as someone they could always look up to and respect.

I felt a lump in my throat and tears welled as each boy, even the shy ones, stood up and talked about their experience on Yingali Station, and how Dave had helped each of them at different times during their stay. Everyone lit a candle in honour of Dave, and Max recited a short poem that touched on life and death.

At the end of the night a special farewell ceremony was organised by Jaripuka. Some of the boys disappeared for a while and came back with their faces and bodies painted according to custom. Jaripuka used the clapsticks for rhythm, singing many ancient songs passed down through many generations by his people. The boys surprised us with some of the traditional dance moves that Jaripuka had taught them during their time here, their eyes bright with the excitement and stirring effect of the movement and what it represented.

The red dust swirled and the flames from the fire caught every movement, casting long shadows that spiralled high into the air. The pride on each boy's face as they completed their dance was obvious. The farewell song, sung by Jaripuka's people when the men went off hunting, was that night, sung by Benjamin and Bini.

Everyone would leave here the next day; some bound for

other places to complete their placements, a couple lucky enough to have job offers. We celebrated quietly for everyone that night, especially when we learned that Max had offered Bini a job at Yingali. Max had really connected with Bini and taken him under his wing.

It was also my last day on Yingali. Jamie was staying on to help with the search for Dave, and Rachel was due to report back to work. Several final briefing meetings had been scheduled with Ed Curren. He wanted to thoroughly dissect again my witness account of activities at Mirna Springs, but more importantly, he was now preparing me for what could potentially be a few gruelling days in the witness box.

I'd be returning to the city reluctantly. I felt a deep sadness for Dave's disappearance and for his family, who had arrived from Darwin and were anxiously awaiting news. I knew I would miss Jamie, but would hold close to me the undeniably precious time that we managed to spend together in that week. It also reminded me with a jolt of the ongoing struggles I had left far behind. I would need to face this head on as I was tossed back into the real world.

Later that night, when Jamie and I were alone, I talked about what happened on the day of the flood. My tears welled as I recalled seeing the upturned jeep, believing that perhaps

Dave and Bini had both perished. Jamie comforted me and held me close. He understood the deep impact this event had on all of us; our little group had felt the loss in such tragic and unforeseeable circumstances so intensely. It was to be several days before searchers located his body. He had been washed several kilometres downstream, and it was only after the floodwaters started to subside that they were able to find him. The Sweeneys and Dave's family were planning to place a monument near the creek in honour of this very special man.

Next morning, there were lots of hugs all round. Max and Lil urged us all to come back for a visit, and Rachel invited them to come down and stay with her when they were next heading to the city. Lil said they would take her up on the offer. Max exclaimed, 'Rachel deserves a bloody medal, and I'll make sure she gets one!' We all regarded Rachel as the true hero of the day. Although she had chosen not to talk at length about her amazing feat, we wanted her to know that her bravery and tenacity on that fateful day would never be forgotten.

As we set off from the homestead, I looked back at Max and Lil waving their final goodbye. I could see why young people who spent time on Yingali wanted to go back and work for the Sweeneys. This extraordinary couple were able to reach out to so many troubled youth, making them feel welcome at their home. Bini was one of the lucky ones; two very special people would be looking out for this young man, providing him with all he needs while he learned the ropes to become the great stockman that he aspires to be.

282

Chapter Twenty-Eight

The trial was due to start in less than a week. My anxiety levels increased drastically whenever I thought about having to face the McCallums in court. I had continued seeing my psychologist Milly, mostly via phone chats, she had been providing strategies to use in the witness box, I wanted to be able to articulate what had happened without fear or anxiety. She emphasised that it was *me;* I was the one who possessed the ability to change my emotions by addressing my rational thoughts. I started to realise that while some things were out of my control, there were many things I could control. I had choices, and rather than thinking that I had to be resilient all the time, I recognised that, just like the next person, I could face misfortune from time to time. It was how I dealt with these challenges that mattered.

After preparing myself for my day in court, I stood back to look at my reflection in the mirror. I looked the part but didn't feel it. Navy blue jacket, white shirt, matching skirt. My long dark hair tied up in a neat bun. I noticed a nervous tic above one eye. I figured with all the trauma I had experienced, there would have to be some signs showing on my face. I looked thin; I had lost weight over the past few months, and my skirt kept slipping down as I walked.

Sighing heavily, I slipped into my high heeled shoes, grabbed my bag and walked briskly out the door. Waiting outside the police escort, who would accompany me into court and stay with me throughout the day - or as long as I would be required to give evidence. By now I was past being nervous, past feeling fearful for my life, and over worrying about all that had happened. I was on automatic pilot now, just wanting to get this over with and move on with my life. I knew these past weeks and months had wreaked havoc with my emotional and psychological health, and decided to have a proper break to refocus my energy back to making a good recovery once this was all behind me.

Even before I stepped out of the car onto the footpath, I could see a pack of journalists and photographers looking my way, waiting impatiently to charge in and report any new development. I knew they would harass anyone unlucky enough to have to run the gauntlet of the pushing, shoving mob. Every one of them out to prove they would do anything to get the juiciest information and the best action shots for their story.

Much to my relief I was quickly shuffled out of the car and taken in through a side entrance. I tried to regain my composure, taking a deep breath before entering the main courtroom.

It didn't surprise me - or probably anyone else - that this case was destined to be a high profile matter right from the very beginning.

The mystery surrounding the missing man, Chad Dimitri, thirty-six years old, an amateur historian with a passion for writing books, had been the subject of much speculation. The case had received major publicity, much of it driven by the family themselves, stories of his disappearance had been reported in most of Australia's major newspapers and television channels. Police alleged it was highly likely Chad was murdered on Mirna Springs Station and his body disposed of on the property soon afterwards. The public were now aware of the charges laid against prominent station owners Tom and John McCallum.

As fifth generation partners of Mirna Springs Station cattle run, there was an unspoken but recognisable degree of importance placed on this dynasty. The original McCallums were true pioneers, and involved in many significant historic community decisions. In fact, old Edward McCallum was a local Member of Parliament for ten years, during which time he ensured changes were made to legislation giving workers on stations more rights and fairer conditions.

Many people were now shaking their heads in disbelief. How could this family have fallen so far from grace, accused of deeds so grave they hadn't even been able to secure bail.

The courtroom was packed. Some people I instantly

recognised, including Chad Dimitri's wife, Maria, who was seated in the front row with a group of people I assumed were family and friends. This case had aroused the interest of a lot of people around the country for varying reasons; some wanted to follow the court case just to hear what would transpire, while others were seeking justice.

I made eye contact with Maria as I walked in. She gave me a slight nod, and I felt reassured. I could do this. This was the opportunity we had waited for – to find answers to a very tragic event, and perhaps later some sort of closure, knowing a court of law had decided the verdict - hopefully, the right one. Only then could some of us start to move on with our lives, albeit as very different people.

The defendants were brought into the court room under guard. I could hardly make eye contact with either John or Tom McCallum. Much later, I was able to stare down both men and they would understand completely that I was not intimidated by either of them anymore.

The associates who worked hand in hand with the McCallums were facing separate court hearings, and had already pleaded not guilty to all charges. They had alleged they were not involved in any way in the killing and eventual disposal of Chad's body - that blame had been placed squarely with father and son.

As the charges were read out and the jury briefed by both defence lawyers and prosecution, it again occurred to me how anyone not knowing anything about this case and the series of events that set this chain reaction into motion could be swayed into thinking perhaps none of this happened at all, or if it did, not in the way police and prosecution had painted it.

Ed told me the McCallums hired a team of highly experienced lawyers who were adept at winning cases that initially appeared unwinnable.

The first witness called by the prosecution was a surprise. I had nearly forgotten about Mack Summers, the friendly helicopter pilot. He was dressed quite formally for his day in court, a business suit and spotty tie. The police clearly regarded his original statement, made some ten days after Chad's disappearance, as significant to the case.

'So can you explain to the court what you witnessed on the road leading to Mirna Springs Station early last year, to be precise, on the 24th of February at 2.50pm, and what were you doing out there at this time?'

'I'm a contract pilot hired by some of the local stations in the far north,' explained Mack in a calm, clear voice. 'My job that day was to fly to Freddie Downs Station, which is situated next to Mirna Springs, to search for lost cattle. I told police on that day I spotted a red Pajero fitting the description of the car driven by the missing man. It had been travelling in a south-west direction, but had stopped by the side of the road. I flew over low to check the driver was okay, but he had just slowed down for a group of emus to cross the road. I saw him drive off again in the same direction about a minute later.'

'What made you think the car fitted the description of the missing man's car?'

'Well, the car was a 2017 Mitsubishi Pajero, red in colour, with a distinctive set of roof racks also painted red and a black roo bar. Police showed me photos of the car, and it matched the one I saw.'

'So, you were near to the turn-off from Mirna Springs Station at that stage?'

'Yes, about ten minutes away by road, give or take.'

The defence lawyer posed no questions.

It took several hours and a break outside in the sunshine to realise I need not be afraid of these people anymore. As I walked to a nearby park, I looked up into the sky and there, among the clouds, a flock of Cape Baron geese, flying in perfect formation, the shape of a V. Such a rare sight in the heart of the city. I could hear their powerful honking, calling encouragement to each other above the city traffic noise. These majestic birds seemed to be calling me, as well as their friends. It was a sign. I decided they were flying for me that day – the V was for Victory. They were telling me I was free, just like them, free to live my life with courage and to do so without fear of reprisal.

Mesmerised, I gazed into the distance for what seemed

like hours, but was only minutes, watching tiny stratus clouds flit across the deepest cerulean sky. I was in a peaceful place, soft grass beneath my feet, dogs running around barking, and the sound of children's joyful voices echoing through the park.

I made my way back to the courtroom with purpose. My head was clear as a bell in that instant, and even more importantly, I felt bravado building inside of me. My heart was beating fast as I ran up the stairs.

I'd been called up as the next witness by the defence lawyer. I took the stand, noticing a sudden tremble in my hands. I looked across at the McCallums. A slight sneer was spreading across the face of the younger McCallum, and it hit me - Tom McCallum was so confident, he really thought he would win this case, and that the odds weren't stacked against him at all. He believed that because he had hired the best criminal lawyer in the state, he would not answer to these serious charges. He whispered a message to his lawyer, eliciting a slight nod. Tom then looked directly at me; his arrogance and total lack of conscience clearly evident. I glimpsed evil then, pure hatred looking back at me.

I tried to remember what my lawyer had carefully advised me during one of our many briefing sessions. 'Just tell the truth Sarah, and try not to get rattled when you're in the box. Remember, you're telling the court what you know in order that justice can be served on behalf of many people. You are representing Chad Dimitri and his family in some ways. This is your chance to do that, and I know that you will want to see the judge and jury reach the right decision.' His words rang in my ears.

'I'll repeat the question Ms Wills, what were you doing at Mirna Springs Station? Can you explain to the court your reason for being there in the first place?' The defence lawyer, Ian Shepherd, a weedy little man in a pinstripe suit, balding pate and an incredibly sharp wit. His piercing brown eyes focused in closely on me, and as he spoke, he waved his left hand around in a sweeping fashion to emphasise his relevant points. He was beckoning the jury to listen to me as I answered his probing questions, which came thick and fast. I knew this was a tactic of his; I had seen how he handled other people in the witness box. As he leaned in towards me I realised that this crafty little man was hoping to make my answers look confused and vague - a strategy designed to discredit the statements I had made previously to the police.

The potent smell of Shepherd's aftershave cologne wafting through the still air was overwhelming, I started to feel slightly nauseous. I wondered if the powerful perfume was another one of Shepherd's tactics, to make people want to speak up and get out of the witness box as quickly as possible.

I had to use every ounce of willpower to concentrate on each question and answer with confidence so that the jury could get a grasp on what really happened to me.

After three hours of gruelling cross-examination I was still in the witness box, but Ian Shepherd was not finished with me yet. His junior offsider, Nick Costa, watched on closely, perhaps hoping to model his own form of ruthless questioning tactics, mirroring his senior colleague's clever strategies.

Shepherd leaned in towards me, asking in a snide tone, 'So you *think* you may have seen some people slaughtering cattle, and just because there was a fence around the area you presumed there was some sort of illegal activity happening on Mirna Springs? It's a bit rich isn't it? You want us to believe that this was an unusual activity, and yet this is a cattle station with live cattle being slaughtered and sold all the time by my clients.'

'Well, if you consider that stolen cattle brought into the property in the dead of night is normal, and me being shot at and chased when I was discovered near the hidden slaughter shed is normal, then I think you are the one who is mistaken.' I think my answer surprised him after that, he abruptly changed tact.

Shepherd left the best until last. For full effect, he read out part of my statement to police.

'So, Ms Wills, you are asking this court to believe that you overheard Tom McCallum threatening to kill you if you were found?' For emphasis Shepherd strutted, completing a full circle across the floor past the jury, bald head shining like a beacon under the fluorescent lighting.

'Yes, that's correct, I did over hear Tom McCallum talking on the phone saying I would be dealt with when they found me.'

'Oh come on, you want us to believe that you overheard a conversation, with you standing on one side of the homestead verandah and my client right around the other side. It sounds to me like a total exaggeration, like a fanciful statement that you've made up to justify your disappearance to your employer and the police.'

'No,' I answered firmly, 'I was in fear for my life on that day and that's the reason I decided I needed to leave the homestead immediately to try to get help.'

'You say that many of the workers were out looking for you, and we understand that when they found you, put you in a safe cottage. I would suggest that they were trying to find you to make sure you were alright, not as you suggest, to do you in.'

Shepherd cackled with delight at this last point. I felt frustrated that perhaps the jury and even the judge may have decided I had dreamed up my escape from danger and that indeed the owners of Mirna Springs wished me no ill will.

'No further questions, Your Honour.' Ian Shepherd had a smug look that said, 'I won that round' as he took a seat again beside Tom McCallum. My chest shuddered involuntarily; a huge sigh of relief.

Ed Curren stood then and asked me if I knew the man pictured on the large screen in the front of the courtroom. An image of the bulldog was highlighted for all to see.

'Yes,' I replied, 'this is the man who found me hiding in the scrub. He captured and assaulted me before helping Tom McCallum lock me in the hut.'

For the benefit of those in the courtroom, Ed named the man as Tony Guzzedi, aka 'rabbit', now deceased.

'It will be alleged the late Mr Guzzedi was part of the syndicate working closely with the McCallums.'

I was shocked at this announcement. I didn't know the bulldog had died, or that he was part of the infamous syndicate. Further documents and information were rendered to the court in support of Guzzedi's involvement with the group.

Following this revelation Ed hesitated, momentarily looking steadily into my eyes. I sensed that something significant was about to revealed. He approached the bench and made a request to the judge. It looked to be about the disc of photographs I had taken during my stay at Mirna Springs; he seemed to want to show them to the court and members of the jury.

Ian Shepherd jumped to his feet. 'Objection your honour, these photos have no relevance to this case, they are simply snaps taken while Ms Wills was lost in the outback. There is no need for the court to view them.' The judge overruled Shepherd and ordered that the 'snaps' be shown.

The significance of these photos couldn't be underestimated: the dread on the face of Shepherd, who clearly knew of the content, became apparent. Tom and John McCallum, on the other hand, may have been told of the content but could never have imagined what was about to be revealed, or how it would ultimately be so damaging to their case.

There was absolute silence in the courtroom as the photos were projected onto a large screen at the front of the room. If anyone had doubted my story before, I knew that after seeing these pictures they would have second thoughts. Each picture told a story: some very clearly showing the ordeal that I had gone through to survive. I had meticulously gathered information about my surroundings, and anyone viewing the shots would understand where I had travelled and. more importantly, what I had discovered each day.

My careful documentation was now being used by the prosecution to prove what had happened to me and the unfortunate Chad Dimitri. With a date recorded on each photo there could be no dispute about the time line and what had happened each day. Just over halfway through, Ed suddenly called an abrupt halt. There, on the hill following my discovery on Old Mine Road, was the shed. There were even close-ups of the men in the shed, and of cattle being slaughtered. The two prominent players - the men in the Lexus - were identified as associates of the McCallums and were therefore implicated in the cattle stealing, and possibly the murder of Chad Dimitri.

Although Ian Shepherd objected to this allegation, Ed argued his point with the judge and jury. He had further compelling evidence proving this was a cattle-stealing gang, and therefore the motive to dispose of someone who discovered the secret was strong.

Next to appear on the large screen was the photo of Chad Dimitri's name carved on the rough wood wall. There was a verbal reaction of shock in the courtroom. Loud sobs could be heard coming from the area where Maria and her family were seated. Ed expertly requested a temporary stop. He stood now, in front of the evidence, and explained police believed the victim, Chad Dimitri, had also been a prisoner in the same hut as me, spending his final hours there before he was murdered. The evidence was compelling.

The photos proceeded. The court saw the hole I created to escape; the time line on each shot clearly revealing how long it took me using just the metal cup to dig my way out. Each picture was telling, and clearly showed that this was a woman who was definitely fighting for her life.

If the photos raised strong emotions in me, they also raised an incredible commotion in the rest of the courtroom. Shouts came from the back of the room.

'You bloody bastards, you are beyond vile, I hope you rot in hell!' I saw the court sheriff removing someone unknown to me, but who clearly had some connection to Chad Dimitri or his family.

Other onlookers had also stood up, and the air of intensity in the room seemed to alarm the judge. The hammer was struck once, twice, three times. He leaned forward and spoke loudly into the microphone. 'Sit down now, I will not have disruption in this courtroom, if you have anything else to say you will be asked to leave immediately. You need to remain silent for the remainder of this hearing.' Another thump of the hammer and quiet was restored.

Being the wily old lawyer he was, Ian Shepherd sensed that all was not well with the defence argument. He called for a recess, respectfully asking the judge if the court could call a break and reconvene the following morning. The judge seemed reluctant, however given the disruptions of the last hour he agreed on the condition that everyone return at the designated hour and there would be no more called breaks.

The McCallums both seemed relieved at the suggestion of a recess, although I couldn't imagine anything worse than being taken back to a prison cell by the court guards. Back in custody, they'd have considerable time to contemplate the day. Just as importantly though, they might be wondering how the judge and jury viewed the new evidence, which could potentially affect their plea of not guilty to all charges.

I was seeking the same thing as Chad Dimitri's family and anyone else who suffered at the hands of these people. I wanted to see justice carried out and those facing court pay a heavy price for what they'd done.

I glanced around the courtroom, making eye contact with Maria, who was sitting at the back with her parents and Chad's brother for support. We both nodded, acknowledging that we were seeking the same outcome: justice for Chad.

I looked over in the direction of the jury. They all looked like normal citizens; some probably had families, careers and mortgages, but for the next few days, and possibly weeks, their time would be taken up listening to endless days of evidence and witness statements in this court, trying to put each piece of the puzzle together, to make sense of what really happened on Mirna Springs - and, crucially, who was responsible for the many crimes committed along the way.

Chapter Twenty-Nine

Four weeks had passed since the start of the court case. Each lawyer had summarised their positions to the court and outlined their preferred outcome. The jury had been out for hours. I nervously paced up and down my patio, phone in hand for any news. Surely by now they must have reached a decision?

Ed told me a no admittance to guilt, combined with no demonstrated remorse by either of the defendants, could go against them with both judge and jury. If found guilty on the more serious charges, they could potentially be sentenced to many years in prison. Given John McCallums age, he would probably die whilst still incarcerated.

The court reporters who frequented the halls of the courthouse, spending hours pacing the pavements, continued to keep the public informed of daily outcomes presented by the prosecution and defence lawyers. The papers were carrying daily accounts, each night the ongoing saga was hard to escape on television. It seemed as though everyone had a vested interest in this case, I sensed that whatever the final deliberation was, and however sensational the story had been, what had finally been revealed during those four weeks would remain a tragic story for many.

I wondered if the Dimitri family would ever see sufficient justice carried out to give them peace for the irreplaceable loss of a husband, father, brother and son. For me, I would sleep better each night knowing these people were locked away for a long time and not able to hurt anyone again. I bore the scars though, of a trauma which could only be described as life changing. I did still have a small hope, however, that some sort of semblance of my early life would eventually be restored and I would move on and rebuild.

The jury was back. In the courtroom I focused my attention on John and Tom McCallum, seated at the front of the court, respective lawyers by their sides. Both men appeared apprehensive. The younger McCallum sat quietly, a pensive look on his face, hoping perhaps, that ultimately, he would be found not guilty and released. If he was hoping that, then he remained completely misguided about the part he played in a long list of corrupt and immoral deeds.

The judge was scathing in his opening remarks. He ordered the McCallums to stand as he read out the charges made against each of them: murder, kidnap, attempt murder, cattle theft, threatening community members, killing stock on farms in the local district.

There were lesser charges as well, mostly to do with colluding with Tim Grant and the illegal activities in relation to stealing water and trying to set up a mine site without proper consultation with First Nations people and landowners in the area.

Finally, the judge asked the jury how they found the defendants in relation to each of these charges. There was an audible gasp throughout the courtroom as the jury announced its verdict: both defendants, guilty of all charges.

In his final remarks the judge talked about the stain that would now mar the good name and reputation that the McCallum's forebears, the first pioneers of the country, had built. The judge said the pair had shown no remorse for their evil and despicable crimes and therefore their sentence should reflect the seriousness and utter depravity of their crimes, which were based on greed and the need for power and control over others. Sentencing was set aside for later in the year.

In the meantime, they were to remain in prison, despite the fact they planned to appeal their sentences at a later date. Ed assured me these men wouldn't be walking free for a long time to come.

We watched as the court sheriff moved towards the men. I couldn't help but notice that for the first time, the younger McCallum looked fearful; the overbearing arrogance displayed throughout the court case absent. John, on the other hand, had clearly conceded defeat. A look of resignation revealed his true conviction. He knew he was guilty and would ultimately pay the highest price - imprisonment, more than likely, for the rest of his life.

As we walked down the stairs we faced a huge mob - journalists, some wielding microphones, others carrying cameras, along with the relatives of the victim, interested onlookers and bystanders. I still had my escort with me but suddenly felt a protective arm wrap tightly around me. I looked up to see Jamie's face, reassuring me with a little smile. Jamie had been called to testify, but much to his relief he was asked only three questions by the prosecutor. The police just needed to verify the day of my arrival in Dillalong, the phone call made after I had arrived at Mirna Springs, and where I had finally been located before being flown out to Adelaide.

Reporters were intent on interviewing the Dimitri family. Maria's lawyer spoke on her behalf. The family had prepared a written statement expressing the deep pain and anguish they experienced following the disappearance of their beloved husband and father. The family were grateful to police and the justice system for the hard work leading up to today's findings, and they hoped a life term would be set with no parole.

Jamie and I walked away from the courthouse together. We were finally going home. I was no longer the state's star witness, a protected person, I was free to live my own life again. No more instructions on where I had to go and what I had to do. The sense of relief overwhelmed me, and I felt a flash of pure joy. 'Penny for your thoughts?' Jamie grinned as he looked deep into my eyes. But I was lost for words.

We walked down the road arm in arm. I had never felt so happy as I did in that very moment.

Chapter Thirty

In the months following the court case, I found myself going back over the events and pondering what would compel a person to turn to a life of crime.

It was tragic knowing the original settlers worked so hard over the years to lay the foundation for the generations that would come after them. That legacy now destroyed by the newest family members, perhaps never to be recovered again.

What motivated Tom McCallum? During the lead-up to the court hearing, he was diagnosed with a Personality Disorder with Psychotic tendencies. Psychiatric and psychological assessments both concluded an underlying mental health issue, which the court needed to take into account before sentencing.

This could partly explain some of the incredibly cunning and almost-believable lies Tom told during the court hearing. The narcissistic and bullying nature of a man who believed he was entitled to everything he wanted, even if people were hurt or killed in the process, was beyond imagination.

Needing to know more I spoke to Milly, who mentioned individuals with this condition can feel intense, uncontrollable emotion, making them not only distressed, but constantly angry. A piece of the puzzle fell into place for me; some of the wild behaviour I witnessed during my stay at Mirna Springs that lacked true reasoning now made sense.

Milly said initially experts considered it an untreatable condition, but there were now new therapies and medications.

Tom and John McCallum risked it all for money, greed and power. Their gamble did not pay off. More crucially, they lost the most precious right of all - their freedom.

I wondered about the fate of the ill-mannered housekeeper, Ronda McCallum, and whether the police had caught up with her. I was still in touch with Connor, and he kept me up-to-date on what was happening. Authorities found the Mirna Springs housekeeper wasn't privy to information regarding the illegal workings of the station, therefore no charges were laid against her.

Ronda may not have been directly involved in the illegal activities on the station, but I had witnessed firsthand a number of deceitful incidents. It was clear to me that she had acted as collaborator and spy, reporting back any information she thought could be of use to them. Along the way she had made herself very unpopular among the workers and townspeople of Dillalong. She had chosen to fall in with her family members and, like them, was renowned for her bullying tactics. How May had been able to condone this woman's behaviour for so long was a miracle, she had no heart. It was a relief to all when Ronda packed her bags and moved on, destination unknown.

But all was not lost, I told myself. Hopefully, Mirna Springs would not succumb to this disastrous event, and someone would eventually take up the reigns and make it work again.

There had been a new development in the ongoing saga of business activities and gang warfare of two syndicates that had been sworn enemies for years. These two gangs continued to jockey for power and control of assets in the far north of the state - districts that they both identified as being "their" territory. Guzzedi was killed by members of the rival gang long before the court case; a bomb was planted in his car by an unknown person. The bombing happened on a busy street in Sydney, and police expressed anger that the gangs were so brazen in their attempts to harm one another that they were continuing to endanger the lives of others. Luckily, no innocent bystanders were injured. Investigations hadn't turned up any new leads. Following the court case, Ed finally explained that it was important I wasn't given advanced notice of Guzzedi's death at the time of the hearing; he didn't want prior knowledge of the killing to impact on the testimony I was about to give.

Munching on toast while scanning the papers one morning, I

was taken aback - there had been another gangland killing. The death of one of the big-time players was reported as payback for encroaching on the other's turf. What was so interesting about this one was that the underworld figure who had just lost his life was one of the men found guilty in relation to the murder of Chad Dimitri, Jack Danver. He was killed inside Yeroon, a high security prison, where he'd been for just a few months. He had placed multiple protests through his lawyer before he was incarcerated at Yeroon; following several death threats, he didn't want to be locked up in a prison where many of his enemies were also imprisoned.

Despite this, Danver was interred in Yeroon, albeit with round-the-clock surveillance. He wasn't allowed out when the other prisoners were around. Nevertheless, somebody managed to make sure that his planned elimination went ahead, despite the safeguards. There was still some mystery surrounding the death; as is often the case, inmates were not willing to talk, probably for fear of retaliation. Authorities hadn't charged anyone with murder, no suspects had been identified, and investigations were ongoing. The paper said there would be an inquiry.

In addition to this story, on the same page, another article appeared that seemed to have an apparent link to the first homicide:

Gangland Feud Fears. Members of a well-known gang

have been questioned over shootings. A shooting in the Sydney CBD has initiated a man hunt to find the perpetrators. Police provided a statement in relation to the shooting and maintained they would endeavour to locate and arrest those responsible for these multiple killings. Resources were to be reallocated to the case in order to catch these gangland figures who had carried out this blatant act at the entrance to a local gym, endangering the lives of onlookers and pedestrians on the street. The three victims were allegedly part of a local well-known gang.

*   *   *

I was getting ready for work when Ed called. 'Hi Sarah, how are you? Have you seen the news today?'

'You mean about Jack Danver losing his life yesterday?'

'Well, yes. I thought you would be interested because this is going to impact your future as well.'

'OK, so I'm listening. Perhaps give me the good news first and then the bad news.'

Ed sounded amused. 'Well no more bad news we hope Sarah! What it means is that the gang members that were threatening you have all either been locked up or killed, even the leaders. Word on the street is that the one or two remaining associates have fled the country for good.'

'What, so you're saying that the gangs have pretty well all

disappeared now, one way or another?'

'Yep, that's right. Basically, this means you're free to live your life without looking over your shoulder all the time.' There was a quiet pause and Ed says, 'You still there, Sarah?' I was holding the phone to my ear but couldn't find the words to answer. I felt quite overwhelmed in those following minutes.

'Yeah Ed, I'm still here. I don't know what to say, except thank you for everything. I couldn't have done this, especially the court case, without your guidance. I'll be forever grateful to you for that, Ed.'

'All in a day's work Sarah, and what's good about this outcome is that the baddies are all taken care of, so to speak.'

We said goodbye. I didn't think I would be in touch with Ed again for a very long time. My life seemed to be finally returning to some kind of normality.

Two months later

It was a beautiful summer's day, and we were swimming in the deep, cool water at Alura Beach, a local haunt where young and old love to hang out. It has a little shelter just by the jetty when the sun gets too hot, and the Boatshed Cafe sells the best gelato on the coast.

We'd come down to the beach with Rosie and some of her family, and it turned out to be such a fun day. As I jumped out of the waves and made my way up the beach, I took a long look at Rosie and her family. They were all on the beach playing volley ball. Shouts and cheers went up as Rosie got one over.

'Hey, that means we're in front,' yelled Rosie.

'Naw, you're cheating again Rosie,' screamed her brother Reece. I sat on my towel laughing and cheering along with them - and of course so did Jamie, who was sitting right next to me. Jamie had been down for more than a week now, and we spent most of our time at the beach or lazing around at home. We had decided we wanted to be together on a permanent basis, and were going to house hunt in the coming weeks. If we found the right one, I would give up my apartment. It was a big move.

I leaned back, feeling the warm towel on my skin. I squelched my feet into the hot sand and pulled them out again in a hurry. How can I describe how I felt right in that minute? Relief, contentment? But no, it was much, much more than that. They say pure joy is the rarest of emotions, but in that tiny instant I felt absolute joy at seeing, hearing, breathing, feeling, just being in this life of mine. I was truly thankful that this was my time. To be alive.

My reverie was disturbed as Rosie's young brother started kicking sand all over us. 'Hey, you guys, we're all going up to the cafe for a gelato, coming?'

I looked over to the sweet face next to mine. 'Hey Jamie, you up for a gelato?'

*   *   *

The following week Rosie rang me up, very excited, to tell me my story had been published along with some of the beautiful photos taken of the wildlife and bush during my journey to Mirna Springs Station and trek to May's country.

When I arrived at the office Callie couldn't wait to tell me the story had raised much interest; some overseas papers and a British Canadian television channel were wanting to do a story on Mirna Springs, they were interested in interviewing Dillalong locals as well. Presenting an account of what really happened out there had opened the doors for change.

I thought about the people I had met in Dillalong. I felt especially happy for Connor, Jane and their family, and looked forward to getting back up that way at some stage in the future.

Five months later

Transformation was already in the wind for the Dillalong community. Local elections had been held, a new Member of Parliament for the Dillalong and Simpson Creek districts voted in. The winning candidate, Diana Carlton, originally from the local district, had already increased her popularity following some very clever and timely responses to local issues. In the few short months she's been in office she has managed to halt plans that were scheduled to divert water to the mining company. What's more, an agreement was reached immediately ceasing the mining lease due to the fragile nature of farming and droughts that have hit the area. Diana has already been to visit all of the affected farms in the area and there are moves afoot to ensure these families are compensated for all of the troubles they have experienced in the past.

I rang Connor and Jane, congratulating them on the good news. Connor predicted a brighter future for himself and his family. He was quite upbeat; they had acquired funding to buy a new herd of sheep, and some ewes were already having their first lambs.

'They will be the future of this place,' Connor said proudly. 'My hope is that one day my own kids will want to take over this property and it'll stay with the family.' They were both excited to be welcoming their first grandchild into the world in a few weeks' time.

One year later

Our wedding day. I was marrying the love of my life, Jamie Landers. Rosie and Mum were fussing over my headdress and veil.

'Oh, you look so beautiful, Sarah, like an angel.' Mum had tears welling in her eyes. We had a big hug and I told her I loved her and Dad so much.

Jamie and I had decided to get married on the boardwalk at Alura Beach. It was a beautiful sunny day. It felt surreal, walking arm in arm down the boardwalk surrounded by friends and family throwing rose petals. Jamie and I were laughing and shedding tears of happiness at the same time. We were surrounded by the people we loved the most, friends and family who wanted to help us celebrate our big day. Later, when I threw my bouquet into the crowd, it was caught by a very excited Rosie.

Three years later

May rang us a week ago. Apart from a bit of arthritis that stops her from getting around so quickly, May is in pretty good health and enjoys having the young ones fussing over her these days. She wanted to let us know that Mirna Springs was coming up for auction. Following a lot of legal battles and red tape, a decision had been made by the courts that the station must be sold to pay legal fees and compensation debts.

May's grandson Joe, is still managing the station, he and the other stockmen had managed to keep the business afloat. May said everything had worked out well for Joe, he'd gained a lot of experience in the role and was promoted by the trustees of the company to the role of overseer. In a stroke of good luck it turned out that following a year of drought, during which time many cattle were lost, there had been two years of good rain. Feed on the station was the best it had been for many years.

The group have now purchased a few hundred extra cattle, and there's so much hope for the future of the property. We were pleased to hear that Benjamin, the young man we had met at Yingali Station, was still working there, alongside his cousin Joe. May chuckled, 'Benjamin's the top stockman at Mirna now.'

John McCallum passed away from a suspected heart attack in prison. No foul play was involved, according to police and the prison doctor. The autopsy report revealed he had been diagnosed with a weak heart almost twenty years ago, and he had done well to live this long.

McCallum had requested that he be buried in the small graveyard at Mirna Springs Station, but his final wish was not granted. He had been found guilty of so many heinous crimes, some occurring on the station itself, and it would be too contentious to allow his burial there. He was eventually buried in Adelaide, next to his estranged late wife Alice, who, unbeknown to father and son, died soon after she left Mirna Springs.

Tom McCallum was still in prison; his non-parole period was set at thirty-five years, so if he survives prison he will be a very old man when he's released. I can't say I feel sorry for him. He never did express remorse for his crimes. He didn't appear to grieve when his father passed away, just commenting that his father introduced him to a life of crime and he would always lay the blame squarely at his father's feet for his current situation.

I still find myself reaching back into the memories of the past to remind myself just how lucky I am to be where I am. Some memories are seared into my subconscious; occasionally they surface and I find myself thinking about how differently it could have turned out for me.

Most days I'm able to dismiss these thoughts or look at them from a different perspective. The past is the past, after all. My life has taken many extraordinary twists and turns over the past three years, and as I take stock I know I have so many reasons to put a smile on my face.

Jamie has resigned from the police force. It was a big decision for him. Since moving to the city he's started a law degree at university and is already into his second year of study. He intends to specialise in representing groups and individuals similar to the youth he had been working with in Dillalong. There's a growing need for these boys and young men to be supported and rehabilitated, rather than put through the prison system. Jamie and some of his fellow students have already set up a support group for troubled youth living in the local area, and community members and even the local council have jumped on board and formed a committee to help address these issues.

There have also been some changes in my career. Since returning from maternity leave following the birth of our beautiful little son Lachlan, I have taken on the role of assistant editor for the paper - a challenging role that I am really enjoying. We are currently preparing a glossy lift-out magazine that celebrates people who live and work in rural communities and outback stations. There are so many people out there who are the lifeblood of the bush, and I'm lucky enough to know a few of them. They inspire many of us, they are very much a part of the Australia that we love.

A new era is dawning for Mirna Springs Station. No one could have ever imagined what the fate of this property would ultimately be, although many of us always hoped Mirna would pass into the capable hands of an individual or family who envisaged a bright future in the cattle industry and the country. New people, new beginnings. They may even start to cleanse away some of the dark history, simply by making a fresh start with the land and gaining the trust of the local people - for those who were aware of the evil deeds that took place there, the name Mirna Springs Station had a different meaning. In time, perhaps this will change.

Max Sweeney called out of the blue, to say hello. There had been heavy rain up Yingali way again, and it had travelled down through the centre, all the way to the Dillalong district. Heavy falls that brought the creeks down were now considered an absolute windfall by the locals. Mirna Springs has never looked greener - the creeks were running again, giving hope to the parched land, starving birds, animals and livestock. The cycle of life goes on.

During a phone call with May, she told me her grandson Joe was still managing the station. Members of the Dillalong community trying to raise the money to buy Mirna Springs and had offered Joe shares in the property if their bid was successful.

So, there was hope that the property might not just survive but continue to run as a profitable cattle station. May gave out a happy giggle when I told her we had a little one of our own now. I looked down at our baby son. 'He has inherited his father's beautiful brown eyes, May. He's an inquisitive little fellow.'

'Ah, so he takes after both of his parents then!' May quipped with a chuckle.

May told me she wants to meet my baby boy, and she also wants me to meet her new great-grandson Bailey. Much to May's joy, Joe finally settled down with his girlfriend and Bailey is her first great-grandchild.

I've been planning a trip up north for some time now. I feel the bush calling me again. The urge to travel north has become stronger; the feeling is hard to pin down. I've told

Jamie it's not just in the mind, it's deep in the heart as well. Of course, Jamie and baby Lachlan will be coming with me.

'So, Sarah, it's a long time since you found my country, when are you coming back here?'

'Soon, May, I'm coming soon. It won't be long now, and I'll be back in your country.'

About the Author

Growing up in the Flinders Ranges South Australia, Karen White developed a deep love of the outback. Her first novel, Finding May's Country, captures the essence of the harsh and unforgiving beauty of a remote and untamed land that is the Australian bush.

Karen developed her love of writing at a young age, often writing poems and short stories for her family to enjoy. Her favourite novel in primary school was the children's classic, The Jungle Book by Rudyard Kipling.

When she's not writing, Karen loves to go travelling to distant parts of the world, bushwalking or spending time in her overgrown native garden.

Port Lincoln South Australia is Karen's home, where she lives with her husband Geoff, two dogs Maisie the kelpie and Mac the west highland terrier.

Karen is a qualified Social Worker, during her career that has spanned several decades she has worked closely with the people of Eyre Peninsula. She describes her community work as being one of the most satisfying and worthwhile roles that she has ever undertaken in life.

This author describes her passion for writing as the perfect fit in her life right now. Karen enjoys inventing complex and intriguing characters in her fictional world. When she writes about dealing with constant danger, she would like the reader to have some hope that everything will work out in the end.

You can find Karen's new book on Amazon and multiple online retailers.